ON KINGDOM
MOUNTAIN

BOOKS BY
HOWARD FRANK MOSHER

Disappearances

Where the Rivers Flow North

Marie Blythe

A Stranger in the Kingdom

Northern Borders

North Country

The Fall of the Year

The True Account

Waiting for Teddy Williams

On Kingdom Mountain

ON KINGDOM MOUNTAIN

HOWARD FRANK MOSHER

HOUGHTON MIFFLIN COMPANY

BOSTON · NEW YORK

2007

For information about permission to reproduce selections from
this book, write to Permissions, Houghton Mifflin Company,
215 Park Avenue South, New York, New York 10003.

Visit our Web site: www.houghtonmifflinbooks.com.

Library of Congress Cataloging-in-Publication Data
Mosher, Howard Frank.
On Kingdom Mountain / Howard Frank Mosher.
p. cm.
ISBN-13: 978-0-618-19723-1
ISBN-10: 0-618-19723-0
1. Treasure troves — Fiction. 2. Vermont —
Fiction. I. Title.
PS3563.O884O6 2007
813'.54 — dc22   2006023568

Printed in the United States of America

Book design by Robert Overholtzer

MP 10 9 8 7 6 5 4 3 2 1

To Phillis

ON KINGDOM
MOUNTAIN

Prologue

In the late summer of the last full year of the bloodiest war in American history, two men in butternut uniforms rode hard into the northern Vermont village of Kingdom Common, yelling and firing their rifles into the air. They galloped across the short north end of the rectangular central green, scattering a gang of kids playing one old cat on the grass under the tall New England elms, waking up the old men dozing on the porch of the Common Hotel. While one man held the horses, the other ran into the squat brick First Farmers and Lumberers Bank of Kingdom Common and demanded, in what a clerk later characterized as a "Rebel-sounding" accent, all of the gold on hand. He stipulated that he wanted only gold, the clerk remembered. Besides his rifle and two holstered pistols, he had eight white linen sacks for the clerks to fill. He made eight trips back outside to the horses, staggering under the weight of each sack. His companion, in the meantime, continued to holler and spout all kinds of threats, damning the Union army in general and Vermont Yankees in particular, and firing his rifle at random intervals. To this day there is a pockmark the size of a half-dollar partway up the granite clock tower of the courthouse, presumably from one of the stray bullets fired by the cursing raider.

The Gray Ghosts, as the two riders would become known in the mythology of Kingdom County, were not long at their work. At most, the robbery took ten minutes. No one had any idea who they were. They might have been Confederate soldiers hoping to divert Union forces to the north or common bandits disguised as Confederate soldiers. Still shouting, they galloped east out of town on the county road, then, it was thought, up the Canada Pike Road over Kingdom Mountain toward the border, five miles to the north. By the time the sheriff, a seventy-year-old Mexican War veteran who, at the time of the raid, was playing checkers at the feed store at the other end of town, had assembled a posse of other graybeards too old for active service and teenage boys too young, the raiders had a good half-hour start. Beyond the border, the pike road was just a faint trace, scarcely more than an animal trail through big woods and trackless bogs and bigger woods still, some of the last true wilderness east of the Rocky Mountains. It was not surprising that the Ghosts got away with their plunder scot-free.

The legend of the Great Kingdom Common Raid, however, was considerably enhanced by two unusual circumstances. First, the nondescript little country bank happened to be one of the wealthiest in northern New England, owing to the deposits of a number of local farmers who had paid substitutes to go to war in their stead and had made huge profits selling provender to sutlers to feed Union soldiers and horses. Astonishingly, the estimated take from the robbery was just under one hundred thousand dollars, all in double-eagle twenty-dollar gold pieces.

Second, so far as anyone could determine, neither of the rifle-toting raiders was ever heard from again, either north or south of the Mason-Dixon Line. Except for a few stray gold coins on the lower reaches of the pike road, not far from the Kinneson homestead, all traces of the riders, their horses, and the stolen gold seemed to vanish from the earth, leaving nothing but the legend of the treasure. The Treasure of Kingdom Mountain.

THE DUCHESS OF
KINGDOM MOUNTAIN

1

Miss Jane Hubbell Kinneson had lived all her life on Kingdom Mountain. Like her father before her, she enjoyed the reputation of being relentlessly old-fashioned. Winter and summer she wore long black dresses made from homespun wool. In the days when she was still farming, she worked her fields with oxen. She still raised most of her own food, and even Miss Jane's manner of expressing herself was old-fashioned. She delighted in using the antique phrases of her father and his Scottish ancestors, calling the brooks on her mountain "burns," the valleys "glens," and the trout "char." During her years as mistress of the Kinnesonville schoolhouse, when families with children still lived on Kingdom Mountain, she referred to the students as her scholars. In recent years she had operated a small bookshop and lending library in the village, which she called the Atheneum, open three afternoons and one evening a week.

For the word "certain," Miss Jane often said "determined." "I'm not entirely determined what to do with you scholars, but I shall give you fair warning. I won't abide slothfulness in the young." "Abide" was another of Miss Jane's favorite expressions. And she loved the word "vex" to denote a frame of mind just this side of anger. "Class, you are late in from recess again. How many times must I tell you that in this short life punctuality is all? Sometimes you vex me beyond human endurance."

As the sole proprietor and last resident of Kingdom Mountain, Miss Jane Hubbell Kinneson was vexed, and mightily so, by anyone who presumed to interfere in her affairs there. She was vexed by King James the First, whom she held personally responsible for the King James Bible. She was also vexed, though perhaps only mildly, by her title in the village, where she was known as the Duchess of Kingdom Mountain. Most of all, in the late winter of 1930, she was vexed by the proposed highway that would cut directly over the top of her mountain, linking Kingdom County and the rest of Vermont with the Eastern Townships of Quebec and Montreal.

Most Commoners, as the villagers called themselves in those days, referred to the new road as the Connector. Miss Jane called it the high road, no one was sure why. Maybe this was another of her beloved Kinneson anachronisms. Or perhaps she thought of the Connector as the high road because it would pass mainly through elevated terrain, skirting the river valleys where the villages and more prosperous farms were located. Then again, she may have wished to distinguish it from the tangled network of country lanes and dirt roads linking the hill farms and upland hamlets of the county one to another in the roundabout manner of the Kingdom of that era, where a straight line was almost never the shortest distance between two points. This much was certain: there would be nothing circuitous about the Connector. And there was no doubt at all that the proposed highway was a vexation Miss Jane Hubbell Kinneson would not abide.

Yet the Duchess was as unpredictable as she was stubborn. At the public hearing for the Connector at the Kingdom Common town hall, she listened to other farmers whose land would be confiscated inveigh against change in general and the new road in particular. She listened to her cousin Eben Kinneson Esquire, the wealthiest man in Kingdom County and the chief attorney for the highway project, present plans and maps and assure landowners that every effort had been made to route the Connector through higher, less valuable terrain. When her cousin Charles Kinneson, the editor of the *Kingdom County Monitor*, pointed out that the Kingdom's hill farmers valued their high mowings and mountain meadows as much as the valley farmers valued their river-bottom land, Miss Jane merely pursed her lips. Maybe she knew that protesting would do no good. Even as she sat in the little town hall listening to the debate, the right of way for the high road was unspooling northeast from the Common with something of the inexorableness of the glacier that, ten thousand years before, had carved out the hills and valleys of what would become northern Vermont. The hill farmers' best hope now, their last hope, really, was that the Duchess, who for decades had held sway over Kingdom Mountain like a Russian empress, and whose words at town meeting still caused grown men whom she had taught as boys to quake in their boots, would speak for them. Wasn't Miss Jane widely believed to have second sight? Perhaps she would prophesy some magnificent catastrophe if the township went ahead with the Connector.

At last Jane rose. Tall and slender, with long, light hair and wide-set gray eyes, still a strikingly attractive woman at nearly fifty, she stepped into the sloping wooden aisle of the hall where, some thirty years earlier, she had delivered her high school valedictory, a scathing denunciation of small-town complacency and provincialism that had shocked the entire room into a prolonged and stunned silence. But instead of the expected denunciation of progress she said only, in her usual direct manner, "I can plainly see that in this instance we shall have to render unto Caesar what's his. In Vermont, at least, this high road will go where it has a mind to go."

While Eben Kinneson Esquire and the town fathers probably did not much relish being compared to a Roman dictator, it was with evident relief that Eben said, "We appreciate your willingness to understand our situation, cousin. Particularly in your case, where this is such a personal matter. Of course we, I mean we the town, will take care to cross your mountain at the very farthest remove from your house and fields."

"You the town will do no such thing," Miss Jane said. "I said, in *Vermont* the high road will go where it wishes. Kingdom Mountain is not in Vermont. Nor is it in Canada. It is an entity unto itself, every square foot of which belongs to me."

"Cousin, as I'm sure you know, that notion has long since —"

"Hear me well, sir," Miss Jane interrupted. "If I spy you or any of your legions on my mountain, I'll defend it by whatever means are necessary."

It is difficult to say how such a declaration might have been greeted elsewhere. With applause, maybe. In the town hall of Kingdom Common on that long-ago March evening, Miss Jane's announcement was met with solemn nods of satisfaction. Eben Kinneson Esquire said nothing more. But not a soul in the room doubted that the battle for Kingdom Mountain had been joined.

2

Many times over the years it had occurred to Miss Jane that waking up in her downstairs bedchamber at the home place was like waking up in a tale by the Brothers Grimm. In the pale dawn light of her fiftieth birthday, on the morning after the hearing at the town hall, she looked out into her kitchen workshop and saw the profiles of her beloved blockheads, Memphre Magog and the Loup-Garou, standing vigil on either side of the door to the porch. She could also make out the shapes of some of the individual birds in her Birds in Strife tableau. Hanging from the ceiling on a slender wire was a sparrow hawk with a limp bluebird in its claws. Nearby depended a red-tailed hawk and a great horned owl, their talons locked in midair combat. Her sharp-shinned hawk was busy defeathering a dead tree sparrow on the windowsill above the soapstone sink. Miss Jane's favorite piece in Birds in Strife was just coming into relief in the early light. It was a northern shrike, carved in the act of impaling a redpoll on the pointed spike of a thornapple branch nailed to the wall above her workbench. Strife, Miss Jane thought, was the way of all birds, and the way of the world as well. John James Audubon had understood that. Many of his best paintings depicted birds in strife. Jackson and Santiago, on the other hand, hardly ever carved birds in combat. Worse yet, they etched in the feathers before painting their birds instead of after, thereby clogging the pinion grooves with paint. Miss Jane Hubbell Kinneson took great pride in being the first bird carver to etch in the pinions *after* she painted. The effect was strikingly lifelike.

Jane sat up and put on her long johns and her red-and-black-checked wool pants, two wool shirts, and two pairs of wool stockings. She padded into the kitchen in her stocking feet, tossed some kindling from the woodbox onto the banked coals in the Glenwood, and washed up under the long-handled metal pump at the sink. The sky in the west was still quite dark. She could make out Orion, locally known as the Voyageur du Nord, about to take a long stride over Jay Peak before disappearing. The Voyageur was a promising sign: a clear day ahead for her birthday adventure.

The oatmeal Miss Jane had kept simmering in a double boiler on the back of her Glenwood all night was a little gluey, but oatmeal stayed with a body until dinnertime. Miss Jane Hubbell Kinneson had eaten her breakfast oatmeal out of the same bowl, white with a blue rim, every morning for nearly fifty years, sitting at the foot of the applewood kitchen table astride the bold yellow line painted down the middle of the floor to represent the international boundary that Kingdom Mountain Kinnesons had ignored for generations. As usual, she ate with one foot in Canada and one in the United States, though the mountain, as she had reminded her neighbors the night before, belonged to neither country. The yellow line was a Kinneson family joke. The border did not exist when her great-great-grandfather, Venturing Seth Kinneson, first came to Kingdom Mountain, pulling in the yoke with his near ox while the off ox, which had cut its foot on jagged ice on the river, limped along behind. To Miss Jane Hubbell Kinneson, and to many other residents of the Kingdom in that era, the border still did not exist.

Thinking about her ancestors reminded Miss Jane of her eighteenth birthday. Hurriedly, she reached for her father's GAR canteen and poured a stiff jolt of Who Shot Sam into her coffee. Then she stepped into On Kingdom Mountain to report the results of last night's meeting to her dear people.

Like her beloved blockheads, Jane's dear people, though life-size, had an otherworldly aspect. Their heads were oblong, their features painted rather than carved, and their eyes were Jane's own wide-set gray Kinneson eyes. There they all were: Venturing Seth and his son Freethinker; her grandfather Quaker Meeting; Uncle Pilgrim, with his long staff in the shape of two intertwined serpents; her father, Morgan, as a young man; and Jane's mother, Pharaoh's Daughter, swaddled in a red Hudson's Bay blanket in the sweetgrass basket in which Quaker Meeting had discovered her as an infant in the ox manger of the barn one Christmas morning.

"Well," Jane announced, "we have met the enemy. I wouldn't say they're ours yet. But they know they have a formidable adversary."

Jane's parlor off the kitchen, On Kingdom Mountain, was a retreat where she could be entirely frank, with her dear people and with herself. Despite her admirable public presence the night before, Miss Jane had been feeling rather melancholy lately. It was not just the proposed high road that had caused the Duchess to find herself at sixes and sevens, as she had recently put it to her dear people. She was also troubled by her failure to win first prize in the North American Bird Carving Contest, not to mention the question of her future on the mountain. Though Jane was as healthy as her own oxen, fifty was not forty, much less thirty, and she really had no clear plan for the future.

"Half a century," Jane mused to her people. It scarcely seemed possible. Time, no doubt, to take stock of one's life. What would she do when she could no longer get by on her remote mountain, with no running water, no electricity, and no children or other close family to help? While Jane blamed only herself and her Kinneson pride for not having a husband and family of her own, her self-indictment was of little consolation this morning.

Then there was the dilemma of the Atheneum. The building, which belonged to the town, was sadly dilapidated. The nails clinching the roof slates in place were rusting out, and several times lately Miss Jane had heard the fingernail-on-a-blackboard screech of a slate pulling loose and skittering down the steep slope, thudding on the grass or shattering to fragments on the long granite steps of the library. The ridgeline sagged from the tremendous weight of the slates over the years. In places the stone foundation had heaved out of true. The Atheneum needed painting, outdoors and in, and the flagstone fireplace needed to be repointed. With the county and the entire country in the depths of the Great Depression, it was unlikely that money would be available for repairs anytime soon. A new highway to bring tourists and jobs was one thing. A library and bookshop was something else.

Jane poured another finger of the beautiful amber-colored Who Shot Sam into her empty coffee cup and tossed it off neat. She believed she could taste, in her hundred-proof homemade twenty-apple applejack, the distinct flavor of each of the varieties she and her father had grafted to the Northern Spy in the dooryard — Duchess of Oldenburg, Westfield Seek No Further, Red Astrachan, Wealthy, Cortland, Alexander, and all of her other favorites.

"I know," she said to her people. "I've been tasting too much of the stuff lately. Well, fine. Sit in righteous judgment, if you're determined to, with your sanctimonious frowns and disapproving countenances. I have to confide in someone, and it may as well be you. What do you propose I should do? Give in to cousin Eben and his cronies? Sell the mountain? Sell you? Eben would have every last one of you in the burning barrel in a Kingdom Mountain minute. As for my Who Shot Sam, a sup wouldn't hurt you now and again, either."

Miss Jane raised her father's canvas-bound wooden canteen, which he had carried all the way to Tennessee and back, in an ironical toast to her dear people and drank straight out of the spout. Now that she had exposed her vulnerability to her hard-shelled Kinneson ancestors, she felt a little foolish. You could bet that *they* would not be caught recriminating with themselves. Not by their relations, not by anyone. Whatever remorse Seth and Freethinker and Quaker Meeting and her father may have had about their own failings, they'd kept their doubts to themselves. Or to themselves and their Maker, King James's Jehovah. Who, Jane believed, had enough shortcomings of his own to regret, though so far as she knew, he never had. What's more, if you couldn't confide in your family, whom could you confide in? At least her dear people were not likely to blab her secrets all over town. At least she could rely on their complete discretion.

Still, she must not repine nor, to paraphrase the Pronouncer of Concord, further dash the hopes of the morning with more 'jack. It was time to stopple up her father's canteen and her self-reproaching thoughts and go fishing. Fishing, and seeing what this special day, as heralded by her second sight, might hold would be the perfect way to mark the anniversary of her first half century on Kingdom Mountain.

3

ALTHOUGH MISS JANE's birthday fell on the vernal equinox, a foot of snow still covered the old Canada Pike between the home place and her five-story barn. The temperature this morning was well below freezing, though the wind was beginning to back around into the south. Spring would have to come eventually, even on Kingdom Mountain.

In the barnyard sat the ox sledge, identical to the pung Venturing Seth and his ox had pulled across the river and up the mountainside a century and a half ago. Standing patiently in front of it were Ethan and General Ira Allen, Miss Jane's matched pair of red oxen. Tall in her red and green lumber jacket, felt boots, and fleece-lined cap with long earlappers, the Duchess touched their flanks with her white-ash goad and they started up the pike. An hour later they emerged onto the frozen surface of Lake Memphremagog.

Memphremagog. The vast body of water stretching deep into Quebec between sheer mountains resembled the big wilderness lakes of northern Maine. This was the lake of the Currier and Ives lithograph reproduction on the door of the iron safe in On Kingdom Mountain, the lake of John Greenleaf Whittier's poem "Snow-Bound," which every scholar who had attended Miss Jane's school could still repeat verbatim. In the Memphremagog Abenaki language the name meant "beautiful summer waters." To the Duchess, the great lake bending north for mile after mile, like a landlocked fjord between the soaring Canadian peaks, was beautiful at any time of the year. Yet it was an exceedingly unpredictable body of water. The mountains served as a natural wind tunnel, and without notice its lovely summer waters, as unruffled as a millpond at sunset, could transform themselves into a maelstrom of five-foot waves. In the winter the ice on the lake was unreliable, two feet thick in one spot, two inches nearby. Had it not been for her moment of second sight a month ago, Miss Jane never would have dreamed of setting foot on Memphremagog this late in the season.

Just ahead of her, on a point of land jutting out from the foot of Kingdom Mountain between the mouth of the bay and the lake proper, were the abandoned buildings that had once constituted the town poor farm. The main building, a hulking, three-story monstrosity topped by a square cupola, had a bleak and forlorn aspect, like a summer hotel whose glory days lay deep in the past. Just beyond, the polished black ice of the lake stretched north to Indian Island, where her mother's Memphremagog people had once come to catch salmon. Miss Jane's ice-fishing shanty sat off the southern tip of the island. To the north lay twenty miles of open water. In all that vast expanse, the fishing shanty was the only sign of human life.

Half an hour later, Miss Jane led Ethan and General Ira Allen into a stand of softwoods on the island, out of the wind. In honor of her French Canadian neighbors, Jane had painted her fishing shanty in splashy pastel colors, sunshine yellow and tangerine, with a cotton-candy pink door and lilac trim around the single window. A coal black stovepipe jutted out of the shiny tin roof. Everything inside the shanty seemed in order, so she began chopping fishing holes in the ice around it with her double-headed felling ax.

A reef extended into the narrows of the lake from the tip of

Indian Island. Beyond it the mountainsides hemming in the narrows plunged down far underwater. When Jane thought of the hundreds of feet of dark, frigid water just below the ice, the bottoms of her feet tingled. She set out half a dozen tip-ups with flags made from strips of old red flannel and baited the hooks with live river minnows she'd brought along in a bucket. Then she went inside and kindled a fire in the small potbelly stove. The kindling came from a bag of wood scraps from her carving projects.

An apple crate sat near the stove for a chair. Beside it was a short club Miss Jane called St. Peter. On the floor of the shanty, along the walls, lay four granite obelisks, each four feet long, with the words UNITED STATES inscribed on one side and CANADA on the other. Miss Jane had borrowed them from the strip cleared through the woods on her mountain to mark the border she did not acknowledge. Their purpose was to weigh down the shanty so that it didn't blow away in the gales that came tearing out of Canada over the frozen lake.

Just as the Duchess started to brew tea in an empty lard can on the potbelly stove, she glanced out the window and saw a red flag snap up. "School's in session," she said, and went outside and pulled in a fat yellow jack perch. It weighed about half a pound and had bright orange fins, an emerald back, and dark vertical stripes on its sides. "Go to fish heaven," she said kindly to the flopping perch, and tunked it on the head with St. Peter. Then she yanked in another one.

"A fine scholar," she said, jerking a third fish out onto the ice and smiling at her habit, increasing of late, of talking out loud to herself. Maybe she needed a cat to keep her company, she thought, as she dispatched the flopping perch to fish heaven. But Miss Jane had never looked into the soulless green eyes of a cat without seeing Satan looking back out at her, and she was wary of inviting the devil into her home at this stage of her life.

After a few minutes the perch stopped biting as abruptly as

they'd started. "School's out for recess," Jane said. "They'll be back after dinner."

As the sun climbed higher, the Duchess shed her lumber jacket and fleece-lined cap. Her long hair, in which there was still very little gray, and of which, truth to tell, she was quite vain, fell down her back. Miss Jane was still as slender as a schoolgirl from a lifetime of constant activity and, except for a touch of arthritis in her hands, remarkably healthy. Yet she had to admit that she was lonesome sometimes. Maybe she should get a cat after all.

At noon she fed Ethan and General Ira Allen the hay she'd brought in a burlap bag on the sledge. She gave them a bucket of water apiece, then got out her pocketknife and skinned and filleted the perch. She shook up the snowy fillets in a brown paper bag with flour and cornmeal and fried them in sizzling butter in a black frying pan on the stove, then sat on the apple crate in the sun streaming through the open doorway and feasted on crispy perch and her own cold baked beans and salt-rising bread, all washed down with black tea. Miss Jane Hubbell Kinneson enjoyed her vittles. She might take most of her meals alone, but she ate well. Into her tea, from time to time, she poured a short jolt of applejack from her father's canteen. Thinking of her father reminded her of the iceboat he helped her build when she was a girl. The boat, which had a big blue and red sail and two iron runners, could attain speeds of well over sixty miles an hour. One winter afternoon, near where the Grand Trunk tracks cut close to the west side of the frozen bay, she and her father had challenged the Montreal Flyer to a race. When they passed the locomotive, the engineer gave them a long congratulatory whistle. That had been a great moment in Jane's girlhood.

She sipped her fortified tea and looked across the narrows at the soaring cliffs of Kingdom Mountain's west side. In places, springs seeping out of the escarpment had frozen to a glittering aquamarine. Once, fishing from a rowboat near the base of the mountain, Jane had asked her father if he could scale those cliffs. He had glanced up at them and said, "A person can do what he has to do."

Twenty-five miles long by eight to ten miles wide, Kingdom Mountain was an anomaly. Unlike the Green Mountains of Vermont and the White Mountains of New Hampshire, its long axis ran east-west rather than north-south. Technically, it did not belong to the Appalachian chain at all but had been formed from the same pink Laurentian granite that made up the Canadian Shield north of the St. Lawrence River. The glaciologist Louis Agassiz, who visited Kingdom Mountain on two occasions, was the first scientist to perceive that it actually belonged one hundred miles to the north, in Canada. It was, Jane thought, a mountain worth fighting for, worth preserving from Eben Kinneson Esquire's road and all roads. On its mile-high summit, above the tree line, perched two boulders that she could see from the fishing shanty. One, flat on top, was called table rock. The other sat atop table rock and was almost perfectly round. Known as the balancing boulder, it was thought to be the largest freestanding boulder in New England, a great glacial erratic decorated on its south side with carvings of caribou, mammoths, whales, and walruses. Whether the Arctic animals had been inscribed before or after the glacier deposited the boulder on Jane's mountaintop was impossible to say. Weathered into the northeast side of the boulder was the outline of a satanic face, known locally as the devil's visage.

Far below the devil's visage, on the lower northeastern slopes of the mountain, lay three glacial tarns called the Chain of Ponds. Like the Upper East Branch of the Kingdom River and the swift, cold burns that ran off the mountain, the Chain of Ponds contained a unique species of blue-backed trout, or char, otherwise found only in a lake on Baffin Island. Beyond the Chain of Ponds a huge, wild bog known as the Great Northern Slang stretched deep into Quebec.

At the south foot of table rock on Kingdom Mountain was a pile of stones known as the peace cairn. It consisted of thousands of rocks and pebbles, many not native to northern Vermont, plus shells, bits of bone, even petrified wood, brought to the mountaintop over the centuries by Miss Jane's Memphremagog Abenaki ancestors. If any criminal or adversary of the Memphremagogs managed to reach the peace cairn, he would be granted sanctuary from retribution. More recently, Jane's grandfather, Quaker Meeting Kinneson, and her father and uncle, Morgan and Pilgrim, had conducted hundreds of fugitive slaves over the mountaintop to Canada. Then there was the legend of the Kingdom Mountain Treasure, which had long since taken on its own life. It was confidently reported in the Common, and wherever else storytellers came together throughout the county, that the Confederate raiders had buried the gold somewhere on Jane's mountain, intending to return for it after the war but, inexplicably, never doing so.

What Jane knew for certain was that the mountain had sheltered and provided sustenance for several generations of Kinnesons and that it created its own weather and seasons, quite sharply different from the weather and seasons elsewhere in the county. It nurtured its own species of trout and, on its summit, several boreal plants and lichens found nowhere else within a thousand miles. Looking up at the peak from the frozen lake, Miss Jane also knew why Eben Kinneson Esquire and the town fathers were so keen on their high road. As soon as the new highway was completed, they planned to purchase the mountain from her for a song and transform it into northern New England's first ski resort — a winter spa, as she thought of it — for ne'er-do-wells from Away with more money than they knew what to do with. The road would pave the way.

"Over my dead body," she said aloud. This the Duchess of Kingdom Mountain meant as much as she had ever meant anything in her life.

4

IN THE EARLY AFTERNOON Miss Jane rummaged through her bag of kindling and found a piece of basswood about six inches long. She moved her apple crate outside into the sunshine, got out her pocketknife, and began to carve, the shavings curling away onto the ice beside her boots. Her jackknife moved in quick, sure strokes. In her hands the stick of wood was swiftly becoming a fish.

Jackson, dunderhead that he was, had once said that he saw the animal he wanted to carve in the wood before he began carving. Santiago had grandly pronounced that his animals came straight from his carving hand. Miss Jane believed that her carvings resided first in her head or, in the case of her dear people, her heart. What you loved you always created from the heart. In the North American Bird Carving Contest, held each summer in Montreal, she had never placed higher than third, behind Jackson and Santiago or Santiago and Jackson. She was quite certain that this coming summer would yield a very different outcome. For this year's contest she had in mind a true marvel, something neither of her two chief rivals would ever think of in the first place.

The little fish Miss Jane was carving had a dorsal fin, a notched tail, and a couple of shallow slashes on each side of its head for gills. She took a small box from her outer shirt pocket. Inside, on cotton batting, were two treble hooks on screw eyes and a single eye hook. She twisted the three-pronged hooks into the bottom of the wooden fish, front and back, and inserted the eye hook under the fish's jaw.

Jane took her felling ax and a short metal casting rod from the shanty out toward the middle of the narrows and chopped another hole through the ice. She tied the carved fish onto the thin wire leader of her line and attached a bell-shaped, two-ounce lead sinker a foot above it. Slowly she lowered the weighted lure into the dark water, where it swayed slightly with the deep pulse of the lake.

Jane's father once told her that before his brother Pilgrim went off to war, he had caught, in Lake Memphremagog, a sturgeon weighing one hundred pounds, a great bewhiskered denizen that had probably worked its way up into the lake from the St. Lawrence River. Miss Jane wasn't sure what might be attracted to her lure, suspended hundreds of feet below in the black and silent depths. Although nothing extraordinary had happened yet, she had little doubt that between now and sundown something important was going to take place. Late one snowy afternoon a month ago she'd been reading *A Tale of Two Cities,* perhaps for the tenth time, when for no discernible reason she had experienced what, over the years, she had come to think of as a Kingdom Mountain moment. An image had come to her, fleeting, unbidden, vivid. In her mind she pictured the colorful fishing shanty, the frozen lake, herself on the ice. Somehow she knew that it was the twenty-first of March, the spring solstice. How she had divined this she had no idea. She simply had. Then the moment passed and she was back with Mr. Dickens, far away and long ago, in the best and worst of times.

As the day wore on, another school of perch cruised by. Miss Jane set her metal rod down on the ice and took a few minutes to pull up half a dozen fish to take home for supper. It was colder now. She put her lumber jacket back on. Occasionally, the spring ice on the lake gave out a tremendous booming roar as a great crack zigzagged through it. What if it started to break up before she and her oxen got safely back to shore? She put this thought out of her head as unworthy of the vision that had brought her here. Miss Jane Hubbell Kinneson believed that when she could no longer trust her second sight, she could no longer trust herself. It was part and parcel of who she was. Yet she knew she should not tarry on the uncertain ice much longer. As she cleared freezing slush away from her line with her tea mug, the blue shadow of Owl's Head across the narrows crept toward her, and the sun angled closer to the mountains in the southwest. Time to go.

Laying her casting rod on the ice again, she fetched the oxen and hitched them to the runnered shanty. They easily pulled it off the ice into the copse of spruce trees on the island, where it would be out of sight of summer boaters. Then she gathered her tip-ups and the bucket of perch and set them on the sledge. "That big fish will be down there for you to catch next winter," she said as she started to reel in her lure.

Abruptly, it stopped. It didn't feel like a snag. There was nothing in the middle of three hundred feet of water to get snagged on. Up through the line came a vibration, a heavy, thrilling weight. "Ah," Miss Jane said.

The word was scarcely out of her mouth before the line was screeching off her reel. "The song we like to hear," Miss Jane told her oxen. "The song of the singing reel."

The fish was headed straight down the lake toward the former poor farm. Soon he would stop to turn the lure in his mouth. When the fish paused for a second or two, Miss Jane lifted the tip of the rod sharply, feeling immense resistance.

She struck again, and the reel shrieked like a bagpipe as the hooked fish headed into the unplumbed heart of the narrows between the mountains, where Memphremagog was rumored to be bottomless. When at last he stopped, Miss Jane began to reel in fast. The dancing rod tip bent out of sight in the water, but the line held and now the fish was coming her way.

Miss Jane was famous throughout the Kingdom for being able to identify each of the ten varieties of game fish in Lake Memphremagog by the way they struck and fought. For once she was stymied. This fish fought too long for a great northern pike, yet it seemed too big for a rainbow trout or landlocked salmon.

At last the mystery fish was swimming in tight circles just below the ice. Each time Jane drew it to the hole it stopped, dead weight. Suddenly, she began to chuckle. The opening, she realized, was too small. Holding her rod above her head in one hand and gripping the shaft of the felling ax just below its two-bitted head with the other, she enlarged the hole in the ice, careful not to cut her line in the process. Then she shrugged out of her coat. Still holding the rod high with her left hand, she lay down and reached into the icy lake water all the way up to her shoulder. Soon she began lifting the thrashing fish up through the hole by its bright red gills. It was a lovely dark silver color. And it was gigantic.

"Upon my word, it's a togue," she said. "You've caught yourself a lake trout, Mistress Jane. Twenty, maybe twenty-five pounds."

While she was pleased to have landed such a fine trophy, Jane could not help feeling let down. Surely, her second sight had not brought her out here on the untrustworthy spring ice just to catch a big fish. But she briskly thwacked the trout twice on the head with St. Peter and shrugged back into her jacket. There were worse ways to spend a birthday than fishing. And the afternoon was not over. Any number of things could still happen. She glanced down the lake. Between the gap in the mountains the sky was the color of her lead sinker. A gust of wind blew a few tiny snowflakes up from the ice, sharp as pinpricks on her face. It was definitely time to head back. First, though, she must clean her fish. One of the earliest lessons Miss Jane had learned from her father was to clean her fish where she caught them. Like closing a farm gate behind herself and cutting her winter firewood a year in advance, it went beyond tradition.

Inside the stomach of the big togue was a brook trout nearly a foot long. Strife, Miss Jane thought. The way of the world. Curious to see what a brook trout found to eat in the wintertime, she cleaned it, too. Its stomach sac was empty save for a coin about the size of a quarter, though how a quarter had found its way into the stomach of a brook trout inside the stomach of a togue was a great puzzle to her.

She rubbed the coin against her wool hunting jacket and held it up in the fading daylight. To her amazement, it was a twenty-dollar gold piece. Turning the double eagle over between her fingers, she made out the date: 1852.

Found money signified that a stranger was coming. Always, when she discovered even a lone forgotten dime in the pocket of an old smock, a stranger had shown up on the mountain soon afterward. Perhaps that was why her second sight had directed her to go out on the ice so late in the year. To lead her to the coin that would alert her to the arrival of a stranger who might help her prevent her cousin and the township from ramming that highway onto her mountain. Miss Jane shook her head over her own foolishness. She had no idea who might visit her mountain, and she needed no help in her battle with Eben and the high road. She really should think about acquiring a cat, she thought. An able, strong cat that lived rough and knew enough to appreciate a barn roof over its head and table scraps to eat in exchange for keeping down the mice. She might even invite it into the house of a winter evening, as long as it didn't jump on her bed. There would be no cats on Miss

Jane Hubbell Kinneson's bed, thank you kindly. She pocketed the double eagle, picked up her ox goad, and prepared to head over the ice toward home.

5

MISS JANE'S LEGS were stiff and cold from her long day on the ice. She had intended to ride at least partway home on the sledge, but the monstrous lake trout took up most of the space. An antic notion occurred to her. From the shanty she fetched a short length of rope, which she ran through the trout's mouth and gills. Taking up the free ends like a pair of reins, she sat down astride the fish on the sledge as if it were a horse or pony. "Giddap," she said, laughing at herself. "Giddap, Ethan and Ira."

Miss Jane Hubbell Kinneson, riding a great silver fish across the ice behind two oxen. What a splendid carving it would make for On Kingdom Mountain. This was more like the adventure she had expected a month ago while reading Dickens.

She had not been under way for long when she heard the storm hissing toward her over the ice. It struck so hard and suddenly that she nearly lost her seat on the fish. The oxen staggered in the blast of wind, regained their momentum, stumbled again. Snow pellets flew through the air around them, sizzling off the ice, bouncing off the steers and the sledge and Jane's clothing.

"Trot," she called out to her team. "Trot, boys."

They moved over the ice. The rime-covered fire tower on the mountain summit disappeared in the oncoming snowstorm. The balancing boulder vanished. And then Miss Jane glimpsed a speck in the sky, headed her way above the frozen lake, and heard, over the wind, a faint buzzing. At first it sounded like the humming of bees in the hollyhocks by her woodshed door on an afternoon in haying time. The buzzing grew louder as the flying object approached, now resembling one of the great winged reptiles that she knew had once terrorized the land. But this creature had a double set of wings and, unlike a bird's wings, or even a flying lizard's, they were fixed in place. It was a bright yellow biplane, racing directly up through the notch between the mountains, attempting to outrun the oncoming blizzard.

Miss Jane could see the aviator plainly now, hands dancing over several levers, desperate to keep his craft aloft. The plane's wings, just a few feet above the ice, tilted wildly back and forth. The oxen looked up wonderingly as the yellow biplane roared by just over their heads. On the underside of the bottom wing, in large black letters, were the words HENRY SATTERFIELD'S FLYING CIRCUS RAINMAKING AND PYROTECHNIC SERVICES BEAUMONT TEXAS. Near the end of each wing was the word DARE followed by an illustration of a dapper red devil piloting a biplane. The aviator, meanwhile, was jabbing downward with the forefinger of one gloved hand, indicating that he wished to land. Instantly, Miss Jane pointed back in the direction from which the plane had come, away from the treacherous open water north of the island. The pilot lifted his left hand and gave her a short salute, his hand snapping straight out from his forehead an inch or two and remaining there for a moment, like an upraised hatchet, then dropping back to the controls. The plane banked hard to the east, toward Kingdom Mountain, nearly clipping the soaring blue and emerald ice wall above the lake. Somehow the pilot managed to turn his craft away from the dark water just beyond the island. Barely missing Miss Jane and the oxen, wings wobbling and motor coughing, the plane labored back into the teeth of the storm.

It hit the ice so hard that both wheels broke off. It took a high, crazy bounce, struck the ice again, and skidded sideways. To Miss Jane's horror, the wind got under it and flipped it up on the bottom left wing at a forty-five-degree angle. It whirled around like a giant top, then turned upside down and, still spinning, vanished in the storm.

Miss Jane was running beside the oxen. In order to breathe, she had to turn her head away from the snow-laden wind, which blew with a force she had never before felt. It drove snow under her earlappers, between her scarf and lumber jacket, up under her mittens at the wrists, down her felt boots.

The oxen were indistinct shadows in the snow, and the big togue on the sledge looked like a fish Miss Jane might have sculpted from a block of ice. Then, as suddenly as the storm had struck, the wind and snow let up. The sky lightened and the mountaintop came back into view. It wasn't a blizzard after all, just a squall. Not far away, standing on the rocky tip of the peninsula jutting out into the frozen bay, holding his limp left arm with his right hand but otherwise appearing unharmed, was the pilot. Nearby, wedged between two table-size plates of shore ice, battered but intact except for its wheels, was the yellow biplane. As she hurried toward it across the ice, a phrase ran through Miss Jane's mind: "Recalled to life." Like Dr. Manette in *A Tale of Two Cities*, the aviator had been recalled to life.

The stranger lifted his left arm with his right hand and repeated his odd, hatchetlike salute, though the movement must have caused him pain, because he winced and immediately lowered his injured arm again to a sling position. A slender man with a dark complexion, dark eyes, and dark wavy hair, he appeared to be about forty. Under his open, fleece-lined leather aviator's jacket, he wore a white suitcoat, a white shirt with a black four-in-hand necktie, and a crimson vest. His white slacks were still perfectly creased, and he wore the first pair of white shoes Miss Jane had ever seen on a man's feet. A thin, dark mustache added to his devil-may-care appearance.

Showing gleaming white teeth, he said in a mild drawl, "Henry Satterfield at your service, ma'am. With thanks for your navigational assistance. I do believe you saved my machine out there. Not to mention my life."

He pointed up the lake with the index finger of his left hand, this time without attempting to lift his arm. Miss Jane looked back over her shoulder and was horrified to see a broad corridor of water stretching from Indian Island nearly all the way back to the peninsula. It occurred to her that *she* might be the one recalled to life. If she had delayed her return by just five minutes, she and the oxen would surely have gone to the bottom of the lake in the breakup.

"And this place would be?" Henry Satterfield said, looking around himself with evident interest.

"This is Kingdom County, Mr. Satterfield," Jane said. She pointed at the mountain rising above them in the dusk. "That's Kingdom Mountain, and I'm Jane Hubbell Kinneson."

"Why, this is just the place I've been looking for," Henry Satterfield said. He paused and shook his head. "Kingdom Mountain is the very place I've been looking for nearly all my life. Do you like riddles, Miss Kinneson?"

"I do," she said. "And Jane will do nicely, thank you."

Henry Satterfield bowed slightly. "Very well, then, Miss Jane. I have a riddle for you. Only I must tell you at the outset that I don't have an idea in the world what it might mean. It's called the Riddle of Kingdom Mountain. My grandfather, Captain Cantrell Satterfield, told it to me. It goes like this."

At that instant Henry Satterfield's left arm dropped limply to his side. His right hand moved slowly to his temple, which, Miss Jane now noticed, appeared to be bruised. Then, before he could recite his grandfather's riddle, and before Miss Jane could reach out and break his fall, he collapsed onto the ice-strewn shore.

6

I$_T$ WAS LATE APRIL in Kingdom County. All of the ice had gone out of the lake, and mud season had come and gone. Miss Jane had turned Ethan and General Ira Allen out of the five-story barn into the water meadow along the river below the hemlock-plank covered bridge. Henry Satterfield had been boarding with her on the mountain for more than a month.

The aviator's injuries turned out to be minor — a sprained left arm, now nearly healed, and what Doc Harrison called a very mild concussion that might have caused some slight temporary loss of memory. In other words, a touch of amnesia, which, Doc assured him, would clear up within a few weeks. In the meantime, he prescribed rest. That was fine with Miss Jane, who was greatly enjoying Henry's company. He turned out to be handy with tools, and besides working on his plane, which the oxen had pulled up the pike to the home place, Henry tuned Miss Jane's Model A Ford truck, jacked up her sagging front porch, and cleaned and oiled her treadle-operated sewing machine.

Within twenty-four hours of the stranger's arrival, the entire Common knew that he had wrecked his yellow biplane on the ice of Lake Memphremagog and was now quartered, along with his machine, in Miss Jane's barn, having politely refused to impose upon her by accepting her invitation to stay in the house. He was a little older than Jane had originally surmised, perhaps closer to forty-five than forty. And word quickly spread that Henry was a veteran weathermaker and stunt pilot who had brought rain to drought-afflicted states from Oklahoma to Oregon and put on flying exhibitions from Niagara Falls to Paris, France, though to Miss Jane he modestly confided that he was actually more of a finder than a maker of weather and had never in his life, so far as he knew, truly *caused* it to rain.

Jane was impressed by his candor and impressed as well by his impeccable manners. Whatever else he might be, Henry Satterfield was a gentleman. It was yes, ma'am this and no, thank you, ma'am that, and, like Miss Jane's deep regard for whatever was old-fashioned and traditional, Henry Satterfield's gentlemanliness seemed very genuine, as much a part of his character as, say, his courage aloft and his curiosity. For the aviator was keenly interested, in a decorous and unintrusive way, about everything on the mountain, from Miss Jane's beloved blockheads and dear people in On Kingdom Mountain to the balancing boulder on the mountaintop. He was interested in the home place, with its spacious kitchen workshop, its curved staircase with the bird's-eye maple banister, and the native butternut casings around the doors and windows. He was intrigued by the five-story barn, said to be the biggest barn in the county, and by the covered bridge over the river at the foot of her lane.

Henry loved Miss Jane's icehouse with its sudden miraculous coldness and the fresh, sharp scent of the blocks of ice she had cut on the river the past winter and the bright yellow sawdust it was packed in. He loved to poke around in her root cellar, filled with the sweet fragrance of binned apples, the earthy odor of potatoes, and the salty tang of smoked hams hanging in nets from the timbered ceiling. He enjoyed reading aloud the motto painted on the pine lintel over the porch door by Venturing Seth Kinneson. "They lived in a house at the end of the road and were friends to mankind." Indeed, as Miss Jane told the pilot, the Kingdom Mountain Kinnesons had assisted not just fugitive slaves but French Canadian and Chinese immigrants slipping over the mountain into the United States from Canada and all kinds of wayfarers overtaken by weather, sickness, and injury, even bindlestiffs and tramps off the Grand Trunk Railroad. No one in need had ever been turned away from the home place on Kingdom Mountain. Jane's great-grandfather, Freethinker Kinneson, had famously remarked that if the horned devil himself came looking for shelter, he would probably feel obliged to take the old gentleman in.

Most of all, Henry was interested in Miss Jane's life and times on the mountain, and in her family stories. Evening after evening, as he sat at the applewood kitchen table while she worked on her latest carving project, a tableau of the birds of Kingdom Mountain, she yarned on to him — how Seth had come to the mountain pulling in the yoke with his ox, how Quaker Meeting had discovered Jane's Indian mother, Pharaoh's Daughter, in the manger on Christmas morning, how her father had walked all the way from Kingdom Mountain to Tennessee during the Civil War, searching for his missing brother, Pilgrim.

As for his own past and family, Henry told Miss Jane that he was born and raised in the East Texas town of Beaumont. His father and his grandfather, who had come from North Carolina, that same Captain Cantrell Satterfield who had passed along to Henry the Riddle of Kingdom Mountain, had run a small ranch. His mother, a schoolteacher like Miss Jane and the superintendent of the local Sunday school, was a woman of Creole ancestry.

It was this revelation, made casually one evening, that the showman was of mixed blood, one-half Scotch-Irish and one-half Creole, that prompted Miss Jane to rise from the supper table, go immediately to the five-story barn, where Henry had been staying with his Burgess-Wright airplane, and personally bring his belongings into the house. Refusing to take no for an answer, she established him in the best upstairs bedroom, where her abolitionist ancestors had hidden fugitive slaves.

Tongues wagged in the Common. The gossips on Anderson Hill, the straitlaced old churchwomen and some of the meddling old churchmen as well, whispered that Miss Jane Hubbell Kinneson had taken up with a man of color. The Duchess, of course, was well aware of the gossip, and she was not happy about it. Say what the Common might, however, it would never be said that a Kingdom Mountain Kinneson extended less than the utmost hospitality to a stranger, particularly a stranger from the South whose ancestors Miss Jane's own people had fought to help liberate. "They lived in a house at the end of the road and were friends to mankind."

But as the hardwood buds on the mountain that spring turned from a ruddy red to the faintest gold, a problem arose. Presumably as a result of the mild memory loss Henry Satterfield had sustained in the biplane wreck, all he could recall of the Riddle of Kingdom Mountain was the first word: Behold.

"Behold," the pilot said aloud twenty times a day, raising an index finger as if preparing to declaim the rest. Often it seemed on the tip of his tongue. But that, unfortunately, was as far as he got. Behold what? Henry had no idea.

At these times a somber expression stole across Henry's face, an expression Miss Jane did not think could be quite accounted for by his temporary amnesia. One rainy evening she asked him bluntly if something was troubling him. After hesitating, he told her that because she had been so kind to him, he could no longer conceal from her that some months ago his former partner, wingwalker, and betrothed, one Lola Beauregard

Beauclerk — Beauclerk pronounced without the *k* — of Lake Charles, Louisiana, had met with a horrible fate. While walking on the lower wing of the rainmaker's biplane in a pair of close-fitting black tights, in a cloudless sky above Tulsa, Oklahoma, Miss Lola had been struck by a freakish bolt of lightning and had fallen to her death in the stockyards below. Since then, Henry confided, he had been derailed from time to time by bouts of sorrow.

Miss Jane, putting the finishing touches on a great blue heron preparing to drive its daggerlike bill through the unsuspecting head of a yellow-bibbed bullfrog, was shocked. All she could think to say was, "Mr. Satterfield, do you like to fish?"

"To fish? Why, yes, ma'am, I do. When I was a shaver, I liked to fish with my granddaddy, the old captain. He was a neat hand to catch catfish with a long cane pole and a cork bob, if I do say so."

"Well, then. If this rain keeps up, let's you and I destroy some blue-backed char tomorrow morning."

"That sounds very agreeable to me. But what, if I might inquire, is a blue-backed char?"

"It's the prettiest fish in all creation," Jane said. "You'll see tomorrow. You will *behold* my beautiful blue-backed char. Perhaps they'll put you in mind of your granddaddy's riddle."

"Let us hope so, Miss Jane," the pilot said. "I have the strongest idea that the riddle could be of considerable importance, perhaps of *very* considerable importance, to both of us."

And once again he lifted his finger like a choir director and spoke the word "behold," and spoke it a second time, and then a third. All to no avail. Henry Satterfield, it seemed, could no more remember his grandfather's riddle than climb into his biplane and fly to the moon.

7

JANE'S KNEE-HIGH rubber barn boots swished through the wet grass, as Henry minced along behind her in his white showman's shoes like a cat trying to keep its feet dry. They each carried a bamboo pole and, in a wicker fish basket, a soup can of garden worms. In a pack basket on her back Miss Jane had stashed a number-four iron frying pan, a box of wooden kitchen matches, salt and pepper and cornmeal and butter, four slices of bread, her wooden flask of Who Shot Sam, and two wooden drinking cups she'd carved from beech burls.

Miss Jane had also brought, slung over her shoulder on a strap, a sharpshooter's rifle, Lady Justice, which her father had carried south on his quest to find his missing brother. Lady Justice was a special gun, with over and under barrels. The top barrel fired seven .54 caliber rifle bullets capable of hitting precisely what a good marksman aimed at up to a mile away. The bottom barrel fired buckshot or a slug and could drop a moose or a black bear in its tracks at one hundred yards. Embossed in silver on the stock was the figure of a blindfolded woman holding up a set of scales. It was a formidable weapon, and Henry could not imagine what purpose it could serve on a fishing expedition.

As they hiked up the pike, here just a single-track lane through disused fields, Miss Jane delivered a schoolteacherly lecture on their quarry. "There is a vast difference, Mr. Satterfield, between a common upstart trout and a char. In Vermont, rainbow trout and brown trout are mere Johnny-come-latelies, imported from afar and not worth our attention. But our so-called eastern speckled, or brook, trout are direct descendants of the char conveyed here from the far north ten thousand years ago by the glacier. Let us admit, however, that char are not the most intelligent of the fishes. Not by a long shot."

Abruptly, Miss Jane veered off the lane, marched over to the nearby burn, flipped her worm into the current, hooked a fish, lost it, rebaited, and hooked it again. This time she swung it, bright and splashing, with a distinctly bluish back, out of the water onto the bank. "A brown trout," she said as she dropped the fish into her basket, "would have learned its lesson the first time I hooked it and not returned for another taste of the same. Char, I'm afraid, even my unique blue-backed char, are quite uneducable."

As they fished down the brook together, the sun came out, retreated behind sailing gray clouds, emerged again. Here in the abandoned farmland west of the home place, Miss Jane's fields were rapidly growing back to brush. Thorn apples, gray birch, poplars, and junipers were springing up where sheep and cattle had grazed not so long ago. The borders of the fields were choked with bracken. One by one, the mountain was reclaiming for itself the farms of Miss Jane's ancestors.

Henry was fascinated to learn that each of the pools on the burn had names. Sheep Meadow Pool. Short Sheep Meadow Pool. Somebody's Home, a sweeping curve with an undercut bank where, Miss Jane told him, a trout always seemed to be lurking. Nobody's Home, a hidden pocket behind a black boulder where last year's tall brown grass leaned out from the banks and touched over the narrow channel. You'd think there should always be a fish in Nobody's Home, Miss Jane said, but there hardly ever was.

Late in the morning they entered the bog between the foot of the mountain and the river, where the stream slowed to a dark crawl between thickset cedar trees. Miss Jane usually timed her fishing expeditions so as to arrive at the spawning pool, where the burn ran into the river, around noon. The pool, about two hundred yards long and thirty feet wide, divided her property on the north from Eben Kinneson Esquire's on the south, where work on the right of way for the Connector had already started. Miss Jane and Henry could hear the rumble of machinery and, occasionally, the shouting of loggers in the distance.

The burn entered the big pool between two low, nearly identical knolls, East Round Hill and West Round Hill. The gap between them was known as the Gate to Canada. On the hillsides grew more cedars, hemlocks, some sugar maples, white and yellow birch, beech, basswood, fir, and spruce. The spawning pool was in the shade nearly all day and had a clean gravel bottom. It was about eight feet deep in the middle and refrigerated all summer long by the icy waters coming off the mountain. Here, Miss Jane announced, for untold centuries the blue-backed char of Kingdom Mountain had foregathered in the autumn to hold their annual matrimonial ceremonies.

A mature butternut tree leaned out over the junction of the burn and the spawning pool. Its crooked lower trunk formed a natural seat where Jane loved to sit while she fished. She knew exactly where the largest fish in the pool were and how to give her wriggling angleworm the most natural drift, moving the tip of her pole directly over her line as it went down the current so that there was no drag on the bait. Miss Jane could always tell the difference between a bite and a snag. A fish vibrated the line. Through the quivering leader she felt connected to the river and to her beloved mountain, past and present.

Henry, for his part, was thinking that cedar bogs, like jungles and frozen wastes, were best viewed from aloft and not meant to be tramped through on foot unless you happened to be, say, a wolf or a panther. He wondered if panthers were native to Kingdom Mountain. Very probably. Bank-fishing the little creek that ran through his father's place with his granddaddy the captain had been one thing. This austere northern wilderness was a different matter altogether. What if he'd had to land here in the trees instead of out on the lake? No one would ever have found him.

As they emerged from the corridor of cedars onto the spawning pool, Miss Jane felt some of the old excitement of coming here as a little girl with her father. Today the river would be up from the rain the night before, and high water usually meant good fishing. But suddenly Jane stopped in her tracks. Both sides of the river had been stripped bare of trees. Not a hobblebush or barberry or lone buggy-whip sapling remained standing. Her fishing tree had been sliced off just above the ground. Both hills were crisscrossed with raw gashes of bluish clay and mud. Just upstream from the truncated butternut, a section of bank had slumped into the burn, washing more mud into the river every second. Piles of evergreen slash clogged the spawning pool, choking off its flow in several places. Two tractors were chugging back and forth across the muddy hillsides, leaving deep ruts in their paths. The Gate to Canada had been clear-cut.

The infuriated Duchess found the woods boss, who wore a green wool shirt over a red wool shirt. On his head sat a blue tuque. In a heavy French accent he claimed to work for Eben Kinneson, who owned the paper mill in Kingdom Landing as well as the land across the river. His woods crew had contracted to clear the right of way for the Connector. Eben had given him a map showing him where to cut.

"Well, you've just cut twenty acres of my prime timber," Miss Jane said. "Without my permission."

Twenty acres? The woods boss showed his tobacco-stained teeth. "Mademoiselle, in one little week we cut ten times twenty acres."

"Yes. But those twenty acres belonged to me."

The boss shrugged. From the side pocket of his wool trousers he pulled a round dollar watch. It was twelve o'clock. He got a case of beer out of a cooler and set the bottles, one by one, on a high yellow pine stump, like Rip Van Winkle's tenpins.

"*À table!*" he called out, waving his crew in.

The boss opened a beer, tipped back his head, and emptied the bottle in four or five gulps. He tossed the empty onto a pile of slash and reached for another.

"The fish, too, will come back," he said. "Mademoiselle."

He winked at the men gathering around the stump. A short man with a black patch over one eye like a pirate laughed behind his hand. Unhurriedly, Miss Jane unslung Lady Justice from her shoulder. Using both thumbs she cocked back one of the two big hammers. In a single swift motion she raised the gun to her shoulder and blasted the beer bottles on the stump into a thousand pieces with a load of buckshot.

Through the ringing in his ears Henry Satterfield heard her say, "If any of you gentlemen see Eben Kinneson Esquire before I do, tell him Mademoiselle Jane Hubbell Kinneson of Kingdom Mountain will be paying him a call."

8

THAT AFTERNOON MISS JANE and Henry set out in the Model A truck for Kingdom Landing to beard Eben Kinneson Esquire in his den. Miss Jane wore her long black driving duster, green goggles, and a black motorman's cap with a leather visor. The truck was painted a shiny black, with green and yellow wheel spokes. She drove with one hand on the big wooden knob of the wheel, also painted black. In her other hand she gripped her flask of Who Shot Sam.

Miss Jane drove fifteen miles an hour at all times, in town

and in the country, with her left tires rolling down the exact center of the road. She took great pride in never having run off into the ditch in her entire motoring career. Unfortunately, the same could not be said of the oncoming motorists she encountered. The aviator, who had survived two years flying Sopwith Camels over Germany for the RCAF during the Great War, rode the ten miles from Jane's mountain to Kingdom Landing with one hand braced against the wooden dash panel.

As they approached the Landing, a truck loaded with pulpwood for Eben Kinneson's Great North Woods Pulp and Paper Company came roaring up behind them. Its horn blared out and the driver gestured impatiently for Miss Jane to move over.

"I think he wants to get by," Henry ventured.

"Let him attempt it," Miss Jane said. "He passes me at his peril."

They arrived at the paper mill, with the pulpwood truck riding their rear bumper, in the late afternoon. The weather had turned sunny, but the sky above the town was hazy with smoke from the factory. Sometimes, when the wind was out of the south, Miss Jane could smell its rotten-egg stench on Kingdom Mountain.

Eben's mill, which sprawled along the Lower Kingdom River, was larger than the whole hamlet of Kingdom Landing. A yellow mountain of crushed sulfur loomed up against the smoky sky. Nearby was a huge stack of sawdust and another of pulpwood. More pulp floated in the river. Two sooty brick smokestacks thrust a hundred feet into the air with the words GREAT NORTH WOODS INCORPORATED painted on them. Thick black smoke poured out of the stacks. Along the riverbank sat several dozen identical wooden row houses.

"In those wretched cribs, Mr. Satterfield," Miss Jane said, "dwell my cousin's peons. What a terrible destiny for my beautiful little butternut tree," she continued, pointing at the mountain of pulp. "I will exact retribution in full measure. Do you doubt it?"

Henry did not doubt it, and said as much. He was relieved that Miss Jane had seen fit to leave Lady Justice back at the home place.

On the hill above the factory sat a building the size of a small castle, white with red tile roofs and soaring turrets. A golf course was laid out beside it, bordered by a small lake. This was Eben Kinneson Esquire's Monadnock House, second in grandeur among northern New England resorts only to the fabled Mount Washington Hotel in New Hampshire. Miss Jane frowned up at it. "How visitors can come to this pestilential town is beyond me. My cousin hopes to add Kingdom Mountain to his holdings and develop a great winter spa there, where roistering layabouts with too much time on their hands will slide downhill on staves by day and fornicate by night. I trust you are not a skier, Mr. Satterfield?"

"No, ma'am, I am not," Henry replied, hoping that Miss Jane would not proceed to inquire whether he was a fornicator.

"Good." Miss Jane steered her Model A with its carnival wheels up to the main gate of the mill. "I mean good that you are not a skier. I have no use for them."

A guard in a blue uniform sat in a white booth hardly larger than a dollhouse. The Duchess rolled down her side curtain. "I am Jane Hubbell Kinneson from Kingdom Mountain," she said. "I wish to see Eben Kinneson Esquire about a criminal act."

The guard stared at Miss Jane, resplendent in her motoring outfit, as though she'd stepped out of another dimension. "Mr. Kinneson isn't in, Miss Kinneson. If you'd like to park in the visitors' lot, I'll take you to see Mr. Brown, the plant manager."

As they walked across the parking lot, the guard had to speak loudly to make himself heard over the deafening rumble of a whirling elevated drum as large as one of the row houses along the river. Inside this gigantic metal cylinder thousands of four-foot-long pulp sticks tumbled together at a furious rate to remove their bark. Nearby was a huge vat, which, the guard explained, was full of acid to decompose the peeled wooden sticks into fibers to make paper. They entered the factory, where endless rolls of snow white paper ten feet wide spun off revolving spools. Immense swordlike cutters snapped off newsprint-sized sheets. The steel-decked floor vibrated beneath their feet in time with the rumbling machinery. Henry was interested in the papermaking process, but Miss Jane was not. As she stalked across the shaking floor, looking neither right nor left, the workers stared at her.

Mr. Brown worked in a glass-enclosed office on the far side of the mill floor. He was a harried-looking man with a green bookkeeper's visor, which, Miss Jane was certain, he wore so that he wouldn't have to look anyone in the eye. "State your business," he said without looking up.

"I shall state my business," Miss Jane replied. "Some trespassing rapscallions who work for this concern sashayed onto my mountain and cut a great deal of valuable timber without authorization. I want you to tell Mr. Eben Kinneson Esquire that Miss Jane Hubbell Kinneson is here to see him."

"Mr. Kinneson isn't here, Miss Kinneson. I believe he's up at his private trout pond."

"Char," Miss Jane said.

"Char?"

"Not trout," she said. "Char. Come along, Mr. Satterfield."

Back across the mill floor she marched, with the white-clad aviator hurrying at her side, past the staring workers, out the door, and beneath the whirling debarker, straight to the Model A. She drove down the middle of the single street of the company town at her usual pace. A coal truck headed their way ran up onto the curb, blowing a front tire with a loud report. For a terrible moment Henry feared that he might have been shot.

PRIVATE ROAD FOR GUESTS ONLY announced a sign beside a steep road winding up to Monadnock House. Without slowing down, Miss Jane swerved onto the private road, very nearly oversetting her high-topped truck.

They passed the horseshoe-shaped lake, where a guest in a tweed jacket was fly-casting at one end. Ahead a golfer, tall and thin, with straight black hair parted in the middle, was crossing the road. He wore a knit sweater and spiked golfing shoes and carried a golfing bag. Miss Jane gave a blast on her klaxon, and Eben Kinneson Esquire scowled at the Model A. Then he continued walking toward the green near the pond.

Miss Jane left the Ford running in the middle of the road and approached the green with Henry in tow. On the hillside above them Eben's resort gleamed in the late-afternoon sunshine. "Golf links," Miss Jane said. "And a private fishing pond. Remark upon all this opulence, Mr. Satterfield. Thoreau, ordinarily the most insufferable of pronouncers and proclaimers, was on one occasion half right. Not necessarily the mass of men, but many rich men, lead lives of desperation. Not so very quietly, either.

"Hello, Eben," she said. "I scarcely recognized you in your fancy footwear. I can remember when you went to school barefoot. This is my friend Mr. Henry Satterfield, of Beaumont, Texas. Mr. Satterfield is a renowned aviator and meteorologist."

"I know who and what Mr. Satterfield is," Eben said with the air of a man who knows everything about everybody.

Eben stepped up to his ball and stroked it briskly past the pin, off the green, and into some cattails beside the lake. He frowned in the direction of the errant golf ball as if it had personally offended him.

"The aim of this game, cousin," Miss Jane said, "as invented by our Scottish ancestors, is to knock the ball into the cup, not the horse pond."

"That is no horse pond but my private speckled trout lake."

"Char," Miss Jane corrected him. "Which brings me to my purpose. Your cutters came onto my land without permission and felled several hundred trees and laid waste to the spawning pool where my blue-backed char have perpetuated their kind since time out of mind. I hold you and you alone accountable."

"You have been offered generous restitution, cousin, for the small amount of land appropriated by the township for the right of way for the Connector. However, I will recommend that the highway be rerouted, away from your trout pool and up the pike road."

"There will be no highway on my mountain, period. What's more, I want you to pay me a thousand dollars for the stolen timber. It will cost at least that much to replant the Gate to Canada with seedlings. Also, I expect you to fill in those ruts, which will turn into little mud-choked rivers every time it rains. Pull the slash out of the burn and the river, dump gravel and sand into the pool where it's been washed out, put some crib dams on the brook, and replace my butternut fishing tree."

"Why, that's absurd. All that would cost many thousands of dollars," Eben said as he headed toward the driving tee of the next hole. "I am a very conservation-minded man, cousin. But I did not rise to become owner of the Great North Woods Pulp and Paper Company by throwing away money. I hear, by the way, that in confronting my crew, you weren't content to rely entirely on verbal persuasion."

"Your crew is fortunate not to be in the morgue. I shall see you in court, cousin."

For the first time since Miss Jane and Henry had arrived at the golf course, Eben Kinneson Esquire smiled. "Court, cousin Jane, is my bailiwick. You will indeed see me there if you persist with this nonsense. Meeting me in court will not be an enjoyable experience, I assure you."

"It may or may not be an enjoyable experience. But I will find satisfaction there."

"You will lose the case and be out your timber and court costs for bringing a frivolous action when generous compensation was proffered." So saying, the attorney approached his teed-up golf ball, addressed it with a confident waggle of his club head, and executed a mighty swing. The ball toppled off the white wooden tee and dribbled five feet.

Miss Jane reached down, picked up the dubbed ball, and, like a housewife tossing spilled salt, flipped it over her left shoulder into the lake. Then she and Henry returned to her Ford.

9

IT WOULD BE INCORRECT to give the impression that Miss Jane Hubbell Kinneson of Kingdom Mountain was a hermit. In fact, she was quite sociable. With the exception of whiskey runners and revenuers who violated her rule of fifteen miles per hour at all times, game wardens, whom she detested on principle, and border officials "whose border didn't exist and never had," Jane welcomed all visitors to her mountain. And she loved going into the village several times a week.

True, Miss Jane's dealings with many of the villagers, particularly with the town fathers promoting the Connector, were somewhat strained. In Kingdom County in those days a certain tension existed between villagers and country people. It was reflected in the rivalry between town kids — townies — and kids from the surrounding farms and mountain hollows, known as woodchucks. Yet the split ran deeper than that. Jane's own high school days had been fraught with conflict, and she readily acknowledged that she had greatly contributed to it by striving to be the best at everything, even demanding to pitch for the boys' baseball nine. Then, of course, there was her shocking valedictory speech. Yet for many years the village had depended on her civic services far more than she depended on the pittance she received for performing them.

Some years Miss Jane made an adequate income from her carved birds and folk figures. Had she been willing to carve waterfowl decoys for hunters, she would have earned considerably more. But this she absolutely refused to do because, though she loved to hunt ducks herself, she regarded the use of decoys as a most detestable kind of entrapment. She made some pin money from the beautiful sweetgrass baskets and white-ash pack baskets her Memphremagog grandmother, Canada Jane Hubbell, had taught her to weave. Miss Jane's baskets were so tightly woven they would hold water. She proclaimed that they would outlast their owner and guaranteed her work by promising to replace any basket that didn't. One day a villager named White, who had bought one of Jane's baskets for his wife, showed up with its crushed remains, demanding a refund. He was a mean man, known for being cruel to his family and animals alike, and it was obvious to Miss Jane that he had somehow contrived to run over the basket with his buggy or that a horse had stepped on it. Nevertheless, she handed him his two-dollar refund without a word. As he was reaching for his buggy whip to lash up his horse, he said in a surly voice, "You said that no-good basket would outlast me, Jane Kinneson."

To which Miss Jane instantly replied, "Mr. White, if you'd died when you should've, it would've."

Miss Jane didn't need much income. She burned her own

wood, ate her own venison, moose, and trout, cultivated a large kitchen garden, cut her ice on the river, compounded her own medicines, walked all over her mountain for exercise, and had no taxes or electric or phone bills to pay. And she did earn a little cash from her various jobs in the village.

For the most part, these were jobs no one else wanted. First, she was the overseer of the poor, the elected official responsible for disbursing emergency funds to the indigent of the township. Usually the local overseer was, by default, a hard-bitten old farmer or tightfisted shopkeeper. But in Kingdom Common, year in and year out, Jane was "put up for election" and unanimously chosen for the job. She was good at rallying family and neighborhood support for the down-and-out and at helping people find work. Often enough, when she ran out of town funds, she assisted people out of her own pocket. In 1930, the year Henry Satterfield came to Kingdom Mountain, Miss Jane was paid a total of eighty-five dollars for her work as overseer. For a number of years she had coached the girls' basketball and baseball teams at the Kingdom Common Academy. When old Coach Sanville died, she took the boys' baseball nine to two state championships. She put on plays, helped with all kinds of fundraisers, and showed movies every Friday night at the town hall. Best of all, she enjoyed her work at the Atheneum, her small free library and bookshop next to the Academy, where, in her capacity as bookwoman extraordinaire, Miss Jane presided over the literary affairs of the village, matching books and readers, helping grammar school children with their homework and highschoolers with their term papers, even sponsoring a series of lectures and symposia. It was one of these events that she planned to surprise Henry with on the evening of their visit to Eben Kinneson's Great North Woods Pulp and Paper Company and Monadnock House.

The Atheneum was housed in an ancient stone cottage,

originally belonging to an ancestor of Judge Allen. When the family moved to the large brick residence on Anderson Hill where the widower judge now lived alone, he had donated the building to the village for use as a library. Although Henry had heard much about the library and bookstore, and about Miss Jane's literary evenings, he had not yet visited the Atheneum and was most curious to see the establishment.

The event was scheduled for seven and, after a quick supper at the Common Hotel, which Jane insisted on paying for, they arrived half an hour early. The Atheneum was not much larger than Miss Jane's former one-room school. It was lighted by a glass chandelier, originally designed to hold candles but now electrified. The walls were lined from floor to ceiling with dark varnished shelves containing thousands of books. Ranged around the room, seated at library tables and in creaky wooden Morris chairs or standing at the shelves poring over the spines of leather-bound sets of authors Henry had heard about from his schoolteacher mother were a dozen or so wooden figures whom Jane referred to as her scribblers and scrawlers.

Like Jane's beloved blockheads and her dear people in On Kingdom Mountain, the scribblers and scrawlers were life-size, with oblong craniums and painted features. One by one, Miss Jane introduced them to the pilot. At a table near the door, bent over an open volume of *Pride and Prejudice,* sat Jane's co-namesake and all-time favorite author, Jane Austen. She had light brown hair and, naturally, Miss Jane's gray eyes, wore a blue gown and a white blouse with lace at the throat and wrists, and was as narrow-waisted as a schoolgirl. Jane Austen had rather sharp features. Henry suspected that she had a sharp tongue as well.

Standing nearby, tall and handsome, was the young poet Robert Frost. Miss Jane told Henry that on several occasions Mr. Frost had visited Kingdom Mountain to botanize with her for alpine plants. And once he had come to the Atheneum to read his poetry. Henry recognized Mark Twain, who had also visited the Common to lecture when Jane was a small girl. She had gone to hear him with her father, who had taken her up to meet the great humorist after his talk. Morgan Kinneson had told Twain that the evening was so hilarious it was all he could do not to laugh out loud.

Slouched into a Boston rocker near the fireplace, his vast girth overflowing the flat wooden arms of the chair, a little gray unkempt wig askew on his large, oblong head, sat a great bear of a man. "Mr. Satterfield, may I present the incomparable Proclaimer of Litchfield, Dr. Samuel Johnson. Doctor, my friend Henry Satterfield." On the lap of the incomparable proclaimer reposed Dr. Johnson's own dictionary of the English language. It was open to the *O* section, the first entry of which, "Oats," was defined as "a grain, which is generally given to horses, but in Scotland supports the people." Through this witticism at the expense of her Scottish ancestors Miss Jane had drawn a firm blue line. Later that spring Henry would learn that she had excised hundreds of sentences, paragraphs, and even entire pages from the books lining the walls of the Atheneum, a process she called "editing down the classics," in accordance with Rule Three of her "Precepts for the Serious Bookperson." There were five precepts in all, and they were posted, in Miss Jane's fine hand, on the inside of the door.

1. Never sell a book for less than you paid for it.
2. But it's perfectly allowable to give books away.
3. Nearly every book should be shorter.
4. "Of making many books there is no end." (Thankfully.) Ecclesiastes 12:12.
5. There is absolutely no money to be made in selling, lending, reading, teaching, publishing, or writing of books. All are labors of love.

"Good evening to you, my friend," Jane greeted a careworn middle-aged scribbler toiling over a mountainous manuscript. "Mr. Satterfield, say how do you do to Mr. Charles Dickens, the most magnanimous and hardest-working novelist of all time."

Miss Jane seemed very fond of all her scribblers and scrawlers, even "persnickety old Henry David Thoreau, Pronouncer and Proclaimer nonpareil." Thoreau, seated on a bench beside a beautiful wooden loon, looked rather somberly at the edition of *Walden* in his hands, in which Miss Jane had summarily blue-penciled out nearly half of the text, including the entire chapter entitled "Economy."

Or, rather, she seemed fond of all of her scribblers with two exceptions. At the rear of the library, near the alcove leading to her shop of new and rare books, was a carved fellow with a high, broad forehead, otherwise quite simian-looking, hunched over a workbench on which lay a half-finished pair of ladies' gloves. "William Shakespeare, Mr. Satterfield," Jane said contemptuously. "The Pretender of Avon and the subject of my lecture this evening." Finally, Jane beckoned Henry into the little annex shop, scarcely larger than a walk-in closet, where, enthroned in a gilded armchair, wearing a crimson robe and a gilt crown, sat "the most villainous impostor who ever set pen to paper. King James the First, author of the King James Bible," which Jane had been assiduously revising for thirty-two years.

Three people showed up for Jane's lecture. Sadie Blackberry, the village berry picker, was a tiny woman in a long dress and a Mother Hubbard bonnet, with a dark, nutlike face and bright black eyes like the berries she was named for. A Number One, the fabled Grand Trunk Railroad tramp who had chalked his distinctive signature on the sides of hundreds of North Country eateries, outhouses, barn doors, and boxcars, had spent the last several years in retirement at the Common Hotel, majestically lifting his hand in greeting to the engineers of the passing trains. And Jane introduced to Henry a tall, distinguished-looking man of about her own age as her longtime friend and fishing partner, Judge Ira Allen.

Miss Jane's lecture was, as she had promised, a spirited attack on William Shakespeare and his benighted advocates. Her thesis was that the seventeenth Earl of Oxford, Edward de Vere, had authored each of the plays attributed to the Pretender of Avon. Henry was baffled by her presentation, and Judge Allen seemed, from his all-too-polite silence, to be skeptical about her theory. "In conclusion," the Duchess proclaimed, glaring at Henry and the judge and beaming at Sadie and A Number One, who were busy washing down her homemade lemon scones with cups of hot tea, "do you think it's even remotely conceivable that this unlettered clown, this low, sneaking, untutored, ill-favored strolling player and glover's apprentice penned the fabled 'Sceptred Isle' piece? No, he did not. Nor any of the thirty-six plays erroneously attributed to him. All were the work of the much-maligned seventeenth Earl." She pointed an accusing finger at the Pretender of Avon and thundered, "You, sir, are a fraud!"

Including a ten-minute digression to attack "the Pronouncer of Concord" and "the Proclaimer of Litchfield," Miss Jane had spoken nonstop for a solid hour. Henry clapped enthusiastically. A Number One emitted a long, appreciative locomotive whistle. Sadie shook her tiny fist in Will Shakespeare's face. Judge Allen congratulated Miss Jane on a most vigorous argument, checked out *The Hound of the Baskervilles,* bought a well-used copy of *The Country of the Pointed Firs,* and went home to read. All in all, for Miss Jane Hubbell Kinneson of Kingdom Mountain, the tea-and-scones literary evening at the Atheneum had been a pretty successful conclusion to a trying day.

10

W HEN HENRY SATTERFIELD, dressed all in white, slender and handsome and smiling amiably, strolled into the Kingdom County courtroom in the Common with Miss Jane a week later, some of the spectators mistook him for her attorney. Henry, for his part, was impressed by Jane's amazingly confident bearing. Arranging her brief at the plaintiff's table to the left of the aisle in front of the judge's bench, nodding familiarly to the spectators and the court clerk, she seemed as much at home here as in her kitchen workshop on Kingdom Mountain.

Eben Kinneson Esquire sat at the defense table to the right of the aisle. For a weekday morning there was a good crowd of curiosity seekers in the courtroom, many of whom had undoubtedly come to get a good look at the exotic southerner staying with Miss Jane.

As usual, Jane wore a black homespun dress, high-buttoned black shoes, and her frayed red and green wool hunting jacket fastened with the large safety pin she called her everyday brooch. Her hair was pulled back into a severe schoolteacher's bun. A cardboard file fastened with black strings lay on the table in front of her. She had also brought along the homemade ash pointer she had used in her capacity as mistress of the Kinnesonville school.

To a medley of clinking, clanking, and hissing from the steam radiators, Judge Ira Allen entered the courtroom. He began the proceedings in genial fashion by announcing that, next to an old-fashioned wood stove, steam was the most even and comfortable heat going, if the loudest. "You, sir," he said, pointing at a talkative radiator in the far back corner. "Are you quite finished? May we proceed?" The radiator behind his bench let out a derisive hiss. "Who asked you?" the judge said, to chuckles from everyone but Miss Jane and Eben Kinneson Esquire.

The large wooden blades of the propeller fans suspended from the stamped tin ceiling whirred around and around. A freight train rumbled through the village. The yard locomotive shifting cars at the American Heritage furniture mill behind the courthouse hooted. Couplings slammed together. Then the mill whistle shrieked out for the 9:30 break. The judge smiled and shook his head. He liked to say that his was a working courtroom in a working town, and that was just the way he liked it. Ira Allen had been born and brought up in Kingdom County and had deep family roots there. Jane had told Henry earlier that morning that she and the judge had vied for the honor of valedictorian at the Kingdom Common Academy. She, of course, had won.

Eventually the freight passed, the yard engine finished making up the local, the radiators subsided into a steady, whispering conspiracy, and the judge called the court to order. He looked at Eben over the top of his reading spectacles. "Where are your clients, sir?"

"I'm representing myself, Your Honor."

"Isn't the new road, the Connector, a town road? Where are the selectmen of the town of Kingdom Common?"

"Your Honor, my clients are exceedingly busy men. Their time is very valuable, so they have asked me to represent them today and to convey their regrets that they could not be here."

"Just how valuable is the selectmen's time, Eben?"

"How valuable?"

"Yes. How valuable per day do you estimate the selectmen's time to be?"

"I should hazard, Your Honor, that their combined time is worth a cool hundred dollars a day."

"Well, Eben, that is very impressive. Please thank the selectmen for conveying their regrets that they could not come to court this morning, as summoned, to explain why I should not grant Miss Jane's request for an immediate injunction to prevent the Connector from infringing on her property. And please convey the following message to them. That, notwithstanding their exceedingly busy schedule, they will appear in person at these proceedings and that, furthermore, I am fining them one hundred dollars per day for each day they miss, starting today, up to the end of this workweek, at which time I will issue a summary ruling in favor of Miss Jane Hubbell Kinneson of Kingdom Mountain."

Here Judge Allen was interrupted by a veritable ovation of clattering from all of the radiators at once. But he was not quite finished. "Also, kindly inform your clients that I am an avid fisherman myself," he said. "An avid speckled trout fisherman."

"Char," Miss Jane said.

"Pardon me?"

"Technically, Ira, there's no such fish as a speckled trout. They're char. Therefore, you are a char fisherman."

"This has not been a banner morning in my life," Judge Allen said. "I am about to go trout — *char* — fishing myself. These proceedings will be renewed afresh tomorrow. Let us all hope that we will get off to a more promising start."

11

Ten thousand years ago," Miss Jane began her testimony the next morning, "Kingdom County was a boreal fastness of soaring mountains, free-running rivers, and dense coniferous forests."

She was standing at the front of the courtroom, gesturing with her schoolteacher's pointer at some crude mountains she'd sketched on a portable blackboard. For all her great gifts as a sculptor, the Duchess couldn't draw a lick, a fact that somehow endeared her to Henry Satterfield, who again sat beside her at the plaintiff's table in his gleaming white suit, newly whitewashed shoes, and crimson vest.

The three selectmen of Kingdom Common, President George Quinn of the First Farmers and Lumberers Bank, Prof Chadburn, headmaster of the Kingdom Common Academy, and the Reverend, from the Congregational church, sat with Eben Kinneson Esquire at the defense table.

At the blackboard Miss Jane stood as straight as the tree her white-ash pointer had come from. As always, she wore black, with no jewelry or makeup. But this morning her light hair cascaded down her back. She certainly didn't look like a spinster schoolteacher, but rather, Henry thought admiringly, like an exceedingly attractive middle-aged woman. And the rainmaker, watching with courteous, unobtrusive interest, was sure that Miss Jane knew it. Showman that he was, Henry Satterfield was quite vain of his own appearance, and he sensed, perhaps, an opportunity here. Exactly what kind of opportunity, however, even he could not have said.

"Ten thousand years ago," Miss Jane repeated, "the place

that we now call Kingdom County would have been scarcely recognizable to us. The mountains were thrice their current height. The forests were uninhabited, even by my mother's Memphremagog ancestors. Now enter the great ice sheet —"

"Objection, Your Honor," Eben Kinneson Esquire interrupted. "We all appreciate the fact that my cousin is an able lecturer. But what bearing does the glaciation of northern New England have upon the town's very generous offer to pay her three times the value of the land appropriated for the right of way and to reroute the Connector around her beloved spawning pool?"

"Jane?" Judge Allen said.

"A gang of Frenchmen in the pay of the Great North Woods Pulp and Paper Company waltzed onto my property without my permission and destroyed the last tract of original forest on Kingdom Mountain. They wantonly despoiled a stretch of river where the descendants of the unique blue-backed char that came south with the glacier have spawned for thousands of years."

"Judge Allen," Eben said, "we must protest. Miss Kinneson's reputation as a venerable fixture of Kingdom County notwithstanding, even she was not here to witness those fish spawning thousands of years ago, and so cannot speak with authority on how long the spawning beds have —"

Crack. Before Eben Kinneson Esquire could finish his sentence, Miss Jane reached across the aisle and brought her wooden pointer smartly down on his knuckles. The astonished attorney gave a yelp and half rose.

"That, sir, is how I dealt with impudence in my schoolroom," Miss Jane said. "It is how I deal with your impudence. Sit down and curb your impertinent tongue."

Eben Kinneson Esquire rubbed his knuckles. A smile played at the corners of Henry Satterfield's mouth, and his dark eyes gleamed. But Judge Allen brought down his gavel with a bang.

"Jane, there will be no more corporal punishment meted out in this courtroom. As for you, Eben, stop your whining. There will be no more unchivalrous references to the plaintiff's longevity, either. Hear me well, my friends. This is not Kingdom Mountain nor yet the august headquarters of the Great North Woods Pulp and Paper Company, Incorporated. It is my courtroom. In it we will conduct ourselves with a measure of civility. Jane, you may proceed with your opening statement. Please do us the kindness of making it shorter rather than longer."

"Kingdom Mountain has always been regarded as a gore," she said quite defiantly, "one of the last in Vermont. In other words, an unincorporated township unto itself. No Kingdom Mountain Kinneson has ever paid a penny of local, state, or federal taxes. The mountain belongs to me and to me alone. I am requesting one thousand dollars as reparation for my timber and an injunction to prevent the high road from crossing my property. Case closed."

Jane sat down at the plaintiff's table beside Henry.

"That's all?" Eben said.

"How long does it take to chronicle a grievous wrong and propose a way to right it? The truth, cousin, need never be long in the telling. The floor belongs to you."

Eben Kinneson Esquire smiled thinly and stood up. Continuing to rub his reddened left knuckles with his right hand, he said, with a superior air, "Your honor, the Great North Woods Pulp and Paper Company and the township of Kingdom Common acknowledge that one of their subcontractors cut a few hundred dollars' worth of timber on Miss Kinneson's property. No doubt some minor alterations were made to the riverine terrain. No documented injury was suffered by the fish. Have any dead fish been exhibited before the court? No. Has the defense produced any witnesses? No again. The Great North Woods Company, however, will produce witnesses. *We* will follow proper courtroom protocol. But why waste the time of the court at all? The town of Kingdom Common has already offered Miss Jane one thousand dollars for the right of way over Kingdom Mountain. Also, the town is willing to route the Connector around my cousin's spawning pool. Indeed, the original right of way map provided to the cutting crew circumvented the pool in question. But instead of referring the matter to me or to the town fathers, Jane Kinneson assaulted my loggers with a deadly weapon."

Judge Allen did not seem much impressed by the last allegation. "Are you ready to call your first witness, Eben?"

Eben's first witness was the Canadian crew chief. With some difficulty, because of Monsieur Thibideau's heavy accent, Eben established that Thibideau had been given a topographical map with the right of way and the condemned property outlined on its contours. The map was produced, and in her cross-examination Miss Jane asked Thibideau to read the legend at its bottom.

The crew chief grinned. "I can't, me."

"Why not? Surely you can read?"

"*Oui*. In French."

Next a college-trained forester, billed as an expert witness for the defense, testified that he had examined the stream in question a few days earlier and found no dead fish.

"A query, forester," Miss Jane said. "Did you secure permission to check the fish in my spawning pool?"

"Certainly. From Mr. Kinneson."

"Let me understand this. My cousin gave you permission to come onto my land to manufacture evidence to use against me in court?"

"Objection, Your Honor," Eben Kinneson Esquire said. "Because of the way that question is —"

"I withdraw the query," Miss Jane said. To the forester she said, "If I see you again on Kingdom Mountain, I won't answer for the consequences."

"Your Honor," Eben said, "the sectors of Kingdom Mountain that lie south of the forty-fifth parallel of latitude, designated as the international border between Vermont and Quebec, clearly belong in the township of Kingdom Common. The township is well within its rights to drive a road over the mountain, connecting the county to the Eastern Townships of Quebec and thence to Montreal. Indeed, the so-called Canada Pike Road running over the mountain has never been officially abandoned by the township. If necessary, my clients can simply route the right of way along the pike road. Miss Jane may own Kingdom Mountain. She does not own the road connecting it to Canada."

"Jane, do you wish to make a closing statement?" Judge Allen said.

"I do," she said. "The woodland splendors of the Gate to Canada have been destroyed. I ask for one thousand dollars as reparation for the cut timber. As for the Canada Pike Road, it's been all but impassable for decades. Neither the township of Kingdom Common nor the state of Vermont nor the United States of America nor the Dominion of Canada owns one square inch of Kingdom Mountain. It belongs to me and me alone.

"There will be no high road," she continued. "I end with a gloss of the famous words of old Cato, who concluded each of his speeches to the Roman Senate, no matter the topic, with the urgent reminder *Carthage delendo est*. Carthage must be destroyed." Miss Jane paused. Then, in a stentorian voice worthy of old Cato himself, she roared out, "*Via alta delendo est*, my good people. The high road must be destroyed."

Judge Allen sighed and retired to his chambers to deliberate. Miss Jane remained sitting at the plaintiff's table with Henry. From time to time she tapped her pointer on the edge of the table and glared meaningfully at Eben Kinneson Esquire, the knuckles of whose left hand were now visibly swollen.

"Well, well," said the judge, returning to the courtroom sooner than expected. "The Canada Pike Road reminded me of a story, folks. You've all heard it said that we Kingdomers don't need to travel the world because everyone worth knowing will eventually come to the Kingdom? Were you aware that in 1904 President Teddy Roosevelt came to Kingdom County?"

"Everyone knows that tale, Ira," Miss Jane said. "Render your verdict."

Unperturbed, Judge Allen continued his anecdote. "Teddy traveled here to testify in person, in a libel suit that he was bringing against the *Kingdom County Monitor*. Old editor James Kinneson had called Teddy a 'porky flatlander' in the pages of the *Monitor* and somehow Teddy caught wind of it and came rampaging up to the Kingdom to join combat. The courtroom was packed. The president said he'd plead guilty to being a bit on the rotund side, but by jingo, he was no flatlander. T.R. pounded the plaintiff's table with his fist and said he'd hunted mountain lions in the Rockies with Zane Grey and written books on the Adirondacks and that he was a country boy and a mountain boy born and bred, and no man jack in the universe could prove differently. Everybody liked T.R. and was highly indignant that Editor K had calumniated him. The jury wasn't out five minutes. In they paraded, finding for the president. There was no doubt, they said, that he'd been libeled." Judge Allen glanced around to be sure everyone was listening. "Then they fined Editor Kinneson five cents. The price, at the time, of a copy of the *Monitor*."

The judge continued, "In the case of Miss Jane Hubbell Kinneson versus Eben Kinneson and the Town of Kingdom Common, I find the town liable for damages to Miss Kinneson's hillside amounting to five hundred dollars' worth of timber."

For a moment it appeared to Henry as though Miss Jane had

adjudicated herself right out of five hundred dollars. But the judge wasn't finished.

"Also," he said, "I find the Town of Kingdom Common and the Great North Woods Pulp and Paper Company liable for causing significant damage to Kingdom Mountain Burn and the Upper East Branch of the Kingdom River, and especially to the spawning bed of Miss Jane's char. Therefore, I rule that under the personal supervision of Eben Kinneson and the selectmen of Kingdom Common, the Great North Woods Pulp and Paper Company will fully restore the stream and river to their previous condition and reforest the Gate to Canada. As for the right of way for the Connector, it's the ruling of this court that the Connector can go out around Kingdom Mountain, as sensible people who wish to travel to Canada have been doing for the past two hundred years. That road is not to impinge on Miss Jane's property."

"Objection!" Eben Kinneson Esquire cried out. "Objection, Your Honor. We will pay for the timber and have a crew replant the hillside. But this court has no legal authority to impose any personal conditions on me or on the town fathers. Or to rule on the right of way."

Down came Judge Allen's gavel. "Oh, yes it does, in both cases," the judge said. "I hereby stipulate that the reforestation and the stocking will be conducted under the direct supervision of the owner of the Great North Woods Pulp and Paper, Inc., Eben Kinneson. Moreover, I intend to be there to volunteer my own services. Other volunteers will apply directly to Miss Jane Hubbell Kinneson of Kingdom Mountain. The work will begin tomorrow at eight A.M., with a one-hundred-dollar-a-day fine for every day of delay. As for the right of way, and the prerogatives of the court, this is the district court of Kingdom County. It has complete jurisdiction over any and all monkeyshines and shenanigans of questionable legality in the county.

You're entitled to appeal the decision, Eben, if you and your clients don't like it. I, for one, don't want that highway anywhere near those blue-backed char or Miss Jane's mountain. Eight o'clock tomorrow morning, gentlemen. Sharp."

12

Half the population of the village traipsed out to Kingdom Mountain the next day to participate in the reforestation project, and for once the weather on the mountain cooperated. It was warm and clear, a perfect day in early May.

The reseeding crew was there by eight, along with Eben Kinneson Esquire. Judge Ira Allen, in his hiking boots and a lumber jacket, worked as hard as anyone. The crew pulled the evergreen slash out of the brook, dumped several wagonloads of clean gravel into the river, filled in the ruts on the cutover hillside, seeded it down with wild grass seed, and planted new fir and spruce seedlings. Eben worked side by side with Miss Jane, Judge Allen, and numerous Commoners. Henry Satterfield, in his gleaming white suit, watched the entire proceedings with a bemused expression. At noon Miss Jane fed everyone baked beans, fried chicken, pickles, homemade bread, and her famous no-egg chocolate wonder cake. The day had the gala air of a barn-raising bee.

That evening, after everyone else had gone home, Judge Allen showed up on Miss Jane's porch with an old bitters bottle he'd found near the Gate to Canada. In it he'd arranged a few yellow woods violets and white and pink spring beauties. Henry saw the judge coming as he was headed out to the barn to inventory the parts he would need to repair his biplane.

The aviator slipped inside the woodshed, leaving the door ajar, while Miss Jane and Ira met on the porch near Jane's Virginia creeper.

"Jane," the judge said, "I want you to know that I expect nothing. Nor did I expect anything when I was considering your case or helping replant your trees. But if you're ever inclined to look down at the village from my home on Anderson Hill, I'd be the happiest man in Kingdom County."

"Why," Miss Jane said after a slight hesitation, "you're a dear old fool, Ira Allen, and come to think of it, I'm no better. What, pray, would a hardscrabble hill farmer like me do with a home in the village? These days I scarcely know what to do with my own home. Still, I thank you kindly for the offer."

There was a lingering moment of silence. Henry peered around the corner of the shed door, but Miss Jane and the judge had stepped out of his line of view behind the creeper.

That night, however, after they had retired for the evening, Miss Jane called up to Henry in his upstairs room through a hole in the ceiling of her bedchamber, "I have an admission to make to you, Mr. Satterfield."

The hole, fitted with an iron grating that could be opened from Henry's room to admit heat rising from the chamber below, seemed to amplify their voices.

"An admission, Miss Jane?"

"Yes. Some time ago, I mentioned to you that Judge Allen and I were school chums."

"You did. No one who didn't know would ever guess it, though. You look, if I may say so, twenty years younger than the judge."

"Pshaw. But it is time for me to 'fess up. Judge Allen and I were not merely school chums. He was, for a time, my admirer."

"I can easily believe that, ma'am."

"One of several."

"I believe that, as well."

"I was too proud, however, to encourage them. In the case of young Ira, who was a fine lad and has certainly turned into a fine man, I was half again too proud to declare myself to him. He married someone else and, though she died recently, I think they were happy together. I also think that he never entirely forgot me."

"I think so, too, Miss Jane," Henry said gallantly. "I do think so, too."

"Thank you again, sir. But why, then, didn't I accept Judge Allen's offer tonight? Don't pretend you weren't eavesdropping. I know better. I would have been eavesdropping had the situation been reversed."

"I don't know why, Miss Jane."

"Well, I don't, either," Jane said, perhaps a bit ruefully. "Henry?"

It was the first time she had called the pilot by his given name.

"Yes, ma'am?"

"When next you fall in love with a beautiful young woman, like the beautiful and ill-fated Lola Beauregard Beauclerk of Lake Charles, Louisiana, you must declare yourself to her. Her answer may be yea, it may be nay. But you must declare yourself. Do you understand me?"

"Yes, Miss Jane."

"No, you do not," she said fiercely. "After your great tragedy, you cannot suppose that you will ever again fall in love. But you will, for that is the way of the world. Strife is the way of the world. So is falling in love. In the meantime, one of us is going to receive an important letter soon."

"How do you know that?"

"I can't say. Any more than I can say how I know that you must declare yourself to the person you love. Second sight is a strange creature. Neither fish nor fowl nor beast of the field nor bird of the air. It's like love."

"How is that, Miss Jane?"

"You must simply trust it. Good night, Mr. Satterfield."

"Good night, Miss Jane."

13

THE IMPORTANT LETTER did not come the following day or the day after that, but Miss Jane remained serenely confident. Sooner rather than later, she assured Henry, the message would arrive. The Texas rainmaker was rather skeptical concerning second sight. But he was far too much of a gentleman to argue the matter with Miss Jane or to point out that if one waited long enough, an important letter or, for that matter, a stranger would almost always arrive.

Henry continued to spend a few hours each day working on his plane. Yet he seemed in no particular hurry to get back aloft and move along. He had no scheduled engagements, he said, until fall, when he was slated to launch a barnstorming air tour in Atlantic City. Miss Jane believed that he had decided to take the summer off to recover from the tragic loss of his wing-walker and intended, Miss Lola Beauregard Beauclerk. And it crossed her mind that perhaps, after his accident on the frozen lake, he needed a breathing space from flying.

The pilot had some music in him. Some evenings he played the fiddle, running through a repertoire of old mountain songs handed down from his grandfather's ancestors in North Carolina, while Miss Jane picked out the chords of "Turkey in the

Straw" and "The Devil's Dream" on her mother's upright piano in On Kingdom Mountain, as her dear people looked on with what seemed like grave approval. Jane prided herself on not being able to sing a note, but she hummed along tunelessly.

Henry could spin a yarn, too. He recounted to Miss Jane how, while trying to become the first aviator to fly around the world, he had crashed in Siberia and subsisted on meat hacked off a frozen mammoth in a cave, dined on nocturnal serpents in Mongolia, and glimpsed a naked, six-armed woman wearing a crown set with rubies and sapphires and riding a tiger in the forests of India. He did not tell her that since his crash landing on the frozen lake and the resulting temporary memory loss, he had sometimes heard his granddaddy, Captain Cantrell Satterfield, talking to him in his head. *What is the delay, boy?* the old man said to him at least once a day. *Are you going to make your run at her or not? Some other jackass could stumble onto the boodle, you know, whilst you're playing the gentleman with the woman.*

"The delay, sir," Henry replied, "is I can't for the life of me recall the two lines of your so-called riddle. It was knocked out of my head by that wreck on the ice."

That's your problem, not mine, said the grandfather, who was as cantankerous now that he was dead as he ever had been in his life, though that scarcely seemed possible.

"Let's have an understanding," Henry said. "We'll leave her out of this."

To which the grandfather pointedly, Henry thought, said nothing.

Henry liked to go into town. While Miss Jane sold and checked out books and held court on literary matters at the Atheneum, he loitered at the feed store and livery stable or sat in the barbershop or out on the hotel porch with the old men, recounting his adventures in the Great War, telling rainmaking stories, talking about the weather. The weather was an increasingly popular topic. It had not rained since the middle of April, and farmers were becoming concerned.

The men at the feed store and barbershop liked the airman for his unassuming ways and friendliness. He was a good listener and never tired of hearing the sagas of the few remaining Civil War veterans on the hotel porch. He especially loved hearing about the Great Kingdom Common Raid, how the Confederate soldiers had robbed the bank and shot up the town, what routes they had taken into and out of the village, what they had carried the stolen coins in.

The women of the Common admired Henry, too. When he came to town he wore a white hat of the style once known as a southern planter's hat, which he courteously tipped to every lady and girl on the street, at the same time bowing slightly. Even the churchwomen from Anderson Hill had to acknowledge that the handsome, mannerly stranger seemed a gentleman born. Children took to him. He could fix a kid's bicycle, which he called a "wheel" in his mild Texas drawl, fashion a slingshot from a forked black-cherry branch and a strip of inner tubing, play the guessing game with three walnut shells and a dried chickpea. Sometimes he let the kids guess which shell the pea was under, sometimes not.

Henry cultivated the acquaintance of Sadie Blackberry, who knew where all the edible wild fruit grew and when it ripened, and of Clarence Davis, the spruce-gum gatherer, who roamed the woods carrying a long cedar pole with a sickle blade on the end. For all his fastidiousness, the rainmaker took to roving the woods on Miss Jane's mountain with Sadie and Clarence. And he befriended the local fish peddler, Canvasback Glodgett, sometimes accompanying him on his excursions up the Lower Kingdom River to Lake Memphremagog, where Canvasback fished from a red rowboat with a long cane pole and a blue and white bobber. He peddled his finny wares through the village in a homemade wheelbarrow, his grating, repetitive calls ringing out from one end of town to the other. "Fish for sale, fish for sale. Fresh, fresh, fresh, fresh. Pickerel and perch, pike and pout, bass and sunnies, but nary a trout. Nary a trout. Pike and pout but nary a trout." Or, "Dogfish, dogfish, two for a dime. Nobody's dogfish eats like mine." And Henry walked along the Grand Trunk tracks, visiting with the now-retired king of the hoboes, A Number One. He even got along with Eben Kinneson Esquire.

"See if you can talk some sense into the hard head of that cousin of mine, Mr. Satterfield," Eben said. "No one's trying to take her beloved mountain away from her. We just want to upgrade the old pike and attract some tourists to this forsaken backwater."

He said it, I didn't, remarked the old captain in Henry's head. *Let's get this show on the road, boy.*

The rainmaker was quick on his feet. Asked about his political affiliation, he joked that he held no man's politics against him and would gladly put on air shows for all comers, even Republicans and Democrats. Yet some said he carried a pistol in the side pocket of his white jacket and had "a history." The pistol part was unfounded. Henry was uneasy around weapons, particularly Miss Jane's Lady Justice, which she had begun taking on their trips to the village. With an eye on its twin barrels jutting up between them as they sailed down the middle of Main Street, Henry said, "I don't really hold with guns, Miss Jane."

"I do," she replied.

Of course, the man had his detractors. From the start, some were suspicious of him, among them the town fathers. President George Quinn of the First Farmers and Lumberers Bank said mark his words, this Satterfield fellow wanted something, though just what George wasn't sure. The Reverend hinted that Henry was not everything he appeared to be, with his dusky complexion and dark eyes and devilish little mustache. Julia Hefner, the church organist and Judge Allen's court stenographer, a grass widow who, according to local scuttlebutt, was Eben Kinneson Esquire's longtime paramour, went the Reverend one better. Julia claimed that in Henry's promenades through the village from barbershop to hotel to post office to feed store, he took care to walk well out around the church at the south end of the village green. She shared this observation with Miss Jane at the library one afternoon. "Why, Julia," the Duchess said, "don't you know that church is the very place you're most apt to find the devil in Kingdom Common? And in the front pew, if not playing the organ."

One afternoon Judge Allen stopped at the Atheneum to pick up a book Miss Jane had recently ordered for him, a new novel by a young southern writer she and the judge much admired named Faulkner.

After paying for the book, he sat down in the Morris chair beside the Pretender of Avon, stretched out his long legs toward the fireplace, and said, "Jane, this is none of my concern. Tell me to tend to my own affairs if you've a mind to. I won't be offended. But you know how highly I regard you."

"I believe we've been over this ground before, Ira," Jane said.

The judge held up his hand. "I'm not appealing my case. It's just that I don't want to see you getting mixed up in something you can't get out of."

"Such as?"

"Well, not to put too fine a point on it, such as harboring or abetting. That kind of thing."

"Ira, have you read the inscription on my front door lintel? 'They lived in a house at the end of the road . . .'"

"'And were friends to mankind.' I know. But that's no mandate from your ancestors to turn Kingdom Mountain into a hideout for a one-man Hole-in-the-Wall gang."

"Is that what you think Henry Satterfield is? Or do you object to my befriending a man of color?"

"I didn't know that he was a man of color. At the risk of offending you further, I don't know precisely what he is, and I'm not sure I want to find out. His heritage has nothing to do with it. The point, Jane, is that I know who *you* are."

"Who am I?" Miss Jane said.

"Well, you're a former schoolteacher, a sterling bookwoman, an artist, and a damn glamorous woman. Moreover, you're loyal to a fault. Loyal to your family, your mountain, and your new friend. Not to mention just about the most pigheaded creature I've ever known."

"Point taken. But surely you don't want me to turn Mr. S. out of house and home?"

"Believe me, Mr. S. can take care of himself. As for what I want, it isn't going to happen, and we both know it. Mainly, I want you to be careful. That's all. Just be careful with all this."

"I have a question for you, Ira. Henry thinks it quite probable that the Vermont Supreme Court will overturn your ruling on the high road. Is that likely?"

"I'm sure Henry would know."

"Come, sir. Cynicism and envy don't become you."

"To answer your question, if I were you I'd engage a good lawyer. My son, Forrest, has just set himself up in practice in Burlington. He'd work hard for you."

"I'll consider it."

It was a still afternoon in the village. The 4:15 from Boston was not due at the railway station for half an hour. Today was varnishing day at the furniture factory, and the pervasive sweet scents of varnish and orange shellac seemed to enhance the quiet. It occurred to Miss Jane that for all the pettiness of the village, she loved her work at the Atheneum nearly as much as her life on the mountain and would be lost without it.

"Would you like to go fly-fishing tomorrow evening?" the judge asked. "That stretch from your covered bridge to the foot of Blue Clay Hill should be good this time of year."

"You're on," Jane said, relieved to be back on familiar footing with her old friend. "You can take the bend pool behind the old cedar still, Ira. I hooked a big one there last week, but I lost him."

The judge nodded. He stood up and walked to the door with his book. "Jane?"

"Aye?"

"I don't dislike Henry Satterfield at all. I just don't entirely trust him."

"And you're jealous of him."

"Point taken," the judge said. Ira Allen was the great-great-grandson of the Vermont hero-outlaw Ethan Allen, and in Miss Jane's opinion he looked uncannily like the statue of his fabled ancestor on the village green. Jane liked and admired him a great deal and did not understand why she had twice spurned his marriage proposals. In the privacy of On Kingdom Mountain, she had wondered aloud to her dear people if she might be afraid to become intimate with a man as smart as herself.

"To go back to the Supreme Court, Jane. They won't let you represent yourself down there. Montpelier isn't Kingdom County, you know."

"That's the truth. And Kingdom County isn't Montpelier yet, either, thank heavens. I'll meet you at the covered bridge tomorrow evening at six o'clock."

14

I'VE BEEN WONDERING, Henry," Miss Jane called up through the vent in her ceiling late one evening in June, in what she had come to think of, quite boldly, as one of their now nightly "featherbed chats."

"What have you been wondering about, Miss Jane?" Henry called back down.

"Has any more of your grandfather's riddle come back to you?"

"No, ma'am, it surely hasn't. Just the 'behold' part."

"I imagine the rest will pop into your head when you least expect it," Miss Jane said. "In the meantime, I hear that you've been making inquiries round town about the Great Raid."

"I have made some inquiries, Miss Jane. I can't help but think that my grandfather, the old captain, knew something about the raid himself, you know. More than once he hinted that if I could ever solve the riddle, it would make me as rich as Croesus."

"Would you like to hear a story, Henry? About my own father and the Great Raid on the bank?"

Miss Jane, who had ears like an owl, heard Henry closing his detective magazine. His bare feet hit the floor, and she knew he was sitting on the edge of his bed in order not to miss a word. "Many Commoners, at the time of the raid, believed that my father, who had just returned from his trek south to search for his missing brother, gave sanctuary to the fleeing bandits. From there the tale acquired a life of its own. Soon the Common was saying that my father found the treasure that the raiders supposedly buried on the mountain."

"From what you've told me of your father, Miss Jane, I reckon that if he had, he'd have given it back to the bank."

"Not necessarily. While my father was honest to a fault, he believed that the gold was already tainted at the time it was stolen."

"How so?"

"Most of it was earned by local farmers who, having paid a substitute to go to war in their stead, profiteered from the conflict by selling oats and hay to Grant's army at exorbitant rates. I too believe that the money was tainted. That's partly why I've never searched very hard for the so-called Treasure of Kingdom Mountain."

"Where would you search, supposing you were inclined to?" Henry said, his voice light, agreeable, conversational. "Up under the balancing boulder on the mountaintop?"

"No," Miss Jane said. "I'd look where it came from."

"Where it came from," Henry said. It was not quite a question and Miss Jane knew he was trying to keep the excitement out of his voice.

"Aye," she said. "When my father died, he left something in a large deposit box at the bank. I know exactly which one. It's the lowermost box on the far left side of the vault, a box nearly as large as my Currier and Ives safe. He established a small fund whose interest would pay the annual rent on this box. In his will he left instructions that it was not to be opened until the one hundredth anniversary of his death. It is assumed by many that the deposit box contains the stolen gold, which my father had, in good conscience, returned to the bank, at the same time assuring himself that, as tainted lucre, it would never be spent. It's just the sort of thing he would have done."

"Because it was ill-gotten gains?"

"Exactly."

"Miss Jane, may I make one more inquiry?"

"Certainly. I will answer it or not as I see fit."

"Fair enough. Do *you* believe the treasure is in the deposit box of the First Farmers and Lumberers Bank?"

"I do not."

"Might I ask, then, what you *do* believe is in the deposit box?"

"A map."

"A map, Miss Jane? You mean a treasure map?"

Something told Miss Jane that this featherbed chat had gone on quite long enough. "My grandfather, Henry, had a little rhyme, perhaps inspired by his unusual name, which he passed on to my father.

> Quaker meeting hath begun.
> No more talking, no more fun.
> He who shows his teeth or tongue,
> He shall pay a forfeit."

"What does it mean, Miss Jane?"

"It means that it is time to go to sleep. Very probably, the map in the vault, if a map it be, was my father's idea of a great joke on everyone obsessed with the treasure in particular and money in general. Good night, Henry."

In keeping with the little rhyme of Miss Jane's grandfather, Henry said good night and nothing more. But his expression suggested that he did not, for a Kingdom Mountain moment, believe that the treasure map in the deposit box of the bank vault was any kind of prank. It was a long time before Henry Satterfield of Beaumont, Texas, fell asleep that night. And when at last he did, he slept fitfully, dreaming of gold and hand-drawn maps and bank vaults dark as midnight. Below in her own bedchamber, Miss Jane lay awake herself, thinking that she had no better idea who Henry Satterfield truly was than she had the day he crashed on the ice at the foot of her mountain. But at last she too drifted off to sleep, dreaming that she and Henry were flying away in his biplane, faster by far than she had ever traveled before, though where they might be headed, and for what possible purpose, she could not imagine.

HENRY

15

I BELIEVE THAT my Burgess-Wright is as airworthy as she's going to be," Henry announced the next morning. "She is, you know, a lady of a certain age. But I think she is ready to be put to the test."

"And then I suppose you'll be on your way, Henry. Well, as a lady of a certain age myself, I must say that I have very much enjoyed your company."

"Let us discuss that after I try out the plane," Henry said. "I have no pressing engagements this summer, Miss Jane. And no wingwalker yet, either."

"You are a brave man to go up again after your terrible mishaps," she said.

It was another fine, dry morning on the mountain, a good day for flying, Henry said. And Jane could see that despite his sorrowful memories of Miss Lola, he was very happy to be going aloft once more. Although she, too, was excited about the maiden flight of the repaired plane, she was terrified that the machine might fail Henry again. Also, she dreaded the moment when he would fly off into the blue and leave her alone on her mountain.

Under Jane's supervision, Ethan and General Ira Allen pulled the yellow biplane out of the barn and down the lane to the water meadow. While she and the oxen watched from the edge of the field, with Miss Jane holding her breath longer than she would have thought possible, Henry, now wearing his leather aviator's hat and flying goggles, spun his propeller, leaped out of its way and into the front seat of the plane, and went bouncing off down the pasture. The plane lifted off the ground, its long wings wobbling, climbed up a few hundred feet, circled the home place twice, and made a bumpy but safe landing.

Henry had warned Miss Jane not to get close to the spinning propeller, but the moment it made its last revolution she ran up to the cockpit. To her own astonishment she heard herself say, "Now it's my turn, Mr. Satterfield. Let's go again, together." She strapped herself into the rear seat behind the rainmaker and, heart pounding, was both petrified and thrilled when, moments later, they jounced off down the hayfield. There was an utterly unbelievable moment when she realized that they were off the ground. Like Daedalus and his overreaching son, Miss Jane Hubbell Kinneson of Kingdom Mountain was defying gravity.

From the start, Jane loved everything about flying. The stomach-flipping jolts and dips, the rushing fields below, the intensifying whine of the engine in her ears as they banked up and up until they could look down on the mountain, the fire tower, the big lake, and the range of jagged peaks beyond. Whoever would have guessed that Miss Jane, born just fifteen years after the Civil War ended, would one day behold her mountain from a flying machine a thousand feet up in the firmament? At first she felt dizzy when the great roaring Burgess-Wright with its twenty-foot-long double wings dived down toward the tilting mountainside below. "Look off at the horizon," Henry called back to her. She did, and the trees righted themselves and Jane felt a keen joy in being alive. She had been born, it seemed to her, to fly.

Calling out over the thundering engine, she named each of the major peaks in the northern Green Mountains, from Mansfield in the south to Owl's Head in Canada. She pointed out the Chain of Ponds on the far side of the mountain and the devil's visage on the back side of the balancing boulder and the vast, swampy Great Northern Slang, which separated her mountain, on the northwest, from the lake. Henry, noticing man that he was, looked carefully at each sector of the mountain, flying low over the Chain of Ponds and the slang, circling Indian Island in the lake, buzzing down to study the peace cairn and balancing boulder, fixing each landmark firmly in his mind.

By the time they landed, Miss Jane was beginning to think of herself as something of an old hand when it came to flying. Afterward she went straight into On Kingdom Mountain and informed her dear people that going up in the Burgess-Wright was the most sublime experience of her life. She was so excited that until Henry called her out onto the porch, she did not notice the message on the slate hanging from a nail beside the door above her great pileated woodpecker knocker.

Mr. Satterfield,

The town fathers of Kingdom Common, in expectation of a favorable ruling from the higher courts, are holding a gala Independence Day celebration on the green in Kingdom Common on July Fourth, to raise funds for the continuation and completion of the Connector highway. Could we prevail upon you, for a modest consideration, to give airplane rides and possibly a fireworks display that evening to help with this worthwhile effort to bring Kingdom County, at long last, into the twentieth century?

> Thank you very much.
> Yours,
> Eben Kinneson Esquire
> Town Counsel

"So, Henry," Miss Jane said, staring at the message, "do you know what this is?"

"I fear, Miss Jane, that it is the letter you have been expecting. It appears as though, despite the judge's ruling, your cousin and the town fathers are not about to give up on the high road."

"That is no letter but an outright declaration of war," she

said. "I am sorry, in a way, now that your plane is airworthy, that you will not be on hand to see the ultimate defeat of my cousin and his cronies. In the meantime, I thank you for taking me on high. Why for pity's sake, what is it, Henry? You look as though you've seen a ghost."

Henry slapped his forehead with the palm of his hand. "There she is, Miss Jane."

"There who is?"

"Not who, ma'am. What. There's the next part of the riddle. *On high*. You thanked me for taking you *on high*."

"Well?" she said.

"Well, what?" Henry grinned as mischievously as one of her former pupils.

"What's the riddle?"

"Oh, the riddle. It goes on like this.

The Riddle of Kingdom Mountain: The Trinity

Behold! on high with the blessed sweet host,
Nor Father, nor Son, but Holy Ghost."

"That's it?"

"That's *part* of it. The part my granddaddy told me. He said I'd have to travel to Kingdom Mountain to discover the other part."

"Well, that's not much help," Miss Jane said. "Never mind, though. It has a promising beginning. I'll tell you what. I'll write it on the message slate."

Miss Jane erased the message from Eben and wrote in its place the first two lines of the riddle.

"What can it possibly mean?" she wondered. "Was your grandfather quite sane, Henry?"

"Some days he was," Henry said. "Other days he'd fall into a black mood and go around muttering about the war and such, mad as a hatter. My father told me he was haunted by what he'd seen and perhaps done."

"A good many were," Miss Jane said. "Including, I think, my own father. That may be why he never told us what, if anything, he found out about his missing brother Pilgrim. He couldn't bear to discuss it."

The Duchess shook her head sadly. Then she repeated the title and first two lines of the riddle aloud. "I know of no 'Trinity' on Kingdom Mountain," she said.

"'Nor Father, nor Son, but Holy Ghost,'" Henry said in a musing voice. "'On high.' Could it possibly have anything to do with your balancing boulder on the mountaintop? That's on high."

"It could, I suppose," Miss Jane said. "It vexes me to be so puzzled by it. I'll work on your riddle, and if I solve it, I'll get in touch with you."

"Why, Miss Jane, are you putting me off your mountain so soon? I had hoped to stay on a bit."

"You had?" Jane was delighted. "You're welcome to stay as long as you like, Henry Satterfield. More than welcome. But I supposed that a traveling man like you would be posting on to wherever as soon as you recovered from the wreck."

"Miss Jane," Henry said, "you saved my skin by directing me to a safe landing on the ice. You nursed me back to health, provided a place for me to rest my head and shelter my machine. I have no pressing engagements. I do have a request to make of you."

"Request away, sir."

"Present company willing, I'd like to stay on here this summer and help you, in any manner I can, to fend off this high road."

Miss Jane, looking out the west window of her kitchen at the mountains, was more touched than she could ever remember being. She did not, truthfully, trust herself to speak at the moment.

"Besides which," Henry said, "we just might, if we put our heads together, cipher out the meaning of this infernal riddle."

"We might at that," Miss Jane said. "We just might at that."

16

Hᴀʀᴋ!" Miss Jane said.

"What is it?" Henry mumbled. He'd been dreaming of an all-nude girlie revue he'd seen some years ago in Columbia, South Carolina. In his dream Miss Jane was prancing about the stage with her schoolteacher's pointer, directing the girls in a sprightly dance. She was attired in a scholarly mortarboard and nothing else, and Henry was unhappy to be wakened from this interesting vision.

"Quick as ever you moved in your life, Mr. Satterfield," Miss Jane called up through the hole in her bedroom ceiling, "meet me in the kitchen."

Henry's first thought was that housebreakers might have gained entry. Still half asleep, he hurried into his white trousers and came bounding down the stairs and into the kitchen, where he grabbed the poker hanging on the back of the Glenwood. He was greeted by no housebreakers, but he could hear the rise and fall of racing engines, which seemed to be coming from the east, on the extension of the old pike road. Then, very distinctly, two gunshots. He thought Miss Jane would certainly want Lady Justice. Instead, she snatched up her scrub broom, a homemade straw besom with which she cleaned her porch, swept her dooryard, and brushed down cobwebs in the barn.

Clad in her nightgown, tasseled nightcap, and wool hunting jacket, she rushed outside just as a large touring car, riding so low that its rear bumper scraped the ground, came sluing into the dooryard. As the car skidded by sideways, klaxon blaring, Miss Jane belabored its hood and roof and the boxes strapped to its rear luggage racks with the scrub broom.

Henry thought that he recognized, behind the wheel of the touring car, the pointed features of the low high sheriff of Kingdom County, Little Fred Morse, as white as an apparition beneath his sheriff's hat.

"And don't come back," Miss Jane shouted, making a home-run swing with her scrub broom and clipping off the ornamental insignia on the hood of the sheriff's car. The whiskey runners bounced down the lane toward the hemlock-plank covered bridge. "Drunkards!" she cried out. "Scofflaws! Wife beaters!"

Nor was she finished for the evening. A minute later a Ford with a star on the driver's door, containing four men in suits and derby hats, came thundering into her dooryard. She served this car the same, tattooing it with the rock-maple handle of her broom. "Private road!" she cried. "Interlopers! Have the law on you!"

"We are the law, woman, we're federal revenuers," the driver shouted as he skidded to a stop at the fork in the old pike, just past the barn. "Which way did those runners go?"

"That way," Miss Jane said, gesturing with her broom toward the bridge. Just as she'd expected, the G-men raced up the other fork, where, some minutes later, Miss Jane and Henry could hear the loud and unavailing whine of their engine as they tried to free the Ford from the burn.

In view of the low high sheriff Fred Lyle Morse's long-standing reputation for looking the other way in matters involving the transportation and sale of illegal beverages, Henry Satterfield was surprised, the following Tuesday afternoon, when Little Fred moseyed into the library, where Henry was reading *Riders of the Purple Sage* next to Miss Jane's carving of the Pretender of Avon, and asked if they could speak privately. Outside on the library steps, the sheriff inquired if he might rent the biplane for an afternoon and evening, along with Henry's services as pilot, to look for moonshine stills from the air along the thickly forested terrain on the border east and west of Lake Memphremagog. At the same time, the low high sheriff said, he and his fishing partner, Doc Harrison, would like to pick up a few cases of Dr. Pinkham's Relieving Bitters in Magog, Quebec, at the head of the lake. Something in the village water supply seemed to be "binding folks up," the sheriff explained, and the best nostrum for this general malady was Dr. Pinkham's elixir, available only in Canada. No one, Fred added, wished to be suffering from constipation and thus be unable to enjoy the upcoming Fourth of July celebration.

While Henry was not entirely certain what the doctor and the sheriff wished him to do, he had no scruples about helping alleviate the unfortunate symptoms in the villagers. The pilot duly made plans to meet Doc and Sheriff Morse the next Friday afternoon at two o'clock at Miss Jane's water meadow.

That night he and Jane conducted a rather long featherbed chat, which Henry initiated by mentioning that his grandfather, the captain, had told him a fascinating tale about his long-ago military service as a border raider. "It seems," Henry said, "that the old rip, who, come to think of it, was then still a young rip, once hid out at a church. He didn't tell me just where the church was located, or which border he was raiding on at the time, but I think we could guess. He did say that the church was near a good-sized body of water. And that when he sneaked into the building and hid in a little closet, the rising sun coming through the colored glass windows shone on a whole wall of crutches and canes and iron leg braces and back braces and collars and every other device designed to outfit the halt. He spent the rest of the day, until nightfall, holed up in that closet, napping and hiding. Evidently it was a holy day, because about midmorning along hitched a whole passel of the crippled and lame and otherwise afflicted. The front door of the church was open, and he could see them scrabbling up the big stone steps on their hands and knees, praying and chanting. And when they got to the top step they flung away their walking sticks and braces and were cured. But my granddaddy said that cured or no, they had to be helped to hobble away by their families and friends or carried off on litters, and one fella sang out that he would skip all the way home like the risen Lazarus or know the reason why, and he made one feeble little hop like a sick jackrabbit and went plunging down the church steps and broke his neck, which my granddaddy said was just about the most comical spectacle he'd ever witnessed."

"Your granddaddy had a singular sense of humor," Miss Jane said dryly. "However, Henry, I believe I know precisely where that church was. It was called Our Lady of Memphremagog and it was in Canada, just over the border from Vermont. People went there from all over the world to be healed."

"Miss Jane?" Henry said. "Do you recall whether that Canadian church had a picture or a stained glass window of the heavenly host? The seraphim and cherubim and such?"

"I catch your drift, Henry. You think your grandfather participated in the Great Raid and hid the stolen gold in Our Lady of Memphremagog."

"It seems possible. The riddle says 'on high with the blessed sweet host.'"

Miss Jane frowned. "I don't recall any frescoes or stained glass depictions of seraphim. But host, you know, could also mean the Communion wafers. They would have been distributed from the chancel box on the dais at the front of the church."

"He wouldn't have hidden it in the box with the crackers,

would he? They'd have found it there when they dumped more crackers in."

Miss Jane thought. "Not in the box. But possibly under it. There would be a space under the dais, you see, between the floor of the chancel and the floor of the nave. If your grandfather had a way to pry up the boards, it's possible he could have left the gold under the raised chancel floor. There's just one problem, Henry."

"What's that?"

"Thirty years ago, Our Lady of Memphremagog burned to the ground, discarded crutches and stained glass windows and confessional booth where your grandfather hid and all. If the gold is there, it has who knows how many tons of rubble on top of it. What's more, the church was believed to be cursed. That's why it burned, they said. God was angry with the priests who had swindled folks into paying for cures they couldn't perform."

But already Henry's head was full of magnetos and wires and batteries and the ringing of alarm clocks. Miss Jane's alarm clock, to be precise, which, along with her scrub broom, he appropriated the following day for the invention she would jokingly call the Auricus Satterfieldicus. With this machine, and with the full approval of his granddaddy, whose commentary Henry continued to hear in his head periodically, he confidently planned to locate, on the site of Our Lady of Memphremagog, the one hundred thousand dollars in twenty-dollar double eagles stolen from the First Farmers Bank, ten percent of which he had decided to give Miss Jane for helping him locate its hiding place. It was, Henry congratulated himself, a very generous disposition and would certainly defray the fee of an attorney to argue her case against the high road in the Vermont Supreme Court, probably with ample left over for her declining years. For whatever else might or might not be said about him, Henry was determined that no one would count a lack of generosity among his shortcomings.

Nothing in his newly found profession of treasure hunting was simple. So Henry was thinking, that Friday about midnight, as he combed through the ruins of the old lakeside shrine with his ridiculous Auricus Satterfieldicus. The luminous dial of the homemade gold detector glowed brightly, but the thin red needle that he had appropriated, unknown to Miss Jane, from the speedometer of her Model A, stubbornly refused to budge. He knew that the Auricus worked. During its maiden operation in the home-place dooryard, he had located several horseshoe nails, a .54 caliber slug from Lady Justice, and a set of false teeth made of tin, which Miss Jane believed had belonged to her great-grandfather. So far, however, all he had found at Our Lady of Memphremagog was the melted base of a brass candlestick and a large round penny coined in 1843 by the Bank of Upper Canada.

In fact, Henry had had the devil's own time just locating the site of the cursed church, though it was only about a mile from the recently cut hayfield where he, Doc Harrison, and Sheriff Fred Morse had landed earlier that afternoon. The wind was now moaning through the tops of the churchyard cedars in a way that the pilot did not find at all comforting, and the waves slapping against the nearby rocky shore somehow reminded him of the chants for the many dead whose obsequies had been held on the very spot he was sifting through. Nearby stood a manure-caked wheelbarrow he had optimistically appropriated from a farmer's barnyard on the way to the shrine.

Keep at her, boy, the granddaddy's voice said with an unpleasant chuckle Henry remembered all too well. *Rome weren't built in a day.*

Suddenly, Miss Jane's wind-up alarm clock, attached to the

end of the broomstick, set up a dreadful clanging. Despite the thrill of knowing he had found the boodle his grandfather had hidden here more than half a century before, Henry jumped half a foot. But this was no time for faint-heartedness. Fetching the garden spade he had brought along for just this purpose, he began to delve into the cindery debris. A foot or so into the scree of burnt bricks and mortar, the handle of the shovel snapped off just above the head. Mindless of his neatly creased white pants, Henry dropped to his knees, like those hopeful petitioners who long ago had crawled up the great stone steps of the church to be made whole. The shovel head scraped against something hard. Wild calculations ran through Henry's head. If he could shovel the gold into the wooden barrow and trundle it back to the plane before Doc and the low high sheriff rendezvoused there with the Dr. Pinkham elixir, he could get out of these forsaken mountains scot-free. He could always send Miss Jane her commission. The shovel head rang on something metallic. An image of a brass-bound treasure chest bursting with coins appeared to Henry. *Nor Father, nor Son, but Holy Ghost.* Of course. That was it. The gold itself was the Holy Ghost.

Out of the rubble Henry wrestled a round enameled metal basin. God Jesus, he thought. Could it be a collection plate? Had he come all the way from Texas to root in the ruins of a country chapel and unearth a collection plate? His grandfather, the captain, certified as a bona fide lunatic at the end, spent his last months on earth toiling feverishly to discover the alchemical formula for turning gold into base metals, on the assumption that he could then reverse the process and, like King Midas, transform all that he touched, or at least all that was metallic, to gold. Could the entire riddle be the insane old officer's idea of a joke? The cumbrous thing he had unearthed had a cover, also enameled. He tossed the basin and cover aside and ran the Auricus over the charred bricks again. Nothing.

The collection plate was the sum and substance of his night's work. Plus the one hundred dollars and fuel for the plane that the sheriff had promised him. Still, if the artifact was a collection plate, perhaps it had some historical value. Knocking the dirt and ashes off the cover and basin, he decided to take them back to the home place and present them to Miss Jane.

Doc Harrison and the low high sheriff, who stood four feet ten inches in his cowboy boots and who wore at all times a .45 Colt pistol whose barrel extended well below his knees, were in a very jolly frame of mind, having already sampled Dr. Pinkham's finest and found it good. Although it was a moonless night, the stars were out, and Henry had no difficulty tracing the long sheen of the lake below back to Kingdom Mountain and setting the biplane gently down in Miss Jane's water meadow, where the glass gallon jugs of Dr. Pinkham's relieving compound were transferred to the rear seat and trunk of the sheriff's touring car. Roof light flashing, siren wailing, Doc and Little Fred roared off over the covered bridge on their errand of mercy. Henry, for his part, gravely presented his artifact from the defunct church to Miss Jane, who washed it off under the pump in the soapstone sink, then began to laugh.

"Mr. Satterfield," she said, "do you know what this is?"

"I thought it might be an old collection plate."

"This, sir, is a genuine porcelain enameled chamber pot. An old-fashioned thunder mug that the priest kept handy to use between confessions or healings."

Still chuckling, she said, "Never mind, it's still a grand find. Look. We'll call it the golden helmet of Mambrino, after the headpiece of the good gentleman from La Mancha. We'll let the Loup-Garou wear it as a crown.

"Here," she said, clapping the old thundermug upside down on the head of her carved wolfman beside the door. "I dub you Sir Chamberpot Blockhead of the North Woods." She continued to smile quite gleefully over her tea and later in bed as she read *Don Quixote,* which she so loved and admired that she had not "edited down" or blue-penciled out a single word of it. As for Henry Satterfield, even after Miss Jane had read him the wonderful passage on Mambrino's helmet, he was deeply chagrined by his misadventure at the site of the sacred shrine of Our Lady of Memphremagog, and more determined than ever to find the Treasure of Kingdom Mountain.

17

COME ONE COME ALL
TO THE INDEPENDENCE DAY GALA
ON THE GREEN IN KINGDOM COMMON
FOR A PICNIC & AEROPLANE RIDES
A HISTORICAL PAGEANT
AND A PARADE
TO BE FOLLOWED BY FIREWORKS AT DUSK
TO BENEFIT THE CONNECTOR
BETWEEN KINGDOM COMMON AND CANADA

The flyers had been printed up by Editor Kinneson at the *Kingdom County Monitor* office, in accordance with Eben Kinneson Esquire's directions. And although no one, least of all Miss Jane Hubbell Kinneson, could have imagined that she and Henry Satterfield would be distributing them by air from the Burgess-Wright, here they were, just a week before the gala, dropping several thousand of the small yellow leaflets on all of the towns within a twenty-mile radius of the Common. Jane still had no idea what Henry had planned and why he was willing to help Eben and the fathers with their fundraiser.

Their featherbed chats notwithstanding, they both kept their own counsel about certain matters. All the rainmaker would say, usually from the hammock he had slung in the shade of the Virginia creeper at the west end of Jane's porch, and often with a significant glance at the incomplete riddle on the slate beside the door, is that they had bigger catfish to fry, and the gala in the Common could be used to this end.

The celebration was all the talk in the village. Besides the biplane rides, there would be an early-afternoon baseball game between the town club, the Kingdom Common Outlaws, and their archrivals from Pond in the Sky, a late-afternoon barbecue, the historical pageant, and, at dusk, just before Henry's pyrotechnics, a reenactment of the Great Kingdom Common Raid.

The drought had held through June, though the oracular old Civil War soldiers on the hotel porch were confidently predicting rain for the Fourth, and indeed seemed to be hoping for it, both to be proven right and to confirm their own deep belief in the unwelcome but inevitable irony that lay at the bottom of all things in this world. To their disappointment, the big day dawned clear. The Common began filling up with celebrants by midmorning. Henry Satterfield's airplane rides started at noon. A landing strip had been cleared on the village green, and everyone, it seemed, wanted to go aloft, from President George Quinn of the First Farmers and Lumberers Bank of Kingdom Common to Canvasback Glodgett, the fish peddler.

The ball game was a great success, with the Outlaws defeating Pond in the Sky 3–2, on Editor Kinneson's ninth-inning home run off the bandstand in deep center field. The smoke from the barbecue mingled with the haze that had hung over the county for weeks, so the picnickers on the green had a rather illusory look, as did the participants in the historical pageant that followed. First came the village's brass marching band, blaring out a spirited version of "The Star-Spangled

Banner." At the heels of the band, a contingent of men dressed in buckskins and carrying flintlock muskets represented Robert Rogers' Rangers, who had come through the Kingdom in 1759 after their bloody raid on Miss Jane's Memphremagog ancestors across the border. Close behind were several of the Outlaws wearing feathered headdresses and war paint and enacting the role of the Memphremagogs who had overtaken Rogers on the shore of the big lake and killed several of his men. There were settlers carrying felling axes; Revolutionary soldiers, including Judge Allen in the incarnation of his famous ancestor, whose statue gazed on benignly from the north end of the common; lumberers and river drivers in red shirts and black slouch hats; a squadron of Civil War veterans in blue; doughboys from the Great War with round helmets and gas masks; even a few modern-day whiskey runners and G-men in shiny black coupes. A Number One tagged along in an engineer's cap, giving out a heartfelt train whistle from time to time. Sadie Blackberry stood waving in the bandstand.

As the procession completed its second circuit, shots rang out east of the village. Two horsemen in gray uniforms came galloping into town, past the hotel, firing rifles into the air. Bank President Quinn, decked out in a swallow-tailed frock coat and a stovepipe hat, who had just locked the proceeds from the gala fundraiser in the bank vault for the night, was taken captive and forced at gunpoint to reenter the bank. The brass band played "Dixie" as one of the raiders stood guard outside the bank while the other rushed inside with flour sacks. Moments later he emerged with the bags bulging and remounted; firing their guns, the two horsemen rode back out of town toward Kingdom Mountain.

In the meantime, unnoticed by most of the spectators, Henry Satterfield had taken off in his biplane. As the raiders galloped away, Henry swooped after them in the Burgess-Wright, just over the treetops, with Miss Jane in the passenger seat firing blanks at the robbers from Lady Justice. The horsemen turned around and, with the plane low overhead, allowed themselves to be herded back into town, hands over their heads. They returned the laden flour sacks to George Quinn just as the biplane landed on the green at dusk to a terrific ovation. Then Henry and Jane and the raiders and President George Quinn shook hands all around.

Not five minutes later, into the twilit summer sky shot multicolored pinwheels, green and pink skyrockets, exploding rainbows. It was Henry Satterfield's fireworks display. There were great pyrotechnic battles in the clouds, volcanic eruptions of vivid primary colors, thunderous explosions high over the church steeple and courthouse tower. A red and yellow panorama swept up the sky above Anderson Hill, resembling the fiery fall foliage on Kingdom Mountain. Then, streaking blue and silver across the northern horizon, there appeared an astonishing reproduction of the aurora borealis, followed by a meteoric shower of yellow sparks like gold coins, falling onto the south end of the green. The finale was a huge American flag, unfurling in the night. The sky went dark. A prolonged detonation seemed to come from all the points of the compass at once. Then silence. The celebration was over.

18

I COULDN'T HELP but think, Mr. Satterfield," Miss Jane called up through the ceiling grate that night, "how much my father would have loved the goings-on today in the Common. Especially the re-creation of the Great Raid and the historical pageant."

"It was a wonderful pageant, Miss Jane," Henry said. He was propped up on three goose-down pillows, reading a story by lantern light in the latest issue of *True Detective*, about two brothers with the rather improbable names of Wendell and Kendell Orbison, who had recently escaped from Leavenworth Penitentiary in a prison hearse.

"Your father was, I believe, a lawyer?" Henry said.

"He was a lawyer and judge and the State Supreme Court chief justice and a farmer," Jane said. "My mother used to say he was the best chief justice and the worst farmer on Kingdom Mountain. It was a joke and not a joke. But even though my dad was no farmer, he was a crack shot and a very good hunter. Every fall he located a good buck on the mountain, and woe betide the unwary moose that wandered down from Canada and into the sights of Lady Justice at any time of year. Father believed that moose compete with deer for the available feed, and he dealt with them accordingly. So too do I.

"About the time I reached my teens," she continued, "my father took it in his head to make me into a hunter. Not just an ordinary run-of-the-mill weekend hunter, either. Dad's idea was to turn me into a kind of Kingdom Mountain female Nimrod, so that I could follow in his footsteps and carry on the Kinneson family tradition of providing meat for their own table."

Henry was not surprised to note, in his copy of *True Detective*, that his own aversion to guns was not shared by the brothers Orbison, who, by the time they ran into a roadblock in Amarillo three days after the breakout, had acquired six rifles, three shotguns, and a Thompson submachine gun with which they fired an estimated two hundred and fifty rounds at the police.

"Miss Jane?"

"Aye?"

"What does the word q-u-i-e-t-u-s mean?"

"Why, it is usually used to mean a death."

The *True Detective* article had ended with the sentence "And so it came to pass that, at a dusty crossroads in the Lone Star State, young Wendell and Kendell met their just quietus."

"Father picked the fall I was sixteen for my initiation into the mysteries of deer slaying on the mountain. The trouble was, opening day of hunting season fell on Homecoming Saturday at the Academy, and Ira Allen had just asked me to the homecoming ball. It was my first real prom, and though it's amusing to me now, it wasn't then. However, once I realized that Ira was impressed that I was going to deer camp, I began to hint to him, scheming minx that I was, that I was an old hand at stalking the roebucks of Kingdom Mountain."

Henry, only half listening, turned the page of his detective mag and began reading the story of a crazed vigilante who had set fire to a churchful of millennialists in Newark, New York. Guiltily, he sneaked a look ahead at the end of the story. "On the Ides of March, in the year of Our Lord Nineteen Hundred and Twenty-nine, John 'Laughing Jack' Before, who had burned up twenty-three (23) misguided devouts and laughed about it, burned in THE CHAIR in Ossining on the Hudson. He did not, at the time of his incineration, appear to be laughing."

"Father's plan was that we would establish ourselves at Camp Hard Luck, on the far side of the mountain, and spend the first afternoon hunting the lower north slopes. I was still angry with him for dragging me along, and quite determined to spite him and myself by refusing to cooperate. The November morning we headed out was very cold after a week of unseasonably cold weather. The three ponds in the Chain of Ponds were iced over from shore to shore, and we walked up to the camp over the frozen surface. In the middle of the afternoon it began to snow. We scouted along a game trail at the foot of the mountain for an hour or so, then Father said the deer would bed down until the snow stopped and we might as well return to camp."

"A wise decision, Miss Jane. But to tell you the truth, hunting has always made me uneasy. It seems somehow akin to armed robbery of the woods, you know. I've never approved of armed robbery."

Miss Jane found this a peculiar statement. Who, other than one of the hardened gunmen Henry loved to read about in his crime periodicals, *did* approve of armed robbery?

"During supper, my father went over his plan with me again. If the snow had stopped by morning I would hike up the game trail beside the big wooden chute that used to convey logs down the mountain to the pond below. There I'd wait, with Lady Justice, while my father drove the far side of the mountain."

"'I knowed that if I pulled that trigger, I'd never again be the same little blue-eyed country gal from Manhattan, Kansas.'" Thus began "The Diary of a Small-Town Gun Moll." Henry wondered. Would the girl's eyes change color if she pulled the trigger? There was a grainy picture on the opposite page of the Manhattan country gal who had fallen in with bad companions. Wearing a baby-doll nightie, she crouched behind a haystack, wielding two machine pistols. The caption read, "Setting a Deadly Ambuscade." A sturdy-legged little filly like that would have been a natural-born wingwalker, the airman thought.

"Have you nodded off, Mr. Satterfield?"

"By no means, Miss Jane. You planned to set a deadly ambuscade on the mountaintop."

"I planned no such thing. I thought about my high school chums, marching around a bonfire on the village green, enjoying cider and doughnuts and one another's company while I was trapped up on that forlorn mountain. What I planned was to spend the morrow sulking. Still, if by some stroke of sheer blind luck I killed a buck, I might, by an act I could only see as barbaric and under utterly false pretense, win Ira Allen's heart,

which I could then wickedly break. That was worth considering."

"And?" Henry said.

"And what?"

"Did you get your deer? And impress your beau?"

"You will find out," Jane called up through the grate, "in due
time. For now, I will let you get back to your literature."

19

AT 8:15 ON THE MORNING after the Fourth of July celebration, President George Quinn strode across the common toward the First Farmers and Lumberers Bank. The barbecue pit
was still smoking, and the green, littered with hotdog wrappers
and bits of fireworks casings and empty Nehi and Coca-Cola
bottles, had about it the slightly melancholy air of an empty
fairgrounds. By any measure, George thought, the fundraising
gala had been a success. Miss Jane seemed to have come round,
the Connector would go forward, and the Common would at
last join the twentieth century. As usual, George got out his
keys, unlocked the front door, and stepped into the lobby. As
usual, he inhaled deeply to catch that first satisfying whiff of
furniture and brass polish, old wood, and money. This morning
what he smelled instead was the acrid odor of powder, which
still hung over the village from the fireworks display the night
before. Why would that scent be stronger inside the bank? The
answer was almost immediately apparent. The massive vault
door had been blown entirely off its hinges, and the emergency
exit at the rear of the bank stood wide open for the entire town
to come and go as they pleased. George actually thought he

might be having a stroke. Not since the Great Raid of 1864 had the First Farmers been robbed or had any patron lost a single penny.

Only later that morning, after it was ascertained that the stacks of greenbacks from the celebration the day before, right out in the open inside the vault for the safecrackers to see and help themselves to, about three thousand dollars in all, not to mention the trays upon trays of silver and the few hundred dollars in gold coins that the bank still kept on hand, were intact, was George able to take a relaxed breath. Whoever had blown their way into the First Farmers had taken nothing but the contents of a large safety deposit box in the lower row of boxes near the back of the vault, rented decades ago by Miss Jane's father, Morgan Kinneson.

"Here's something," Henry said that afternoon, holding up his *True Detective* for Miss Jane to see. He was lounging in the porch hammock with his white hat pushed jauntily back on his head, like a teenage boy on his first ice cream soda drugstore date. On the yellowish page of the magazine was a touched-up black-and-white photograph of a biplane swooping low over a little town that looked to be somewhere on the Great Plains. Standing on the dreary street below, by an automobile with a star embossed on the door, were two men in uniforms, firing Tommy guns at the aircraft. Obviously the photograph had been staged. The headline read COURTEOUS CLYDE OF THE CLOUDS STRIKES AGAIN.

In his best recitation voice, cultivated at the knee of his schoolteacher mother, Henry read aloud the following paragraph.

The so-called "Courteous Clyde Barrow" of the Clouds has not been professionally active in his old stomping grounds for several months. The polite robber/pilot, renowned for saying "please, sir" and "thank you, ma'am," has not been seen in Oklahoma, Kansas, or Missouri since robbing a string of banks in that region in an 18-month period ending this past March with his near-capture in Tulsa. "Courteous Clyde" — his true identity is not known — has developed a unique *modus operandi*. Stealing a local automobile, he then robs the bank, drives to a field outside of town and is met by a biplane flown by his bonny ("Bonnie"?) bride, or partner, described as an exceedingly goodlooking young woman. The couple has endeared themselves to the populace of the "dust bowl" states by quite literally "papering" the towns they target with some of the currency taken from the bank. Also, Clyde generally takes with him into the bank a sack which, when the more important business has been transacted, he thrusts across the teller's counter, requesting that it be filled with "silver dollar cartwheels for the children," which he then showers down upon the local schoolhouse in a gleaming cascade just before flying into the "blue yonder."

As reported in our April issue, after a spectacular midday robbery in Tulsa, in which "Courteous Clyde" landed on the main street of town in front of the Wheatgrowers' Savings and Loan, which he promptly and politely proceeded to rob, he was fired upon by one Charles "Choctaw Charlie" Flying Eagle, age 14, returning to town with his .22 rifle from a successful prairie dog hunt. It was thought that "Bonnie" may have been struck by one of the bullets.

We are told that Clyde is much missed by this magazine's dust bowl readers, if not by the bankers of the region. Follow-up reports on his whereabouts will be printed in future issues of *True Detective*.

"Well, Miss Jane, I am clearly in the wrong line of work," Henry chuckled. "Think of the opportunities I've missed out on. This Courteous Clyde fellow is one up on me."

He closed his magazine, flopped back in the hammock, and pushed his white boater down over his eyes as if preparing to take an afternoon snooze.

"Are you a betting woman, Miss Jane?"

"I am not."

"No, of course not. But if you were a betting woman —"

"Which I am not."

"Which you are not, but if you were, you could bet your last dime that Courteous Clyde, whoever he may be, would not have left three or four thousand dollars in cash to lie fallow in the Common bank but would have taken it to redistribute from aloft."

"Why would *anyone* who broke into the bank leave the cash?"

"Well, *anyone might* leave the cash in order not to draw down the G-men on himself. If they don't even know what was stolen, you see, they can't be expected to investigate too zealously."

Miss Jane looked at Henry, his hat tipped over his face, and was quite sure that she did see. Just what he had found in the bank vault, if her suspicions were correct, was evidently going to remain a mystery. It seemed clear to her, however, that her friend the judge had been right about Henry Satterfield. There was little doubt in Miss Jane's mind that for the past three and a half months she had been harboring a professional bank robber on Kingdom Mountain.

The drought continued. Commoners and farmers had begun to use the word now: *drought*. The first cutting of hay had been sparse, and at this rate there would not be another. In the meantime the Connector, despite Judge Allen's ruling that it could not infringe upon Miss Jane's property, came closer and closer to the mountain. One morning near the end of the month a gigantic steam shovel appeared on a flatbed of the

Boston to Montreal freight. That afternoon the machine began widening the cut at the foot of Blue Clay Hill, where the Upper Kingdom River pouring out of Lord Hollow joined the East Branch from Kingdom Mountain. Miss Jane could stand on her porch and watch the progress of the right of way by the dust clouds rising above the oncoming construction. It was evident that the town fathers and Eben fully expected the Supreme Court to decide in their favor, though the case was not scheduled for another month. In accordance with Ira Allen's recommendation, Miss Jane had hired his son, Forrest, to represent her. She hinted to her dear people in On Kingdom Mountain that if they were willing to lend their assistance, she still had a surprise or two up her sleeve for Montpelier.

She was contemplating these surprises, with some considerable satisfaction, one morning while touching up the bright red cockade on her pileated-woodpecker door knocker, when she realized that for some time she had been staring at the completed riddle on the slate beside the door.

The Riddle of Kingdom Mountain: The Trinity

Behold! on high with the blessed sweet host,
Nor Father, nor Son, but Holy Ghost.
The soldier stands vigil, where the rood is rove,
Over the golden trove.

"I reckon it wasn't a map in that bank strongbox after all," Henry Satterfield remarked from the hammock. "It was the rest of that jingle. At least that's what came to me last night in a dream. I somehow was holding a letter in my hand, written by my granddaddy to your father, thanking him for a certain long-ago service. Then down at the bottom, why, there was the balance of the riddle. Your second sight must be catching, Miss Jane. But I would like to ask you a question. What's a rood?"

"I believe that a rood is a rather archaic term for a cross. I'm surprised that you, with your newfound second sight, didn't divine its meaning.

"Henry," she said suddenly, "do you fear ghosts?"

"Ghosts? No, ma'am. I learned in the war it wasn't the poor dead I needed to fear but the quick. Particularly when they spoke German and were trying to shoot me and my machine out of the sky."

In fact, that was not entirely the case. Ever since he was a boy, growing up with his storytelling granddaddy in the haint-infested bayous of East Texas, Henry had been quite terrified by anything having to do with the supernatural, though he was not about to admit as much to the practical-minded Miss Jane Hubbell Kinneson.

"A very sensible reply, sir. I'm glad you don't. For I'm afraid that if you're still interested in helping me, a rather somber task lies before us. Not to put too fine a point on it, I need to make a little transfer."

"What kind of transfer, Miss Jane?"

Jane thought for a moment. Then she said, "For reasons I shall explain in good time, my grandparents chose not to be buried in the family plot in Kingdom Mountain Cemetery but across the pike in what has long been known as the paupers' field. It is an arrangement I have never been comfortable with, and less so now that we are being threatened with this high road. I would like to transfer their remains to the family plot."

"I Jesus!" Henry exclaimed, sitting bolt upright and nearly tipping out of the hammock.

"If you'll agree to help me with the transfer," Miss Jane said, "I will help you try to solve the riddle. Here." She reached into her dress pocket and withdrew the double eagle she'd found in the stomach of the trout and now carried as a good-luck token. She said, "I think you know what this is. Never mind just where I found it for the time being. No, I want you to keep it. We'll call it earnest money. What do you say? Shall we strike hands on our partnership?"

This may have been the single inducement Miss Jane could have offered Henry to persuade him to assist her in what he could only regard as a most ghoulish task. Somewhat reluctantly, he extended his hand. Yet while Jane could not be sure, she thought Henry held her hand in his for just a moment longer than customary in a purely business transaction. Or maybe that was wishful thinking on her part.

20

LATER THAT EVENING the low high sheriff drove out to Miss Jane's home place, and he and Henry walked down the lane to the hemlock-plank covered bridge. The sheriff spit tobacco over the wooden railing into the river and said, "This little bank matter, Mr. Satterfield, puts a law fella in a pickle. So I need to ask you a question. Did you ever hear tell of a fella name of Clyde?"

"I have known a few Clydes in my day," Henry admitted.

The low high sheriff, the crown of whose sheriffing hat came up to the middle of Henry's white sport jacket, said, "Have you ever knowed one goes by the name Courteous Clyde? Courteous Clyde of the Clouds?"

"I read up on him recently," Henry said. "He sounds like quite the ticket. Showering schoolchildren with silver dollars. Robbing banks with an airplane."

The sheriff nodded. "Well, here is how it is. If you can help me keep Courteous Clyde of the Clouds and his ilk away from Kingdom County, I will not prosecute this latest banking transaction in the Common too hard. After all, nothing of value seems to be missing from the vault."

"I don't reckon you'll be seeing Clyde away off up here in these mountains, Sheriff. No, I think I can safely say you won't see him again."

"Again," the sheriff said.

"At all," Henry corrected himself. "I meant to say you won't see him at all."

After a minute the sheriff said, "Do you like to fish?"

"I do," Henry said. "Do you?"

The sheriff allowed that he liked to fish. Then he said, "If Clyde ever did come here, or was thinking of it, I wonder why? Whatever would draw him clear up to the dead end of nowhere?"

"Oh, just to relax, to have a little getaway for a few weeks, I imagine. Just until the hay-fever season is over. Then I imagine your Courteous Clyde would be off to bigger and better things."

"Well, the judge has a message for Clyde. Should you happen to bump into him."

"The judge?" Henry said, feeling a chill race up his back. "Judge Allen?"

"That would be the one. Judge Allen would like you to get word to Mr. Clyde that if he, or any fella whosoever, was to harm a hair on Miss Jane's head, or mislead her in any way, or trifle with her heart, or make off with anything belonging to her — them were the judge's exact words, Mr. Satterfield, *to make off with anything belonging to Miss Jane* — Clyde would never be able to run so far or fly so fast that Judge Allen wouldn't find him."

Fred Morse looked at Henry. "It wouldn't do," he said, "to underestimate the judge. He and Jane go back a long way."

"Please tell the judge he has nothing to worry about," Henry said. "Please tell him that from what I have read about Courteous Clyde, his intentions are always those of a gentleman."

The sheriff seemed satisfied. His hat nodded up and down. Then as if to seal the matter, he spit into the river just below a leaning soft maple, the first tree on the mountain to turn red in the fall. A blue-backed char about sixteen inches long came up to investigate and, so fast Henry could not quite follow the motion, the low high sheriff drew his long-barreled .45 sheriffing pistol and shot off the trout's head. "That's how I like to fish," he explained as he started down the bank. "They don't suffer that way. I don't like to think of them flopping around on the end of a sharp hook, suffering." His voice sounded far away in Henry's roaring ears.

Fred labored back up the bank in his high-heeled cowboy boots, holding the mostly headless fish by its blue-tinged tail. "I like to eat them, too," he said. Then he added, "It's that consarned water."

"Did you get wet? Fill your boot?"

The sheriff shook his head. "No. It's that hard water over in the village. Folks are getting bound up again. I'd like to hire you to take I and Doc back up to Canady this Friday. For another batch of Dr. P."

"I believe that can be arranged," Henry said.

"I thought it could be," the sheriff said amiably. "Keep in mind what the judge said, if you will. Keep in mind that I like to fish. And how."

"Oh," Henry said, "I'll never forget it."

21

Henry Satterfield seemed out of sorts or, as Miss Jane put it, at sixes and sevens, after ambling down from the outhouse past the drought-stricken hollyhocks and golden glow early the next morning and seeing, in Jane's barnyard, her yoke of red oxen hitched to a sledge. On its flat bed were two long-handled spades, an iron bar, a coil of stout rope, and Pharaoh's Daughter's sweetgrass basket. Though the temperature was already over seventy, and Henry had been looking forward to this day for reasons of his own, yet another chill ran through him.

After breakfast they headed west out the pike road behind the thumping sledge. Miss Jane wore a long dark dress, high black rubber barn boots, and, despite the warm weather, her red and green wool lumber jacket, fastened at the top, where it was missing a button, with the oversized safety pin. She walked as straight and tall as any woman in Kingdom County and briskly, too, so that Henry, who had no great love for walking if he could ride or, better yet, fly, had to hurry to keep up with her and the oxen.

The pike road hooked up the mountainside through Jane's former sheep pasturage. Ahead was the original homestead of Venturing Seth Kinneson. Here, in 1775, he had thrown up a one-room log house in the wilderness where he had lived for a few years with his family before building the home place. Under the poplars marking the site of his first pitch, a red rose bush was blooming. Perhaps Seth's wife, Huswife, had brought it with her from Massachusetts.

They continued along the overgrown road behind the oxen,

passing cellar holes and barn foundations. In the disused fields between the abandoned farmsteads, buttercups and daisies were giving way to steeplebush and meadowsweet. Already, high summer had arrived on Kingdom Mountain, though the prolonged drought had imparted to the foliage the parched and withered look of early fall, and the trees and shrubs were powdered with a compound of dust and fine ash from forest fires to the north.

A mile west of the home place the lane ran through the northeast edge of the cedar bog near the two cut-over hills forming the Gate to Canada. In a spongy region more water than dry land they crossed a plank bridge over Kingdom Mountain Burn. Downstream from the bridge the quick highland brook slowed to a creeping flow, winding darkly under cedars and hemlocks and losing itself a dozen times over in slangs and beaver backwaters before entering the river at the spawning pool. The bog water was tea-colored and icy cold. The backs and sides of the blue-backed char that lived here were dark as well. In the winter Miss Jane cut cedar fence posts and rails in the bog and skidded them out over the ice with Ethan and General Ira Allen. Some of the biggest bucks in Kingdom County bedded down in the bog by day, emerging to feed in the abandoned fields on the mountain after dark. To Henry Satterfield the bog was a forbidding place. Miss Jane had told him stories of unexplained disappearances and the loup-garou that had dwelt here since time out of mind, the monstrous werewolf that devoured wayfarers overtaken by darkness. She had carved a dozen of these creatures and sold them to folk-art collectors the world over.

"This was my wild young uncle's favorite place in the Kingdom," Jane said as they stood on the bridge and looked out at the bog. "Pilgrim Kinneson was as much at home here as the moose and bobcats."

"What did Pilgrim do that was wild?" Henry prompted.

"Oh, not so very much. He took a few char and deer out of season. My father told me that Pilgrim was a very neat hand with a gill net. And with a jacklight and a musket, too. I suppose he brought a little whiskey over the border. That was before he went off to war."

"Miss Jane? Has anyone ever truly disappeared in the bog?"

Jane hesitated. Then she said, "I know of just one who did. A girl. A young woman, actually. It was early winter, and the ice under the snow was uncertain. It was supposed that she drowned, but no one really knew. They never found the body."

Miss Jane shook her head. "Hand me that iron bar from the stoneboat if you will, please, Henry. We need to borrow a plank from the bridge."

She inserted the end of the bar under one of the twelve-foot-long planks and pried it up. The wood was damp and punky, and the square-headed nails pulled out easily. She pried up the middle and far end of the plank, and together she and Henry slid it onto the ox sledge.

As they emerged from the cedars into a scrub field, Miss Jane pointed to the top of a lone tamarack tree on the edge of the bog. On its topmost spire perched a red-tailed hawk. Beneath the tamarack was a barberry bush. Suddenly the hawk tilted its head forward and dived, talons extended. A snowshoe hare, brown for the summer, bounded out of the bush. It screamed once, then hung limp as a cloth as the red-tail silently carried it out of sight into the bog.

Jane bent over and picked up a tuft of brown hair near the barberry. "In the winter Monsieur Lapin would be white and camouflaged by a foot of snow. The hawk never would have spied him."

"Bad luck for the rabbit," Henry said.

"Good luck for the hawk," Jane said. "Strife, Mr. Satterfield. It's the way of the world. Gee up, steers."

As they headed up the mountain under a bluebird blue summer sky, Henry said, "I noticed you called the rabbit Monsieur Lapin. It reminded me of growing up in East Texas. Visiting my Creole grandma and grandpa over in Louisiana."

"That's what my family's neighbors, the Thibeaus, called the rabbits they snared. My father told me that for the first few years after coming here from Canada, the Thibeaus subsisted on rabbits. Rabbits and partridges and char. Whatever they could catch or snare."

Miss Jane pointed at a shallow cave in the mountainside. "That's where they wintered over the first year. With a cow and a logging horse and a few chickens and five children. Pamphille Thibeau worked on the far side of the mountain, cutting logs for my grandfather's sawmill. Oh, they lived a hardscrabble life, Henry. Dad and Pilgrim were attending the Kinnesonville school at the time. On the first day of the term all five of the Thibeau children showed up at the schoolhouse knowing not a word of English among them. But they all turned out to be very able scholars. Manon, the oldest girl, was just Pilgrim's age."

The pike road wound up past the Thibeaus' cave, which ran back into the cliff about fifteen feet. Actually, it was less a cave than a shelter roofed by a rock overhang.

"After a few years, Pamphille bought a peddler's wagon and painted it red and yellow," Miss Jane said. "He traveled the borderlands from farm to farm selling household wares out of that painted wagon. Manon used to go along to translate for him. But the Thibeaus were always regarded as different by some people. They spoke a different language, their main holiday was New Year's rather than Christmas, and they said their prayers on a string of beads. One night soon after they shifted here from Canada, some Commoners paraded up the mountain in white sheets and burned a cross in front of the cave. Manon raced cross-lots to our place, and my grandfather rode up and confronted the rabble."

"With a gun?"

Miss Jane shook her head. "He didn't need a gun and wouldn't have brought one under any circumstances. He was a Quaker. He just reined in his horse and ordered the ruffians to leave the mountain straightaway and not return. Then for good measure he named them all by name, sheets or no. He knew well enough who the instigators were. From there it was an easy matter to surmise the names of the riffraff who would follow them. As for the Thibeaus, they hung on for a time. But two of the children perished in an epidemic, another boy was lost in the Civil War, and yet another was killed in a lumbering mishap. Then Pamphille and his wife died. Eventually, the mountain claimed them all."

"Maybe that's where the treasure is buried," Henry said. "In the cave."

Miss Jane shook her head and smiled. "I'm afraid that the only treasure is the mountain itself, Henry. That's a treasure worth preserving. Come up, boys."

She clicked to the oxen, and they proceeded up the mountainside above the Thibeaus' cave.

SALADA TEA. The black letters painted on the inside of the window stood out sharply. Below them, like an afterthought, were the words KINNESONVILLE GENERAL STORE AND POST OFFICE.

Miss Jane and Henry stood on the listing porch of the former store in the deserted hamlet. Cupping their hands around their eyes to cut down on the reflection, they peered inside at the empty shelves. Set into the wall behind the counter were forty wooden cubbyholes where forty families had once received their mail. But Kinnesonville had been tenantless for more than a decade. The store had not been a working store for longer yet. The five or six houses still standing were overrun with bittersweet and wild grapevines. If the high road went through, they would be burned to the ground.

"When my father was a boy, Henry, he came here every Saturday morning to pick up the *Farmer's Weekly Companion*. The *Companion* ran pirated installments from Charles Dickens's novels, and the line of people waiting for the next installment often stretched all the way out the door and down to the pike."

Across the road from the store was the one-room school over which Miss Jane had once presided. Next to it was the Kinnesonville church. The steeple, which had blown off in a hurricane, lay rotting in a wild raspberry patch like the fallen turret of a cursed castle. It was said in the Common that the church bell, long since sold for scrap iron, still tolled to lead lost hunters out of the cedar bog.

"Miss Jane, where did all these folks go?"

"Some moved out west where the farming was better. The more ambitious of the young people flocked to the cities. As for the old folks and the rest, well, Henry, they went where I and thou and the oxen must now go if we're to accomplish our day's work."

She pointed at the cemetery on the ridge above them. "Walk on, gentlemen," she said to the steers.

22

LIKE MANY ANOTHER New England cemetery, the Kingdom Mountain graveyard enjoyed one of the finest views for miles around. You could look west over the Green Mountains, stretching from Mount Mansfield and Camels Hump in the south all the way to the tall Canadian peaks in the distant north. Off to the southeast, just visible in the hazy air that had hung over the region for more than two months, the Presidential Range of the White Mountains loomed larger still. *On high,* Henry mused. The riddle specified that the golden trove was *on high.* Unless they went up to the mountaintop, to the peace cairn and the balancing boulder, they couldn't get much higher than they were. Furthermore, if a rood was a cross, a cemetery was a likely place to find one.

Surrounded by its antebellum iron picket fence, the graveyard contained no more than one hundred and fifty stones. None were in any way prepossessing, just gray granite markers two to three feet tall and as unadorned as the lives of the people whose final resting places they marked. Through the middle of the cemetery ran a row of mature sugar maples. Each March and April for many years, Jane had unsentimentally tapped the cemetery maples. In the northwest corner of the graveyard grew several old-fashioned varieties of apple trees. Near the orchard stood an elm with a swinging oriole's nest. Two new graves, which Jane told Henry she'd hired Clarence Davis, the local spruce-gum picker, to dig a week ago, lay waiting under the elm. A pair of robins searched for worms on the fresh mounds of earth beside them.

Just across the pike from Kingdom Mountain Cemetery was

the paupers' field, where Jane's grandparents were buried beneath two plain granite markers. Otherwise, the paupers' graveyard was a place of cedar. It was enclosed with cedar rails. The cedar-pole gate was hinged to upright cedar fence posts. Most of the thirty or so grave markers were made of cedar as well. Some of the crude wooden tablets had fallen over into the grass. Long neglected, they marked the graves of the mountain's outcasts and unknowns.

QUAKER MEETING KINNESON, 1805–1864. Below Jane's grandfather's dates was the word FATHER. Beside Quaker Meeting's stone was his wife's. JANE KINNESON. MOTHER. It had always seemed odd to Miss Jane to see her own name on her grandmother's gravestone.

In order to give his friend some time alone with her ancestors, Henry ambled off to read the inscriptions on the cedar markers. UNKNOWN DIED ON THE RIVER. And carved crudely on a fallen tablet, A CANUCK LUMBERJACK DIED FIGHTIN. Beneath Died Fightin's marker a woodchuck had tunneled a hole into the hillside. Nearby was the Thibeau plot. The graves of the children were designated by lozenge-shaped wooden markers no larger than breadboards.

The Duchess handed Henry a shovel. "This is just one more job of work on the mountain, Mr. Satterfield," she said stoically. "Taking care of family."

Jane set about digging methodically, like a woman spading up her kitchen garden in the fall. Henry, with his white showman's shoes and crimson vest, worked fitfully, in the unconvincing manner of a man not accustomed to physical labor. Yet there was something eager and anticipatory in his expression. Perhaps he merely wanted to get the transfers over with, Miss Jane thought.

Unlike the firmly packed blue clay of the river valley, the soil on the ridge was light glacial till. They were down to the coffins by noon. To Miss Jane's relief, both were intact.

She fetched the oxen and unhitched the stoneboat at the foot of her grandfather's grave. As Henry watched, she pried one end of the casket up at an angle with the iron bar, then wedged an end of the borrowed bridge plank under the raised casket. She wrapped the heavy rope they'd brought with them around the coffin and snubbed it off with a neat half hitch. The other end of the rope she ran over the top of the jutting plank and fastened to the pulling ring of the ox yoke.

Miss Jane clicked to the oxen. "Softly, boys."

As the animals eased forward, Quaker Meeting's coffin slid up the canted plank. Like a well-balanced seesaw, the plank with the coffin on top tipped down onto the bed of the stoneboat. Jane repeated the process with her grandmother's coffin, then clicked to the oxen and drove them out of the paupers' field and across the road into the cemetery proper, where she glanced up at the hazy sun. "I call this a fair morning's work, Henry. Let's take our nooning."

They ate on the burnt grass under the lone elm tree beside the new graves. As Miss Jane unpacked the sweetgrass basket, it seemed strange to Henry that she could sit so comfortably beside the last earthly remains of her grandparents and sprinkle salt on her hard-boiled egg and munch homemade baked bean sandwiches laced with maple syrup from the cemetery maples. But they were both hungry in the way people who have done hard work outdoors usually are, and after all, as Jane had remarked, she was just taking care of family.

"Family ties are of considerable consequence in my part of the country as well, Miss Jane," Henry said. "But with your permission, I wonder if I might make a rather personal inquiry?"

"Permission granted," Miss Jane said.

"Would you want me to" — Henry paused for the slightest moment — "view the remains? To spare you the pain?"

"Why, Henry Satterfield, whatever can you mean? I know very well whose remains are in those boxes. And I'll assure you that I don't care to view them. Why would you think I might wish to?"

Henry inclined his head toward Miss Jane, bowing slightly. "Why, indeed, Miss Jane," he said. "Why, indeed, now that I think of it. It was a passing whim. Forgive me."

"You've done nothing at all to be forgiven for, sir. If you truly thought I wished to verify the remains, it was a kind offer."

Suddenly Miss Jane's gray eyes were amused. "I do believe, Henry, that you suppose my grandfather found that so-called treasure and somehow arranged for it to be buried with him."

Henry bowed again in acknowledgment of Miss Jane's deduction. But she shook her head and said no, she was certain that if Quaker Meeting had ever stumbled on the loot from the robbery, he'd have returned it to the bank, ill-gotten gains from profiteering on the war or no. "And that's assuming that the treasure was ever buried on the mountain to start out with," she added. "Which I've always much misdoubted."

"Oh," Henry said very gravely, "I believe it was buried on the mountain, Miss Jane. I do believe it was. That, you see, must be the import of the riddle. However, as far as your grandfather finding the boodle and not returning it, I take your point. That would be very unlikely."

Miss Jane unwrapped another sandwich and handed it to the aviator, then folded up the brown butcher paper to use again. "So, Mr. Satterfield. No doubt you will remember this day in later life. Picnicking with your peculiar Vermont friend in Kingdom Mountain Cemetery whilst moving two graves."

"My friend, yes. But peculiar? Far from it."

"Oh, yes," Jane said. "I was a peculiar child, a peculiar, if capable, teacher, and I am a peculiar friend. You and I both know it."

Miss Jane seemed so proud of being a peculiar friend that Henry caught himself on the verge of acquiescing. Then, despite himself, his eyes swiveled back to the coffins. He must and would find a way to look inside them, even if he had to play grave robber and return under cover of darkness to re-exhume them.

Miss Jane handed him one of her famous cartwheel molasses cookies. "This puts me in mind of the day I got the receipt for these cookies, Mr. Satterfield. It was a very warm afternoon in the spring of the year back when I was keeping the Kinnesonville school. I happened to glance out the window, and for a moment I thought that a caravan from *The Arabian Nights* was winding down the valley. It was the Barnum & Bailey circus train, en route to Montreal. One hundred cars painted bright yellow and blue and red. When it stopped to take on water at the Kingdom Mountain tank, I let the entire school out. They were doing some minor repairs to the locomotive as we arrived, and it was such an unseasonably warm day that the circus master directed that the elephants be allowed to cool off in the river. Twenty performing elephants of all sizes were led out of the cars and into the big pool below the trestle. The circus master was very accommodating to the children. He pointed out Jumbo, the world's largest elephant. And he had one of the cooks give each of my scholars a huge molasses cookie. Those circus cookies were the best I ever ate. Before the train departed, I got the receipt."

"Well, Miss Jane," Henry said, lolling out with his sleek dark head propped on his fist and his elbow resting on the grass, "it just goes to prove what the old judge said."

"What might that be?" Miss Jane inquired.

"That if you but wait long enough, the world and everyone in it worth knowing will travel to Kingdom Mountain."

Henry plucked a clover blossom and held it on his tongue to

extract the sweetness. "Miss Jane," he said, "I'm truly sorry that the new highway's coming. Regardless of the higher court's decision, I am quite determined to help you stop it."

Miss Jane nodded, but her eyes had the abstracted expression that sometimes came into them just before one of her Kingdom Mountain moments.

"What do you see?" Henry said.

"I don't really see anything. It's more of an idea taking shape in my head. I just had the idea that years from now you might come here with a new wingwalker, a beautiful young woman who would like to hear a story."

"What story would I tell her?" Henry said. "How I moved some graves with Miss Jane Hubbell Kinneson?"

Miss Jane smiled and shook her head. "A young woman, Mr. Satterfield, would like to hear a love story. Hark now. I'll tell you one. When my uncle Pilgrim was home for the summer holidays from his medical studies at Harvard, he fell deeply in love with Manon Thibeau, the eldest daughter from the family I spoke of who dwelt in the cave. Manon was by all reports a beautiful woman and as much in love with Pilgrim as he was with her. But now enter my grandparents, Quaker Meeting and Jane Kinneson, who were appalled by the idea of a son of theirs courting a French Canadian girl. From the start they opposed the match."

"I thought your folks liked the Thibeaus. What about your father driving off those white-sheeted cowards who came to burn them out?"

"Protecting a neighbor and his family from a craven mob was one thing. Countenancing a marriage between their son and a Catholic girl was an altogether different matter. Manon's parents felt the same way about their daughter marrying a Protestant. Both sets of parents honestly believed that if Pilgrim and Manon married outside their faith, they and their children and all their descendants to come would burn in Hell forever."

Miss Jane looked at the weathermaker. "In the fall of that year, Manon vanished."

Jane sat looking silently down the mountainside. Then she said, "Manon, Henry, was the girl I told you about who disappeared in the bog. The Thibeaus didn't place a grave marker for her because they kept hoping she'd show up. But she never did. After she vanished, Pilgrim ran away to war, and we heard nothing of him until his commanding officer reported him missing in Tennessee."

Henry thought for a few moments, sucking on another clover blossom. "Miss Jane? Where in Tennessee did Pilgrim turn up missing?"

"Near a town called Gatlinburg. It was thought he'd been captured by Will Thomas's Cherokees and taken back up into the mountains of North Carolina. But we never learned his fate for certain. When he came up missing, my grandparents, in their despair, turned against the very doctrines they had cleaved to when Pilgrim and Manon wished to marry. First they withdrew from the Presbyterian church. Then they renounced the religion of their ancestors altogether. Finally they insisted on being buried in the paupers' field with the French Canadians and outcasts and unknowns."

Miss Jane stood up. "But times change, Mr. Satterfield. And I have a role in all this, too. My role is to rectify what I can by reuniting family and neighbors. And in matters that I can't rectify, at least to bear witness to all that has happened. And to do so without judgment. I thank you, sir, for your help in this matter. And Henry? The gold isn't in those coffins. They're as light as feathers. Go see for yourself so you won't lie awake nights wondering."

23

JUST OUTSIDE THE cemetery gate, an iron pump stood on a granite millstone. The pipe from the pump ran through the hole in the stone to a well deep under the ground. This well had long been believed to be fed by an underground aquifer of glacial meltwater ten thousand years old. The well water, the coldest and purest in all Kingdom County, was called Easter water because for more than one hundred years people from Kinnesonville and the surrounding farms had gathered here on Easter morning to pump water for washing and drinking. It was thought that the Easter water washed away sins, assuaged guilty consciences, and reconciled grudges between family members and neighbors. How this tradition started no one knew. But for many years Presbyterians, French Canadians, and even a few Kingdom Mountain freethinkers had made their pilgrimage here on Easter Sunday, often in a spring snow-storm, to draw the healing water from deep in the heart of the mountain.

"Just how deep is this miracle well, Miss Jane?" Henry asked. Inclining his ear close to the opening, he dropped a pebble through the hole in the millstone.

"Deep enough, Henry, so that if that's where the raiders dumped the boodle, that's where it will stay till Gabriel blows his trump."

When Miss Jane filled a blue flower vase from an ancestor's grave with brook water and primed the pump, the pressure pulled back on the handle like a big trout. She loved thinking that the icy water that gushed out of the rusty metal spout might have come straight from a glacier. She filled the vase and returned to the two coffins, which she and Henry slid, one at a time, down the plank into their new graves. They could not have been much lighter if they were empty, Henry thought, but now he was terribly worried that the gold might be deep in the impenetrable granite core of the mountain, submerged in the well beneath hundreds of feet of glacial water.

Miss Jane picked a few clover blossoms and dropped them onto the coffins. Dipping her fingers into the brimming vase, she sprinkled Easter water over the rough wooden lids. A mourning cloak butterfly, so recently emerged that its blue and yellow wing bands still glistened, landed on one of the coffins and sipped at a droplet.

"Shoo," Miss Jane said to the butterfly. "It's too late in the day for you to be out and about. Go back to sleep till morning."

She and Henry began to fill in the graves, though not before the showman fixed a last lingering look on the coffins, as though he'd still like to look inside, just to be sure of what he already knew.

"They'd be much heavier," Miss Jane said to him again. "Let us get on with the work at hand, shall we?"

Just before leaving the cemetery, she patted down the fresh dirt on the two graves and repeated, quietly, "Go back to sleep, my dears. No one will disturb you again."

The granite markers of her grandparents' graves were not large, and it was not hard to dig them out of the ground, tip them onto the stoneboat, and move them across the pike to the main cemetery. Then they went back to the paupers' field once more to fill in the empty graves, Miss Jane taking care to shut and fasten the cedar gate behind herself. There were no longer any cattle or horses or sheep on the mountain to wander into the paupers' field. Closing gates behind herself was simply something Jane's father had taught her to do when she was a small girl. It went beyond habit.

The wind was gusting out of the north, sweeping down from Canada over Cemetery Ridge, as it had since long before there were any people on the mountain, alive or dead. As they threw the dirt back into the holes, Henry could feel blisters beginning to form on his hands.

"A harsh and forlorn place, this mountain," Miss Jane said when they were finished.

"I'd have liked to see it when it was all cleared to fields and pasture," Henry said.

"Perhaps you will."

Henry looked at her, but all she said was "Let's head home."

They started down the mountainside, the oxen walking faster now. Kinnesonville looked even emptier, the bog below darker and more forbidding. Back at the home place Miss Jane fed and watered the oxen, then made supper. She and Henry ate at the applewood kitchen table, a plain country supper of sausage, toasted homemade bread, fried potatoes, coffee, and apple pie. Afterward Miss Jane surprised Henry by asking him to join her in On Kingdom Mountain. Most evenings they sat visiting on the porch or in the kitchen.

From the Currier and Ives safe, Miss Jane removed a cardboard box containing her stereopticon, a wooden device about a foot long. At one end was a binocular eyepiece with thick lenses, and at the other end a rectangular pasteboard card mounted with two identical photographs was placed in a wireframe holder. When viewed through the lenses, the twin photographs formed a single picture in three dimensions.

From the box, Miss Jane selected a card, which she inserted into the holder. To focus the device, you moved the frame like a trombone slide. As a girl, Jane had loved repairing to the parlor with her folks after a holiday meal and viewing slides of the

Grand Canyon, Niagara Falls, and other exotic places. She and Henry Satterfield had looked at some of those photographs before, but tonight what came into focus when Henry peered through the eyepiece was the home place. In front, by the gate, was a box-shaped wagon drawn by a white horse wearing a straw hat with two ear holes. On the side of the cart were the words PAMPHILLE THIBEAU PEDDLER. Beside the horse stood a smiling man with a hat like the horse's. Viewed through the stereopticon, Pamphille Thibeau looked strikingly lifelike. Beyond him the home place gleamed with fresh white paint, against which the family motto on the lintel stood out clearly. Over the gate was a wooden trellis covered with blossoming roses.

Miss Jane handed Henry another slide. It was a formal tableau of people in old-fashioned suits and long dresses posing in chairs on the lawn in front of the home place. Behind them children of various ages were arranged on the porch steps.

"The man with the beard sitting in the Boston rocker beside the woman in an identical rocker is my grandfather, Quaker Meeting," Miss Jane said.

Quaker Meeting Kinneson looked gravely out of the picture as if he were viewing Henry Satterfield rather than vice versa, and Henry did not quite measure up. The pilot had no difficulty imagining this stern old patriarch facing down the nightriders who had terrorized the Thibeaus on the mountain. Or forbidding his son Pilgrim to marry Pamphille's daughter Manon.

For the next hour, while the wind rose, Miss Jane handed Henry one slide after another from the history of her family.

"County Champions," she said. Into view came a dozen schoolboy ballplayers wearing baggy homemade uniform pants and shirts and homemade caps with rounded bills that made their faces look like those of grown men. The champions were perched on the railing of the Kinnesonville school porch. Some wore old-fashioned baseball gloves with pockets as thin as pancakes and fingers as thick as sausages. "That's yours truly," Miss Jane said, pointing to a pretty, long-legged girl with light hair. "I played first base and batted leadoff, where I could put my fleetness to advantage."

"Circus Train," Miss Jane said. "I snapped this one." The Barnum & Bailey train sat on the siding by the water tower near the high trestle. "Jumbo, World's Largest Elephant" stood knee-deep in the big pool below the trestle, spraying his back with cool river water.

Miss Jane handed Henry a slide of the Kinnesonville church, its toppled steeple miraculously reattached. On the church lawn people were eating at trestle tables. "Church Supper."

Next came a photograph of the Kingdom River in the spring, packed with logs from bank to bank. Downriver more logs were flying high into the air. Men in calked boots and checked shirts watched from the bank. "Dynamiting the Jam." Henry wondered if one of the dynamiters was Died Fightin.

"Blueberrying" showed a young man and a young woman in berry bushes up to their waists. The girl had long dark hair and a heart-shaped face. She was wearing a white blouse with a high lace collar. Even before Miss Jane named the berry pickers, Henry was sure that this was a picture of Pilgrim Kinneson and Manon Thibeau.

Next came two photographs of the south side of Kingdom Mountain, cleared to fields where originally there had been only woods, and woods were once more fast encroaching. Miss Jane showed Henry farmers sitting on chopping blocks with dogs at their feet, hunters standing beside heavy buck deer hanging from dooryard maples, logging horses skidding gigantic tree trunks through snowy evergreen woods, men in suspenders and felt boots holding court around the stove in the Kinnesonville store, their expressions as deliberate as those of Supreme Court justices.

In one photograph taken on a stormy winter day, people in sheepskin coats and fur hats were lined up in front of the post office and store. The queue stretched along the porch past the window with the SALADA TEA sign and down the steps and out into the snow-filled street. "Waiting for *David Copperfield*."

The last slide, "Armistice Day," showed the people of Kingdom Mountain marching in a parade through Kinnesonville. The procession was led by a three-piece brass band. Miss Jane said no one dreamed that in less than two weeks the town would be struck by the influenza epidemic that would kill one of every two men, women, and children in the photograph. Through some quirk of light or exposure, the eyes of the marchers looked white and spectral. "I call this 'Ghosts,'" she said.

For a time it was quiet in On Kingdom Mountain, as if Miss Jane's dear people, too, were spellbound by the family photographs.

Then Jane said, "I thank you, Henry. For your help today."

Henry shrugged and started to leave the parlor. But Miss Jane held out the boxes with the stereopticon and slides. "These are for you."

"I don't want a reward, Miss Jane. I was glad to help."

Jane tucked the boxes under Henry's arm. "Show them to your next beautiful young wingwalker," she teased.

Henry thanked her and started up the stairs toward his bedchamber.

"Mr. Satterfield," Jane said just before he reached the top of the stairs, "the photographs aren't a present. They're a legacy. You see, there is no one else here on the mountain to leave them to."

Outside, the wind was blowing against the weathered clapboards of the home place. In the graveyard on the mountain it blew harder still, over the granite and cedar markers and the newly dug graves. Yet there were no ghosts on Kingdom Mountain that night. Only stories, some of which, like Pilgrim's fate and Manon's, might remain mysteries for all time to come.

24

"Speaking of stories, Miss Jane, I believe that you were going to finish telling me that deer-hunting yarn you'd started."

It was the following evening and they had just settled in for their featherbed chat, which they had both come to look forward to greatly. Almost, Miss Jane thought, like a long-married couple. Or two young lovers in a fairy tale, kept apart by a high wall or, like Pilgrim and Manon Thibeau, by wrongheaded families.

"Was I?" she called up through the vent. "Where did I leave off?"

"You and your father were at the camp, and you wanted to shoot a deer to impress your beau, Ira Allen."

"For goodness' sake, Henry, he wasn't my beau. I was far too strong-minded to declare myself to any beau. But yes, I did want to impress him. As I was telling you, it was still snowing hard when my father and I turned in for the night. Early the next morning, well before it was light, I woke to the smell of camp coffee and bacon and bread toasted on the camp stove. It had stopped storming, but the snow was a foot deep. Right after breakfast I started out with Lady Justice and six bullets, quite excited, now that I was doing it, to be hunting the mountain on my own. I walked carefully because I couldn't see what was beneath the snow, up the game trail above Pond Number Three beside that great wooden log chute. Two small deer had gone up the mountainside ahead of me that morning. I followed in their tracks, walking slowly so I wouldn't perspire and then take a chill on my stand, which Father had cautioned me against. I came out on top of the mountain directly below the balancing boulder. From that close the devil's visage resembled nothing at all."

Henry was sitting on the edge of his bed, the better to hear the story. He had spent much of the day lying in the porch hammock and speculating where he would have buried the stolen gold if he'd been with his granddaddy, the old captain, and his comrade-in-arms. Under the peace cairn? Beneath the floor of Camp Hard Luck? Was the camp even there in 1864? Listening to Miss Jane's story, Henry shut his eyes and saw double eagles dancing on the inside of his lids.

"I walked around the huge boulder," Miss Jane continued, "and admired the carved pictures of the caribou and whales and walruses. From here I could look down on the home place and the lane to the river, which was still open and steaming, and then on along the valley to the village. I could see much of northern Vermont and New Hampshire and deep into Canada. I counted thirty-six peaks, all pink on top from the sunrise reflecting off the snow.

"Three deer went over the mountaintop that morning, two small does and a medium-sized buck with a six-point rack, not a deer to impress anyone with. For lunch I ate meatloaf on homemade bread, pickles, and mother's chocolate cake. Afterward I sighted Lady Justice in on the fire tower, which was still covered with rime.

"Then, in the pale November sunshine, I fell asleep. For a moment or two after I woke I didn't know where I was. I must have slept for a good while, because the sun was nearing

Mount Mansfield, far off to the southwest, and it was colder. How could I, the last of the Memphremagog Abenakis, have fallen asleep on stand? I was mortified.

"That's when I saw the deer. It had been there, pawing up moss under the snow below the fire tower, for some time. It was huge, with massive antlers. I never stopped to think what I was going to do next. I drew a bead, and when I clicked back the hammer, the buck heard the noise and bolted. I fired once, levered in another shell, fired a second time. My second shot hit the animal in the back left leg. It collapsed but was up again immediately, plunging down the mountainside out of sight. Henry, I felt terrible. What would my father say when he learned I'd wounded the deer and let it get away? How, for that matter, could I live with myself, knowing that I'd wounded that animal mainly to impress a young man? To persuade him that I was something I wasn't, at least not yet, a hunter capable of bringing home a great trophy. All, *all* was wrong. This whole adventure was wrong, and in it I thought I saw all that was wrong about our living on this mountain. Isolating ourselves in a wilderness that none of us, really, was suited for. Right then I made up my mind that I was not going to let the mountain trap me the way it had trapped my father and his father and grandfather. Deeply ashamed, angry with my family and with myself, sick at heart that the deer might die an agonizing death in some blowdown, I started down the mountain after it. In the hour of remaining light, I was determined to track the animal to its bed and put it out of its misery."

Henry was somewhat disappointed. This story did not, after all, seem headed toward any revelation about the treasure, though you could never be sure just where Miss Jane's stories were going until they got there and he was, admittedly, eager to hear whether she had succeeded in putting the poor deer out of its misery and winning Ira Allen's heart.

"At first the buck stayed in the trail I'd followed up the mountain that morning. It was easy to track him by the blood in the snow. About halfway down the mountainside, he veered off into what we called the Limberlost, a very wild and forbidding region that had always made me uneasy. Follow him there I must, though. The deer zigged and zagged, around gigantic boulders broken off from the mountaintop eons ago, around barberry thickets, the tiny red berries bright in the slanted light, the animal's blood on the snow brighter still. He crossed several seeps trickling off into Bad Brook. Just at dusk I came into a clearing near three old American chestnut trees that had somehow survived the great blight that left scarcely one chestnut standing from New England to Georgia. The wounded buck stood under one of the chestnuts, with his profile to me. I counted eight points on one side of his rack, nine on the other. I thought again of my father, who at just seventeen had had a huge responsibility: to find his brother, missing in Tennessee. I had a small responsibility: to finish the deer I'd wounded. I raised Lady Justice and did so with a shot straight to the heart, and not long afterward, my father appeared in the clearing. Working quickly, we dressed out the deer and put its liver in Father's pack basket. He never mentioned the wound in the buck's leg.

"When I asked him how we would ever get the huge deer back down to Camp Hard Luck, he thought for a moment, then said we'd give him an old-fashioned bobsled ride. That's just what we did. We dragged the buck over to the log chute, which was covered with a few inches of snow, and together we hoisted him onto the steep incline and gave him a shove. Down he went, whizzing along at a terrific rate of speed. Half an hour later we retrieved the animal from the frozen pond below. One of the tines on his right antler had snapped off when it hit the ice, so now he had eight points on each side. We dragged the carcass up to the camp and hung it by the horns from the heavy beam extending out from the roof peak.

"That night it snowed again, Henry. As we built up the fire in the camp stove with the sweet-smelling yellow birch and sugar maple in the woodbox, I asked father point-blank whether, on his trek south, he had found any trace of Pilgrim.

"'Daughter,' he said, 'I walked a thousand miles and more in search of my brother. I saw terrible things for a young man of seventeen, or a man of any age, to see. When I returned home, I had no further wish to view the world beyond Vermont. I vowed to myself that I would never leave again, and if I could prevent it, no Kinneson would leave Vermont to sacrifice himself, or herself, for whatever cause, ever again.' My father's way of ensuring this, insofar as he could, was to leave me the mountain in trust for my direct heirs, they to hold it in trust for theirs, and so on, in perpetuity."

"With respect, I think your father did you no good service with such a stipulation, Miss Jane."

"I think that you are right, Mr. Satterfield," Jane said quietly.

For a time neither spoke. Then Henry said, "But what about young Ira Allen? Was he impressed with your great hunting feat?"

"I think he was," Miss Jane said. "Though perhaps the deer impressed him more than I did. As the seventeenth Earl wrote, the course of true love never did run smooth. Not entirely smooth, at least. Ira was, and is, the least envious person I've ever known. Yet I think that when he first saw that big deer, he was just a little envious of it and of me for shooting it. How could he not be? When it came to hunting I was an amateur who'd had a huge stroke of beginner's luck. Still, I'm glad I finished it. As I've said, Henry, my real mistake with Ira was never declaring myself. *That* is always a mistake."

25

For a long time that night Henry lay tossing in his upstairs chamber, dwelling on Miss Jane's story and his grandfather's riddle and the treasure. "Behold! on high with the blessed sweet host." The line ran through his mind like the refrain of some old hymn that he did not care for but could not dislodge from his thoughts. Suddenly he sat up. He stood and, as if in a trance, went to the west dormer window and looked out toward the lake and the mountains beyond. Little Lord Jesus Asleep in the Hay! In the cupola of the abandoned town farm, two miles to the west, was a flickering light. "On high," he muttered. "The blessed sweet host." The poorhouse cupola was surely "on high," looming three stories into the air and commanding a heavenly view far up the lake into Canada. That was it, Henry thought. The treasure lay concealed beneath the floor of the cupola, where, Miss Jane had told him, runaway slaves once hid.

It seemed to Henry, as he hurried into his white suit, that this was the moment he had been born for. Shoes in hand, he tiptoed downstairs and, ever so stealthily, let himself out the door, not failing to give his little salute to the two-headed Memphre Magog beside the door and, opposite him, the Loup-Garou wearing Mambrino's golden helmet. Fetching Miss Jane's big barn lantern and the crowbar they'd used on their excursion to the cemetery, he noticed that his hands were trembling slightly.

As the excited weathermaker posted along over the old pike through the dark woods, past cellar holes and barn foundations of Kinnesons long since moldering in their graves, toward the big lake and the abandoned town farm, he could not stop thinking about ghosts, haunted houses, and specters. Weren't the sites of the hidden treasures he'd been reading about nearly always haunted? The idea of creeping through a dark and empty building rumored to be frequented by the long-dead gave him great pause. A man who had fought the Hun four or five thousand feet above German soil, who had worked as an itinerant bank teller specializing in withdrawals at the end of a fiddle case, and who had flown around the known world putting on aerobatic exhibitions should not be daunted by tales designed to entertain children of a winter's evening. Henry thought of the shining gold coins sacked up under the cupola's floorboards and quickened his pace. Now that he had deciphered the mad old captain's riddle, he could not let someone else, quick or dead, beat him to the boodle.

From high on the mountain something howled. A wildcat, maybe. Or a poor hare taken by a fox or an owl. Henry recalled the frightful story Miss Jane had told him about Rogers' Rangers, returning from their retaliatory raid on her ancestors, surprised on the lakeshore very near where Henry now found himself. Three of Rogers' men had been slaughtered and their heads used as makeshift bowling balls. A sensible man would go back to the home place and return for the treasure the next day, in the bright and reassuring morning sunshine, with Miss Jane. What if, so far from discovering the gold, he encountered the dreaded Lady of the Lake who was said to flit through the forlorn premises of the old manse and lure young men to a watery death? Though Henry's heart was no longer in this enterprise, his white shoes, just visible in the darkness, carried him swiftly along, closer and closer to the poor farm. What did Miss Jane love to cite? *Alia jacta est.* Yes. The die was cast.

As he approached the peninsula near where he had wrecked his biplane on the ice, the poorhouse towered up before him, its ornate scallops and gingerbread and gables all pale and strange-looking in the thin moonlight. He could hear the waves crashing on the stony beach. The light in the cupola flared, then nearly went out, like a wavering beacon. Someone *on high* was up to no good, Henry was certain of it. He realized that he had no plan for getting rid of the intruder. Maybe he could frighten off whoever it was with the crowbar. If attacked, he supposed he could use the bar as a weapon, though that would be more his granddaddy's style than his. Once he had witnessed Captain Cantrell Satterfield, CSA, Retired, harry two little black girls away from his favorite fishing stump with a sugar-cane machete.

The front steps of the home were granite, but the wooden porch planks had rotted through in places. The door stood partway open, and in the moonlight Henry could see broken bottles strewn over the hallway floor. Only when he was inside the hulking shell did he light his lantern, which cast unsettling shadows on the cracked plaster walls and ceiling of the hallway. Just ahead a circular staircase ascended to the upper floors. Somewhere a loose shutter banged. It occurred to Henry that he had no way to transport the gold back to the home place. He wondered if, for caution's sake, he should rebury it somewhere on the mountain. It was important that no one other than Miss Jane catch wind of his discovery. Pausing on the second-floor landing, he wondered again what the "Holy Ghost" in the riddle signified. *Nor Father, nor Son, but Holy Ghost.* Could it be the resident apparition, the Lady of the Lake? He took a furtive glimpse out the landing window and was terribly startled to see, peering back at him, a spectral figure dressed all in white and holding a lantern. His realization, a moment later, that he had been frightened by his own reflection did little to allay his terror. On up the creaking steps he fled. The stairs to the cupola rose dark and forbidding ahead of him. After falling in love with Robert Louis Stevenson's *Treasure Island,* he had, at Miss Jane's suggestion, been reading his way through Stevenson's boys' adventure tales. Recently he had finished *Kidnapped*. He thought of David Balfour's crazed uncle Ebenezer sending David up the crumbling steps of the old tower, ending in thin air.

Here, now, the grandfather's voice said. *Catch a-holt of yourself. Do you want that loot or don't you?*

Up, up the narrow steps he went, chivvied on by the relentless captain. The door to the cupola was closed, but when he lifted the latch, it immediately swung open to reveal eight or nine dogs blocking his way. Henry was so flabbergasted he nearly forgot to be afraid. Together, the dogs represented a dozen different mixed breeds: Border collie crossed with spaniel, retriever with boxer, a flop-eared blue hound with the legs of a poodle, a shepherd with the head of a Newfoundland. The room was so brightly lit that spots danced in front of Henry's eyes, and he thought he must be seeing things.

A diminutive figure, his back to Henry and dressed in a paint-spattered smock, was painting, by lantern light, a replica of Kingdom County on the floor of the cupola. In the painting, Lake Memphremagog stretched north through the mountains into Canada. Above the gleaming lake loomed Kingdom Mountain and, on the summit, the great balancing rock with the animals carved on its face. To the south, surrounded by green and leafy hills, lay the village of Kingdom Common. But at the far northern end of the lake, a huge glacier, gleaming silver, blue, and crimson in the lowering sun, was advancing on the Kingdom.

In the Common it was high summer, while on Miss Jane's mountain fall had arrived and the slopes were a riot of red and orange. Farther north it was spring, with the early blush of small gold leaves covering the mountains. Stretching south from the great glacier at the Canadian end of the lake, the surface of Memphremagog was frozen, and a winter gale was blowing in from the west. Grazing at the foot of the glacier were two benign-looking mastodons.

At last the painter stood up, turned around, and noticed Henry, standing stock-still in his white suit. He grinned and made a small sideways motion with his hand, and instantly the menagerie of fantastically colored dogs lay down with their heads on their front paws. Still grinning, the man peered up at Henry, who, without quite knowing why, reached into his pants pocket and brought out the old gold double eagle Miss Jane had given him as a good-luck piece. He flipped it end over end to the painter, who caught the coin in his mouth like one of his own dogs, removed it, examined it carefully, and put it in the pocket of his many-colored smock. Nodding rapidly several times, the painter knelt down again and began, with great rapidity, to paint a new scene on the side of Kingdom Mountain. By degrees, in the flickering lantern light in the old cupola, there appeared on the far side of the mountain a tall tree, quite unlike any Henry had ever seen. At the foot of the tree stood a soldier in a gray uniform, pointing a long-barreled pistol up into the thick green branches above. Whatever he was aiming at was invisible. When Henry tiptoed past the dogs and pointed into the foliage, the man shrugged.

"It's not here, sir," a voice behind him said. Whirling around, Henry came face to face with an apparition in a white gown, a long trailing white nightcap, and a hunting jacket. It could only be the ghostly Lady of the Lake, come to fetch him to her watery demesne.

"Henry!" Miss Jane said from under the nightcap. "What ails you? You look as if you'd seen your old captain himself. I said the gold isn't here. Hand me that bar. I'll show you."

Carefully, in order not to spoil the newly painted scene, Miss Jane pried up a floor plank. Except for a few old rags, the space below, where fugitive slaves were rumored to have been hidden, was empty.

"It's got to be here somewhere," Henry said, holding his lantern down near the hidey-hole while Miss Jane stared at the painter's representation of the butternut-clad soldier pointing his pistol into the branches of the strange tree. Then she replaced the plank, tipped her nightcap to the artist, and said, "Come, Henry. Our friend has work to do."

All Henry could do, however, was to shake his head wonderingly, as though he still thought that the treasure must be hidden "on high" in the cupola. The artist, for his part, continued to paint under the watchful eyes of his silent dogs.

Over the next several days, the mysterious dog-cart man, as he came to be known from the small red wagon pulled by his mongrels and containing his paint cans, brushes, and a bedroll, did great works in Kingdom County. Although the artist was deaf and mute and could not say where he had come from or why, he painted as though his very life depended upon putting his bright and primitive and entirely arresting scenes, which mixed past, present, and even perhaps the future, up on the sides of local farmhouses and machine sheds and little general stores smelling of cheese and harness leather and kerosene and gossip. On the outside of Miss Jane's hemlock-plank covered bridge, below the patent medicine advertisements, he painted a trout like no trout ever painted before, with a blue back and a broad band on its side consisting of an entire rainbow of lavender, pink, orange, yellow, and green. In the corner of its jaw was a beautiful red and white Duchess of Kingdom Mountain wet fly like those Miss Jane tied during long winter evenings and sold on commission at the five-and-dime in the village. On the brick wall of the First Farmers and Lumberers Bank he painted a tableau of the Kingdom Common Raid, with a few gleaming double eagles spilling out of the bulging linen tow sacks slung over the backs of the raiders' galloping horses. Eben Kinneson Esquire hired the dog-cart man to paint, on the south side of his great Monadnock House resort, a snowy slope with a few brightly dressed skiers whizzing down it and, above an alpine-looking lodge, a brand-new highway. On Miss Jane's barn he depicted Venturing Seth coming across the frozen river, pulling with his ox; Freethinker, guiding a family of fugitive slaves over the mountaintop; and Quaker Meeting discovering Jane's infant mother, Pharaoh's Daughter, in the sweetgrass basket in the ox manger. While his dogs watched patiently, heads on their paws, ranged in a semicircle, the dog-cart man added a blue-clad soldier, presumably Pilgrim, shackled and rail-thin, being led through the woods by a Confederate soldier. Where they were going, and why, was a mystery.

"He's prophesying the past, Mr. Satterfield," Eben Kinneson Esquire told Henry when he saw the tableau on the barn. "Only on Kingdom Mountain!"

Most intriguing of all was the painting the dog-cart man made on the huge sliding door at the top of Miss Jane's high drive leading to the hayloft. It was an autumn scene in Kingdom County, and the people of the village were gathered at the annual Harvest Festival on the fairgrounds. Miss Jane, unmistakable in her black dress and shoes, was standing on the racetrack in front of the grandstand, waving at Henry, who swooped low over the grounds in his yellow biplane, his left hand cocked in a jaunty salute. Viewed from the home-place porch, it seemed quite evident that the plane was landing and that Henry was waving hello to a very happy Miss Jane. Yet if you viewed the same scene from the covered bridge, it appeared that the plane was taking off, Henry's salute was a farewell wave, and the expression on Miss Jane's face was stricken. Just how the dog-cart man achieved this dual effect was impossible to say. It had taken him no more than twenty minutes to complete. Ultimately, all of the artist's paintings had a mysterious quality. You could unravel only so much meaning from them. Like Miss Jane and her anarchistic east-west-running Canadian granite mountain, they were what they were. No one, least of all their silent creator, could explain what they signified.

26

THE DROUGHT THAT SUMMER was the worst anyone could remember. After normal rainfall in early April, not a drop of rain fell during the next three months. The clover and timothy grass, even the tough redtop, which flourished where no other grass would grow, turned brown and died back before it was half a foot high. The red and orange Indian paintbrush and white daisies and blue roadside chicory, the black-eyed Susans and butter yellow cinquefoil, withered without ever blossoming. One by one, wells ran dry. Strong pasture springs that had never failed in one hundred years slowed to trickles, then gave out altogether.

For the first time since Seth Kinneson had arrived on the mountain, much of Kingdom Mountain Burn dried up. Miss Jane's char congregated in the few pools left, their bluish backs jutting out of the water. She and Henry drove them into a net and transported them to the river in milk cans. There was a constant eye-watering film in the air, day and night, from Canadian forest fires to the north, and the woods of the borderlands were tinder dry. In mid-July Miss Jane had begun manning the wooden fire tower on the mountaintop, watching for smoke. Occasionally Henry would go with her, but the fearless aviator was uncomfortable with heights when not in his plane. Climbing the rickety steps made him dizzy. As he clung to the shaky rail of the observation deck, his eyes smarting from the smoke, the sun as red and flat through the haze as an over-heated stove lid, it was all the rainmaker could do to glance down at the balancing boulder and the peace cairn. Through the haze and smoke he and Miss Jane couldn't make out the steam shovel and horse-drawn earthmovers and scrapers working in the valley below, though they could hear the rumble of the machinery and, from time to time, the boom of dynamite where the construction workers were widening the old road. What did Eben and the town fathers know about their pending appeal to the Vermont Supreme Court that Miss Jane didn't? It was inconceivable to her that they would be allowed to set one foot on her property without her permission, much less push a road over her mountain.

The new highway had become an end in itself, as absurd as its name. What earthly good would it do anyone, this Connector connecting nothing to nothing? Even if the high court were to rule in the township's favor, the concrete two-laner seemed without purpose. No new road was coming down from Canada to join it. The Great Northern Slang would continue to be an impenetrable barrier to any highway north of Jane's mountain. Yet the work on the right of way proceeded apace, and the clearing along the county road continued all that month. As often happens in small towns and, it is rumored, perhaps elsewhere as well, everyone seemed keen on this ill-advised, costly, and pointless project, confusing it with progress. By late July the right of way had reached the riverbank just across the covered bridge from Jane's property. It was time, she told Henry, to take measures. It was time to put "Eben and his boys" on notice.

One still summer morning Miss Jane invited Henry to accompany her and Lady J to the fire tower, where she announced that she planned to sight in her rifle in case, in the ensuing battle she now felt was inevitable, they had to "fall back" to a defensive position atop the tower. In preparation for this exercise she had spent the past two days cutting out life-size cardboard figures of construction workers, the town fathers, and Eben Kinneson Esquire. The previous evening she had tacked these effigies to the row of swamp maples and black willows along her side of the river just below the covered bridge.

Henry had not been looking forward to this latest escapade. What if Miss Jane missed the silhouette of Eben and plugged, instead, the mild-mannered clerk of the works for the right of way? As they climbed up the shaky steps of what Jane had taken to calling her "little redoubt" on the mountaintop, the smoke from the forest fires to the north was so thick that they could barely make out the spectral figures of the derby-hatted workmen and their horses and mules across the river, not to mention the rather childish outlines tacked to the maples and willows on Miss Jane's side. She estimated that as the crow flew, the paper targets were about a mile away and that over that distance a bullet fired from Lady Justice would drop six feet.

Miss Jane jacked a .54 caliber shell into the chamber of her father's rifle and rested the stock on the observation deck railing. Had he not been holding on to that same railing for dear life, Henry would have clapped both hands to his ears. As it was, he let go with one hand and covered one ear when she touched off her first round. Across the river, a hammerheaded construction mule — an intemperate animal named Sal who, the evening before, had tripped across the bridge while Henry was bathing in the river and had chased him, buck-naked except for his white hat, all the way up to the home place —

dropped down stone dead. *Now we're talking,* Henry's grand-daddy said in the rainmaker's head. There was a panicked flurry as the construction workers dived for cover behind their road scrapers and dump wagons. Miss Jane squinted at the willow, just downriver from the bridge, to which she had affixed Eben's likeness. A large splinter had flown off the tree trunk beside the cardboard figure. "I failed to adjust for windage," she said.

"Right in the breadbasket," she announced as her second shot ripped squarely through the midriff of the paper attorney. "Let them reflect on that before they cross the Rubicon. We will pick them off like the Visigoths they are, Henry. *Via alta delendo est!*"

She fired again.

"Miss Jane, you have shot and, I fear, killed a mule."

"Aye. It's that evil-tempered animal with the white patch on its forehead that harried you home last night. Forgive me, Henry. But the sight of you posting up the pike in your birthday suit with that misbegotten creature at your heels and you clapping your hat over yourself like Adam with his fig leaf was so comical I laughed out loud. Step up, now. Try your hand at this good sport."

"I'll pass, thank you just the same," Henry said, as she politely held out Lady J stock first.

Miss Jane shrugged. In the scant time it took her to jack the shells into the chamber, aim, and fire, she hit two more of the cutout figures. The construction crew were sprinting back down the right of way across the river. "Go it!" the Duchess chuckled.

"Miss Jane, I beg you, desist," Henry cried out. "For God's sake, ask yourself the question my mother taught me to ask myself when I was a shaver. Ask yourself what Jesus and his chosen twelve would do in this fix, and do accordingly."

"What Jesus would do?" Miss Jane said, astonished. "I have no earthly idea what Jesus would do. Jesus had no property to defend. Nor, so far as I know, a .54 caliber sharpshooter's rifle with a shotgun barrel attached below for close work. No, Henry. The question is not what the outspoken young Nazarene would do but what I must do. As for the twelve fawning slackers, his so-called disciples, I neither know nor care. I don't give a fig for a single one of them."

"But Miss Jane," Henry protested, "Jesus believed in turning the other cheek."

The Duchess coolly blew away the last curling puff of smoke emerging from the upper barrel of Lady Justice. "I do not," she said. "If I turn the other cheek, it will be to lay it lovingly on the curly maple stock of Lady J and blast the high-road Goths off the face of the earth. But what do you say, Mr. Satterfield? What would the horned red devil do in my situation? How would *he* advise me, practical-minded old fellow that he is?"

"He would offer you some way out of this pickle, no doubt. And it would be a poor bargain on your side. My granddaddy, the captain, learned that. He was a dreadfully tormented man. Come, now. Let us descend. You have sent your message, as intended."

On their way down the mountain, the two friends continued to speak of lofty matters. "One of these evenings, Henry, I must show you my Kingdom Mountain Bible," the Duchess said. "I have not scrupled, you will discover, to revise a good deal of the New Testament as well as the Old. The four Gospels, as told by Matthew, Mark, Luke, and John, are pretty well marked up in my Kingdom Mountain Bible. First I eliminated from the conversation of the young schoolteacher — for I have no doubt that he was no nail driver but, with his great love of hearing himself talk, a schoolmaster — all references to Hell, of which there are many in King James's corrupt version. Hell is a vicious notion put in Jesus's head by his lunatic cousin, John Baptist. John Baptist was a very bad influence, sir. Here comes he, rampaging out of the wilderness in a hair shirt, gobbling locusts, citing wicked old Isaiah, and putting all kinds of grandiose notions in his young relation's head. I have no more use for John Baptist than for Sneaking Saul. Ha! Watch out for that hobblebush, Henry. It tries to trip me up every time I come this way."

"You mean King Saul, Miss Jane? My mother used to read me the story of King Saul and how the boy David soothed him with his harp."

"That is a different and altogether more appealing Saul. I mean the tax collector who changed his name to Paul after he was struck by lightning on his way to Damascus and rendered daft. I refuse to call him Paul. Sneaking Saul he was, Sneaking Saul he remains. Once a tax collector, always a tax collector, Mr. Satterfield."

Partway down the trail, they stopped at a spring bubbling out of the mountainside beneath a tall yellow birch tree growing on top of a pink granite boulder. The upper roots of the birch reached down over the boulder, clasping its sides in an iron embrace. As they drank the icy spring water from their cupped hands, Miss Jane told Henry that she could detect in it the faint wintergreen flavor of yellow birch bark. Sitting at the foot of the boulder, they continued their conversation.

"What are your thoughts on the Sermon on the Mount, Miss Jane?"

"It is unimpeachable as it stands. In my Kingdom Mountain Bible, I only tacked on a few womanly sentiments that no man could be expected to think of. Whatever else he was, Jesus, you know, was very much a man's man. The Bible needs a woman's touch here and there. I added, for instance, 'Live each day not as if it is your last, but as though it is the last day of the lives of the people you meet.' And 'Cherish the miracle that is you.' Also, I thought it a good idea to include 'To immerse oneself in the natural world is to share a universal thread with every living thing.' Jesus, you see, was far more interested in people than in nature or animals. It was quite wrong of him to curse the poor barren fig tree. And to send those innocent hogs to their death over the cliff! Come to think of it, I doubt he would have been much fazed by the fate of the hammerheaded mule this morning. Every generation should have its own Bible, Henry. Thomas Jefferson was revising the New Testament along somewhat similar lines to mine when he died."

"I wonder if our friend the high sheriff will come calling about the mule?"

"Not if he knows what's good for him," she said, smiling.

"You have a wonderful set of teeth, Miss Jane."

The Duchess, who had taken excellent care of her teeth all her life and was quite vain of them, was pleased and amused.

"And a lovely complexion, Miss Jane."

In fact, Henry could not help thinking, when he looked at Miss Jane's lovely honey-colored face, of the golden Treasure of Kingdom Mountain.

"I suppose it is the Indian blood in my veins. The tawny part, I mean. My mother, you know, though she had no Indian ways at all, was the last of the full-blooded Memphremagog Abenakis."

"And, if I may say so, Miss Jane, an excellent pair of gams."

"Gams, Mr. Satterfield? What under the sun do you mean?"

"Your l-e-g-s, Miss Jane. What a stunning wingwalker you would have been."

"Why," she said, turning quite pink and standing up, "they take me where I wish to go, I suppose. You are as bold as Thomas Tubberty. If I didn't know better, Henry, I might suppose that you were sparking me. But now let us direct our l-e-g-s to hie us down to the home place. If the sheriff is imprudent enough to come calling, I wish to be there to greet him accordingly."

27

I<small>T WAS NOT</small> the sheriff of Kingdom County who showed up at the home place that afternoon, but Eben Kinneson Esquire and the town fathers in Eben's new dark Buick, appearing, through the haze, as spectral as a hearse. In the smoky air the mountaintop seemed to float just above the home place, as it sometimes did on chilly fall mornings when a thick band of fog rising from the river obscured all but the treeless summit. Even Eben found the levitating mountain unsettling. He wondered if the illusion, which was also visible on certain icy winter mornings, might put off prospective investors and skiers.

Miss Jane and Henry met the visitors in the barnyard, Jane carrying Lady Justice. "We'd like a word in private with Mr. Satterfield, cousin," Eben Kinneson Esquire said.

"Mr. Satterfield had nothing to do with my little skirmish with the mule this morning, cousin," Miss Jane replied. "That was entirely my doing."

"We did not come out here about a dead mule," Eben said. "We wish to consult with Mr. Satterfield on a purely professional matter."

"Oh, Miss Jane is no stranger to my profession," Henry said, slightly bemused. "Consult away, gentlemen."

"It's this confounded drought, Mr. Satterfield," George Quinn said. "Last night the Reverend here had a dream."

"A very foreboding dream," Prof Chadburn said. "Tell them, Reverend."

"I was fishing in the Kingdom River," the Reverend said, though it was well known that he was no fisherman, "when seven kine, fat-fleshed and well-favored, came up out of the pool below the High Falls behind the hotel. And seven other kine came after them, poor and ill-favored and lean-fleshed. And the lean and ill-favored kine did devour the seven fat kine."

Miss Jane had always regarded the Reverend as a pompous moron. Now she was sure of it.

"Horsefeathers," she said. "It was that half an angel food cake you packed away for a midnight snack, Reverend. You might better have flung it out the window to your ill-favored kine."

"I should think that you, Miss Jane, of all people, would appreciate a prophetic dream," the Reverend said in an injured tone. "The point is, if the drought is to end we need intervention. That's why we've come to consult with Mr. Satterfield. You are a rainmaker, are you not?"

"Oh," Henry said with a dismissive wave, "I don't make rain so much as I follow it. I don't reckon that I ever slap *made* it rain in my life. Sometimes I have seen wet weather coming and nudged it along, so to speak. Coaxed the clouds this way and that and maybe encouraged an electrical storm to follow my plane. Rainmaking is an uncertain and hazardous enterprise, I'm afraid. Like many another human enterprise."

George Quinn said, "More of our farmers are going under every day, Mr. Satterfield. The whole county is a blasted dust bowl. We would very much appreciate it if you could nudge some rain our way. We would be prepared to compensate you for whatever hazards may be involved."

"Sir," Eben Kinneson Esquire said, "if you can nudge or cajole or inveigle or conjure some rain our way, we will take that rain any way it comes. We are prepared to make it worth your while. For an all-day and all-night soaker, we would be willing to pay you one hundred dollars."

That evening after supper, having completed the final figure in her water-bird sequence — a fine individualistic bittern, its neck and head extended straight up as if getting ready to let out its distinctive pumping gurgle — Miss Jane started carving a new bird, she did not say what. While she worked, Henry told her about a new red Gee Bee Racer plane he'd had his eye on for some time. "True, it would not have quite the maneuverability of my old Burgess-Wright," he was saying. "Single-wing craft never do, of course. But it would more than make up for that in speed. Nor would I need to replace poor Miss Lola. Wingwalking would be out of the question with the single-wing. I wonder if I might take a quick gander at your revised family Bible, Miss Jane. The one you mentioned to me this morning?"

"Certainly," Jane said, though she couldn't imagine what her Bible might have to do with the new plane. From the Currier and Ives strongbox she fetched her huge black King James Bible, which she had been revising since the age of eighteen.

Opening it to the book of Genesis, Henry read the word "Horsefeathers" beside the story in which King James's Jehovah changes Lot's wife into a pillar of salt. "Just the sort of tale a despot would make up," Miss Jane had neatly penned in the gilt-edged margin of the page. "God did no such thing."

"Horsefeathers" was Miss Jane's most dismissive pronouncement. It adorned the margins of Genesis, punctuated the wild outcries of the Old Testament prophets, and accompanied the mainly crossed-out text of Paul's stern letters.

Henry, who had wished to reread the story of the Great

Flood for clues as to how he might engender enough rain to earn one hundred dollars toward the down payment for his cherry red Racer, was keenly interested in Miss Jane's Kingdom Mountain Bible. "Horsefeathers," he read again beside the entirely excised story of Noah. "How, pray, Mr. King James the First, would all the animals have fit into the ark?"

"Why nothing could be simpler, Miss Jane," the pilot said. "As my mama told me when I asked her that very question, there were far fewer animals in Noah's day than in ours."

"On the contrary, Henry, there were far *more*," Miss Jane replied. "We've exterminated half the species on earth since then."

Henry turned to the New Testament. Jesus, he thought, would know how to make it rain. Searching for some kind of incantation, he read in Miss Jane's bold handwriting, beside the passage in which Jesus says "I have no mother or brothers or sisters," "For shame. Mary is your mother. James and John your brothers. It's wrong, young man, to renounce your family. Family is everything."

"I wonder."

"You wonder what, Henry?"

"I wonder if Jesus mought be hinting here that *all* men and women are brothers and sisters?"

"If so, he picked a very poor way to say it," the Duchess said. "To deny his mother after everything she did for him! Don't you see? If we deny our family, we deny ourselves."

"Maybe he was just multiplying it, like his loaves and fishes. But what are you carving now, Miss Jane? Who is that tall gentleman?"

"It's an archaeopteryx," Miss Jane replied. "Half bird, half lizard. They discovered the petrified remains of one in Mongolia not long ago. I intend to enter him in the North American Bird Carving Contest in Montreal next month. Here, I'll tell you what. We'll call my archaeopteryx Noah. The Noah of Kingdom Mountain. Then we'll ask him in person how King James's Jehovah made all that rain. It was a cruel and unusual punishment, if I do say so."

During the next several days, while Henry pored over Miss Jane's family Bible for a clue to how to bring rain, she worked very rapidly to finish her Noah of Kingdom Mountain. Her strokes were short and sure as she tapped her beechwood mallet on the brass-bound wooden handles of her Sheffield chisels. She defined Noah's eyes and beak with a U-shaped veiner. Periodically, she stopped to remove the rough burr on the inside of her knives with a Kingdom Mountain slipstone lubricated with sewing machine oil. On the wall above her tool bench, her hook-nosed skew knives and concave fluters gleamed in the lamplight. The kitchen was fragrant with the scents of sawdust, resin, oil, varnish, and paint. Her beloved blockheads, Memphre Magog and Loup-Garou, seemed to watch attentively as the clear white basswood chips fell about Jane's high-buttoned shoes and the Noah of Kingdom Mountain took shape.

At first Noah looked like a Gila monster with wings. Then, with her crooked knife, Jane sculpted out his sweeping cockade, which she painted a fiery red. She gave him a sharp yellow bill bristling with reptilian teeth, and piercing green eyes.

"My father used to tell me that every stranger who traveled to Kingdom Mountain should be welcomed as if he were Jesus in disguise. We'll welcome our good Noah thusly and see what he advises us to do about the rain."

Thumbing through the newly arrived Sears, Roebuck catalog, Henry shook his head over Miss Jane's latest wonderment. At the same time he had an idea for one of his own. He would need to borrow Jane's Model A truck for an hour or two the next morning, he said.

28

THE FOLLOWING DAY Henry drove into Kingdom Common. At the foot of Blue Clay Hill he passed the steam shovel, a coal-fired steam bulldozer, and a large construction crew of men, mules, and horses, widening the county road for the new highway. In the drought the road was so dusty that Henry couldn't see fifty feet ahead. He crept along in the Model A, glad to be driving himself and not riding with Miss Jane. At the post office he filled out a money order, enclosing an extra two dollars for return postage. Five mornings later he returned to the Common to pick up the item he had ordered, and that evening after supper, when Miss Jane walked into the kitchen from a fly-fishing excursion with Judge Allen, she saw, sitting beside the soapstone sink, a brand-new battery-operated Sears radio with an auxiliary shortwave band. Kneeling next to it, nearly beside himself with exasperation, was the rainmaker.

"It's a present for you, Miss Jane. And a means for hearing when weather's on the way," Henry said. "The trouble is, I can't bring in a single station. Only this infernal crackling static."

"Why, Henry Satterfield," she said, "don't you know that —" She sat down at the table and began to laugh and, to Henry's amazement, continued laughing until tears came to her eyes. "Don't you know," Miss Jane said, wiping her eyes and gasping for breath, "that there's no radio reception in Kingdom County? We're all shut in by mountains and —" She began to laugh again until it occurred to her that she might be hurting Henry's feelings. "I'm sorry, Henry. The radio was a most kind thought. But I'm afraid we'll never hear a blessed word out of it."

The rainmaker was undaunted. The next morning he returned to the village. At the commission-sales auction barn he bought several large spools of used fence wire, which he transported up the old Canada Pike in the back of Miss Jane's truck, unwinding the spools and joining the lengths of wire end to end as he proceeded. With the help of Jane's oxen, he dragged the last spool up the steep pitch above the tree line and ran the wire to the top of the wooden fire tower. Before descending, he fastened the end of the wire to the railing around the observation deck.

That evening Henry proudly announced that Miss Jane was in for a wonderful surprise. She replied, rather ungraciously, that she had reached a point in her life where she could do quite nicely without surprises, wonderful or otherwise. The high road had been surprise enough to last the rest of her natural life.

"Someone," Henry said, "has a mite of trouble accepting a gift. Or a compliment, I might add. Someone is afraid that it might indebt her to someone else."

"Someone else," Miss Jane said in her best schoolteacherly fashion, "should tend to his own affairs."

While someone and someone else conducted this dialogue, Henry hitched the mile-long fence-wire antenna to the battery-operated radio. From the console came loud static, then banjo music. A moment later a broadcaster with a southern accent announced the call letters of a station in Lookout Mountain, Tennessee. Henry spun the big dial and picked up a preacher in Wheeling, West Virginia. Finally he found a man with a resonant voice giving the national weather forecast. And though there was as yet no end in sight to the drought that had settled over the entire Northeast, someone and someone else could not help grinning at each other. When rain did come, they would be the first to know.

"But do you think it will rain, Henry?" Miss Jane said worriedly.

To which he replied, "With respect, ma'am. It always has."

Out of nowhere one evening a shabby little gypsy carnival appeared in the village. Every two or three summers it seemed to materialize on the fairgrounds on the south edge of the Common as suddenly as if it had fallen out of the sky, with a few colorful, ragged tents, a precarious Ferris wheel, a fortune-telling booth, a Wonders of the World exhibit, and an ancient merry-go-round. The carnival was under the management of a longtime friend of Miss Jane's named Mr. Foxie Romanoff.

The following evening Miss Jane and Henry drove into the village to attend the carnival. They had their fortunes told, and Henry bought Jane a cotton-candy cone. They rode the merry-go-round, several of whose wooden animals Miss Jane had replaced for Mr. Romanoff over the years. The gypsy, who was not really a gypsy but a former tailor from Poughkeepsie, New York, who had grown weary of his sedentary profession and traded his needle for life on the open road, escorted them into the Wonders of the World tent and showed them, for twenty-five cents apiece, the mummy of a young woman known as the Bride of Ramses, which he had purchased from a failing Hungarian circus the year before. Inscribed on the lid of the sarcophagus were the words "This is the Beloved Bride of Ramses II, who, when her husband died, chose to join him in the underworld rather than live on alone. All the best stories are about love."

That evening, when they arrived at the home place, Miss Jane fetched her great Kingdom Mountain Bible out of the strongbox. In the margins of the book of Proverbs, she wrote, in the elegant Palmer handwriting she had taught to two generations of students at the Kinnesonville school:

Always dwell in a west-facing house.
Close all gates behind yourself.
Declare yourself to the person you love.
All the best stories are about love.

That night Henry called down through the grate, "Tell me, Miss Jane. How did you come to revise the King James Bible in the first place?"

Jane, now working her way through *Bleak House* again, and thinking how like the opportunistic and detestable Mr. Tulkinghorn her cousin Eben Kinneson Esquire was, slipped a bookmark into her novel and laid it on the coverlet beside her. Though far from short, *Bleak House*, like *Don Quixote*, had required almost no editing down. Page after page in her edition was as pristine as the day it rolled off the press. It was a pity, she had thought many times, that the same could not be said of her volumes of Thoreau, the Pronouncer of Concord; Samuel Johnson, the Proclaimer of Litchfield; and so many other pronouncers and proclaimers whose pronouncements and proclamations she had been obliged to blue-pencil over the years. King James and his pernicious Bible were the worst of the lot.

"About the time I reached the biblical age of adulthood, Henry, twelve or thirteen, I began to realize that very little of the King James Bible made a particle of sense. In particular, I couldn't swallow the loving, all-powerful father who allowed his only begotten son to be strung up on a cross and tortured to death just to prove a point. And blasted two whole cities — infants, toddlers, and all — from the face of the earth to punish a few bad apples. Not to mention slaying the innocent firstborn son of each Egyptian family. I have always been partial to the Egyptians, you know, given my mother's first name. No, sir. This madness had to be the work of King James, not a just and magnanimous deity, and must not be allowed to stand. When I turned eighteen, I had a most unfortunate experience with

King James the First and his Bible. That is when I decided to revise it and his detestable Jehovah. In my Kingdom Mountain Bible, old Jehovah is a jolly, good-natured fellow. He helps his dear people when he can and doesn't stand in their way the rest of the time. Sometimes their shenanigans amuse him or make him happy or sad. That's all right. Every family, you know, should write its own revised Bible."

"What did your folks think about you, at the age of eighteen, undertaking to revise the Bible?"

"My mother died when I was sixteen. My father, the chief justice, was a freethinker. He encouraged me in the endeavor."

"They must have been very good parents."

"Indeed they were, though not without their own little Kingdom Mountain particularities. Pharaoh's Daughter was educated at Mount Holyoke and named me after my father's mother, Jane Kinneson, and her own mother, Canada Jane Hubbell, who left her in the barn in the sweetgrass basket. Also, I believe she had in mind her favorite author, Jane Austen. As for my father, besides being a lawyer and a judge, he was a born teacher. He taught me most of what I know about the mountain. He farmed part-time because he loved the mountain, and he was wonderful with animals and a good hand to raise a crop. But my father had no head at all for the business end of farming. If he raised cabbages and kept them through the winter to capitalize on the spring cabbage market, why, come spring, the bottom would invariably fall out of cabbages. If he switched milk buyers, the new buyer would fail and he'd have to go back to his old creamery, hat in hand. He supported the farm with his income as a lawyer and judge.

"What's more, Father, who had so much patience when it came to teaching me the ways of the black bears and blue-backed char, and how to read Caesar and Virgil, had no patience at all for fixing machinery. He took it into his romantical head that all his agricultural difficulties would be solved if he could raise and combine his own grain. That was a most dubious proposition on Kingdom Mountain, with its brief frost-free growing season. Everyone, including my mother, warned him against the project. Nothing would do, however, but he must buy a combine. He found one advertised in the *Farmer's Home Companion,* a magazine my mother detested because it put just such ideas as raising his own grain in my father's head. The thing belonged to a rancher in North Dakota, and had been converted from a ground-driven thresher pulled by thirty-two horses to a steam-powered wonder said to cut, thresh, and winnow thirty acres of grain a day in a single continuous process. He purchased it, had it shipped east by rail at a great expense, and drove it home from the station. If I live to be one hundred, Henry, I'll never forget the day it arrived, accompanied by a plume of coal black smoke and a great dust cloud. It had four iron wheels, each taller than a man and studded with spikes, and more gauges and levers and gears than a steam locomotive. The wooden threshing blades were eight feet long and four feet high. The boiler was as large as a good-sized culvert. As my father drove it up the lane, he gave a great blast on its steam whistle. But once ensconced on the threshing floor of the barn, it never started again. No matter. My father painted it fire engine red with blue wheels and a canary yellow boiler. He called it the Samuel L. Clemens, in honor of Mark Twain's typesetting invention that wouldn't set type. I called it King James's Jehovah because all it ever caused was trouble."

"What became of it?" Henry inquired.

"It's still out there on the threshing floor, where, I can assure you, it will remain. The thing is beyond repair."

"I was just wondering," Henry said. "For our little weather-making venture. There's nothing people like better than a rain-making machine. I have built them from the most extraordinary things — a gasoline-powered washing machine, a wrecked Model T Ford, even a windmill. Of course, it is all for show.

When the rain at last approaches, I start up my inventions, and everyone is happy. Furthermore, that way I would not have to go up in my plane at all during an electrical storm. Like the storm in which poor Miss Lola Beauregard Beauclerk met her q-u-i-e-t-u-s."

"It all sounds rather fraudulent," Jane said, opening up *Bleak House* again. "Rainmaking machines and such."

"Oh, I have told the town fathers as much. But if they persist, what can one do? Permit me to look at the combine, Miss Jane. I promise I won't fly into an electrical storm."

29

EARLY THE NEXT morning Miss Jane found her friend sitting on the threshing floor of the barn surrounded by pistons, levers, gauges, and engine parts. Nearby was her big barn lantern, out of kerosene. Evidently the rainmaker had been working on King James's Jehovah most of the night. As exasperated as she was, something about the man's unswervable determination appealed to the Duchess. She could see him flying to Siberia, Tibet, China, and India, dining on the frozen remains of a mammoth, encountering a many-armed woman on a tiger, and who knew what else.

The rainmaker worked straight through the day. At noon Miss Jane brought him cucumber sandwiches and a jug of switchel, cold spring water spiked with a dash of vinegar and a touch of molasses. For supper she cooked him a whole apple pie from the Early Yellow Transparent tree behind her house. He refilled her barn lantern with kerosene so he could toil into the night. Miss Jane remarked that if King James's Jehovah had taken such pains to get mankind right, instead of cobbling Adam and Eve together in a single day, the world might not be in such a fix.

"I've always said as much myself," Henry replied, peering through a metal valve at the Duchess as if observing her through a telescope. "There are those who will blame some great agent of evil, as it were. But if more care had been taken with us to start out, why, what toehold could the great enemy of man find?"

Stop the palaver and get on with the job at hand, soldier, said the captain's voice, which had been advising Henry more frequently lately. *And I don't mean fiddling with that wheat gin. You should be up on her mountain, looking for the treasure I've all but put in your hands.*

It occurred to Henry that the granddaddy, whom his mama had said was wickedness incarnate, was enjoying every moment of this maddening search for the missing gold. He would not put it past Cantrell Satterfield to misdirect him deliberately. What he could not understand was why the old officer had not returned to Vermont to raise it himself. An optimist by nature, Henry believed that with Miss Jane's help he was quite close to solving the mystery of the riddle. In the meantime, if the town fathers were foolish enough to pay him one hundred dollars for pretending to make it rain, he'd gladly oblige them.

Henry asked Miss Jane's permission to bring the radio, attached to its antenna, out to the barn so that he could listen for oncoming weather while he worked. The same compulsion to continue in a straight line that had impelled him over some of the most difficult and dangerous territory on earth in his Burgess-Wright drove him to complete his repairs in less than a week. In the grain bin down in the machine's innards he found an owl feather, a few shards of petrified wood, a snake fang, and a dime-store ring with a scratched glass stone.

On the sixth night of his labors, Henry and Miss Jane listened to the weather forecast from Chicago. A broad system of thunderstorms was progressing from west to east over the Great Lakes. If they stayed on course, the storms would reach northern New England in thirty-six hours. Moreover, the first hurricane of the season was gathering off the Cayman Islands. This struck Henry as a very good omen, since he had read, in an adventure story from Miss Jane's Atheneum called *Sunken Treasures of the Deep,* that the fabled buccaneer Edward Teach had scuttled a treasure ship some leagues north of Grand Cayman Isle, and the connection between the pirate, the hurricane, King James's Jehovah, the hundred-dollar fee for bringing rain, the new red plane, and the gold from the Great Kingdom Common Raid, though extremely tenuous to Miss Jane, was stunningly clear to the rainmaker.

The following day, while Henry fine-tuned the combine, the dog-cart man painted its name, King James's Jehovah, on the collecting bin. How he knew the name was a mystery. When Miss Jane, in her capacity as overseer of the town poor, asked him to sign a relief voucher, the painter shrugged and made an *X.*

That evening, hillbilly hoedown music from Lookout Mountain blared from the radio with frenzied intensity. Banjos rang, fiddles screeched as if bowed by demons. Later, preachers from Wheeling and Memphis called down damnation on the transgressors of the drought-parched land. Heat lightning flickered over the Green Mountains, and the forecast called for dangerous electrical storms approaching from the west, to be followed by the lashing tail of the hurricane. The wind roared in the forest on the mountain, and Commoners stumbling home from the hotel barroom that night heard keening voices in the sky. Some swore that the old Kinnesonville church bell tolled out from the ghost town high on the mountain. Henry promised Miss Jane that the next day, come hell or high water, he would start King James's Jehovah and they would drive it down to the Common, to arrive triumphantly with the rain.

The following morning was hazier than ever. Through the smoke the rising sun turned the entire mountain blood red. By noon the sun had shrunk to the size of a fiery penny. The fire tower on the mountaintop drifted in and out of view. Sometimes it seemed fifty miles away, then for a few moments it hovered directly over the home place. In the early afternoon the entire mountain seemed to come unmoored from its bedrock. It rose majestically, then descended and matter-of-factly reseated itself like a proper mountain. Once during the Civil War the image of a battle being fought by a Vermont regiment in Pennsylvania was imprinted in the sky above Kingdom's summit, and in the Common speechless onlookers had watched loved ones fall. Cannon fire from the transposed battle was heard as far away as Bethlehem, New Hampshire. The balancing boulder had levitated hundreds of feet into the sky and slowly rotated one hundred and eighty degrees so that the devil's visage, now gazing down on the smoky battle, was visible from the village. Then the illusion vanished.

Late that afternoon the sky to the west turned black. The radio reported that torrential thunderstorms were hitting the Adirondacks, just across Lake Champlain from Vermont, with unprecedented fury. Henry told Miss Jane that they would now, for the first time, start King James's Jehovah, which they had pulled out into the barnyard with Ethan and General Ira Allen. As Miss Jane ran for her driving duster, goggles, and motorman's cap, Henry set the bulky radio on top of the combine's grain bin to track the progress of the oncoming storm.

To his chagrin the rainmaker could not seem to activate the machine. "Confound you, sir," he told it as he threw this gear and depressed that throttle and the storm clouds sailed closer. The water in the boiler bubbled. Coal black smoke poured out of the tall stack. But the valves stuck, the steam seemed to be blocked, and there were so many levers, gears, wheels, cylinders, switches, and dials that even the mechanically minded aviator, who had repaired superannuated locomotives in Siberia and three-hundred-foot-tall windmills in Tibet, not to mention his own biplane more times than he could count, had no luck at all starting it.

"Wait here, ma'am, if you will, please," Henry said as he trotted down the lane toward the hemlock-plank bridge. At the foot of the hill he dashed across the water meadow toward his plane. Too late, Miss Jane perceived his design. Despite his promise never to fly into an electrical storm again, he was going aloft to guide in the rain.

"No," she shouted. "No, Henry!" But the yellow biplane was already bouncing over the pasture and lifting off.

Horrified, Miss Jane watched the Burgess-Wright gain altitude. Henry was flying due west toward the gathering thunderheads. Through the smoky film the receding plane looked nearly colorless.

As he ascended above the Green Mountains, clearing the top of Jay Peak by scant feet, a jag of lightning struck Miss Jane's own mountaintop with a thunderous explosion, igniting the wooden fire tower like a gigantic Roman candle. A yellow sphere of electricity about the size of a basketball raced down the wire antenna from the flaming observation deck of the tower to the combine, which gave a deep coughing roar.

Jane clamored aboard King James's Jehovah. She yanked one lever back, jammed another forward, ratcheted a third sideways. The huge blades clattered into motion, and the machine made a bounding lurch.

Miss Jane Hubbell Kinneson, decked out in her motoring regalia, clung to the wheel for dear life as Jehovah rumbled through her flower garden, threshing up her pink and white summer phlox, Delft blue delphiniums, and multicolored zinnias, along with her prize Harison's Yellow rose, which she had kept well watered from the river, morning and evening, all summer.

In the water meadow a dozen seagulls in off Lake Memphremagog to take refuge from the storm froze in terror. Several were summarily clapped up by the combine. The machine jolted across the covered bridge just as Eben Kinneson Esquire and the town fathers approached from the opposite direction in Eben's Roadmaster. The astounded lawyer had no choice but to drive off the road into the pool below the bridge.

Like its stern namesake descending on a coven of idolaters, King James's Jehovah veered west down the Connector right of way, threshing up a hedgerow of young poplar trees. An oncoming dump truck took to the ditch. The combine clapped up a YOUR TAX DOLLARS AT WORK sign and half a dozen free-ranging Rhode Island Red chickens pecking in the road in front of the Currier farm. At the junction of the Connector and the road to Lord Hollow, the steam shovel operator took one look at the oncoming juggernaut and drove his shovel over the bank.

A four-horse hitch hauling a wooden road scraper went galloping down the road in front of the combine. More gulls flew along behind, snapping up panicked grasshoppers flushed out of the ditches. Now Eben and the enraged town fathers, drenched to the skin, were overtaking the machine in Miss Jane's Model A, which they had commandeered from her dooryard. A Border collie and two nanny goats from the Kittredge farm joined in the chase. Six first-calf heifers in Ferlin Sanville's pasture stampeded through their fence and were not found until three days later, fifteen miles away, on the main street of Pond in the Sky. Sadie Blackberry, searching futilely with Clarence Davis for any edible wild fruit in the drought, looked up as King James's Jehovah went by and immortalized herself in the mythology of Kingdom County by remarking, "Don't mind that ruckus, Clarence. That's just Miss Jane Hubbell Kinneson in a rainmaking machine." From nowhere a Morgan horse appeared in the right of way, running hard in front of the combine.

"Whoa up, you blackguard! Whoa, you destroyer of the innocent!" Miss Jane commanded. But the wrathful Jehovah, having long bided its time for just such a campaign, had a mind and will of its own. Preceded by the galloping Morgan, followed by a yapping, bleating, coughing, crowing, shouting procession of dogs, goats, town fathers, construction workers, gulls, and farm boys, not to mention the low high sheriff, who had been lying in wait for speeders at the foot of Blue Clay Hill, the machine was not to be deterred from its mission.

The clerk of the works for the Connector, setting up his surveying instruments on the outskirts of the village, saw something never before seen through the eyepiece of a transit. Then the runaway combine brushed past him, eating up his overalls and leaving him standing in the roadway in his drawers just as the first big raindrops started to fall. Without fanfare King James's Jehovah ate the WELCOME TO KINGDOM COMMON sign on the edge of the village. Miss Jane gave out a lusty cheer. The Bronze Age deity himself, King James's I Am That I Am, incinerating Sodom, atomizing Gomorrah, drowning every last one of his own dear creatures save sanctimonious old Noah and his two-by-two menagerie, could scarcely have acted with more purposeful malice than the long-dormant thresher, now bearing down on the commission-sales auction yard, bulling over the pole fence and consuming auctioneer Bumper Stevens's prize fighting rooster, Calvin Coolidge. The ancients on the hotel porch leaped out of their cane-bottomed chairs and ran inside, retreating faster, Editor Kinneson said in that week's *Monitor*, than the Vermont regiment that turned tail and fled at the first battle of Bull Run. "Perhaps," the editor wrote, "Miss Jane Hubbell Kinneson may be forgiven a brief moment of triumphalism, in view of what is at stake for her, as the avenging 'Jehovah' smartly executed a left flank maneuver and headed down the ball diamond on the village green, breaking up a practice session of the local nine. She struggled valiantly to prevent the thing from committing manslaughter."

Jehovah was unstoppable. No one, including the Duchess, had the faintest idea how to halt it. It ate second base and the pitcher's rubber, leveled the mound, toppled the chicken-wire backstop, and continued across the street toward the Congregational church lawn, where the Reverend was changing the weekly message. He got as far as THE LORD GOD IS AN ANGRY G before, as if to prove his point, the berserk combine gobbled up the bulletin board. Whistle screaming, it proceeded down U.S. Route 5 straight for the fairgrounds, where the carnival was encamped. Miss Jane could hear the calliope music over the thresher's engine.

Then, just before what would surely have been a catastrophic collision, the runaway machine gave out a final sigh and stopped beside Mr. Foxie Romanoff, who was operating the Ferris wheel, filled with children, in the rain.

Mr. Romanoff looked up at Miss Jane, covered from head to toe with soot and dust. "What would it set me back," he said, "to acquire that ride for my show?"

Miss Jane thought for a moment. "I'll trade it to you, even steven, for the Bride of Ramses."

That's when they spotted Henry Satterfield, coming on in his plane just ahead of the onrushing storm. The lightning and thunder shook the old Burgess-Wright like a toy. The wings and guy wires were alive with blue electrical current, and the same unearthly violet light played over the aviator's hands on the controls as he cleared the looming water tower just west of the fairgrounds. Miss Jane could smell ozone in the approaching rain, as well as something singed and sulfurous, as if the electricity in the air had scorched the airship. As it came in over the fairgrounds and landed beside the Ferris wheel, she ran up to the plane carrying the coffin of Ramses' Bride, stashed it behind the jump seat, and hopped in. Just as she and Henry took off, the deluge struck.

The Commoners on the bluestone sidewalk in front of the brick shopping block, the pensioners back out on the hotel porch, a few ballplayers scampering across the green with mitts and bats tucked under their arms, looked up and, through the welcome torrent, saw the plane overhead. They could just make out the letters on the bottom wing, HENRY SATTERFIELD'S FLYING CIRCUS RAINMAKING AND PYROTECHNIC SERVICES BEAUMONT TEXAS. The roar of the engine combined with the thunder as the Burgess-Wright banked sharply east out of town over the new right of way, now fast becoming a muddy stream. Henry landed in Jane's field and rolled into the barnyard, up the high drive, and through the big open sliding door onto the wide wagon ramp between the hay bays. Only then did the rainmaker and the Duchess look at each other. Bedraggled, grimy, scarcely recognizable, they both began to laugh. Once started, neither could stop laughing until they collapsed in each other's arms. Miss Jane got out her wooden flask of Who Shot Sam, took a long drink, and offered the canteen to Henry. They were still laughing as she told him how the fire tower had been struck and set on fire, how the glowing ball of electricity had run down the fence-wire antenna and activated Jehovah. She described the way the steam shovel had plunged over the bank like some frightened prehistoric creature. Henry told Jane how he'd found the rain and then just gotten back to the village before the storm. Finally, Miss Jane explained that she'd traded King James's Jehovah for the Bride of Ramses.

"What on earth for?" Henry said, still laughing.

"I haven't the faintest idea," Miss Jane said. This set them off again.

"Have another sip of Sam, Mr. Satterfield."

"This 'jack is beginning to rise to my head," he said. "I'd call it potent stuff."

More laughter as the rain drummed furiously against the barn, which shook with each thunderclap.

"Henry," Jane said, "do you know what we need?"

"Besides more applejack?"

"Yes. Besides more applejack, you and I need a good bath. Now tell me. Have you ever gone skinny-dipping in the rain with a duchess?"

"Why, no," Henry said, half choking and still laughing, so that his last jolt of Sam started to come back up through his nose, causing him to whoop all the harder. "But I should very much like to."

"Why, then," Miss Jane said, polishing off the applejack and climbing, somewhat unsteadily, out of the airplane, "let us see which of us can reach the river first in that glorious state in which" — and here she began to laugh again, so hard that the gallant aviator had to help her with her dress buttons — "we were created."

30

SOME HOURS LATER, dry, warm, and very much in the state in which they were created, lulled by the steady rainfall and the wind in the trees on the mountain, quite sober now from their plunge into the river, Miss Jane Hubbell Kinneson and

Henry Satterfield lay close together in her bedchamber at the home place. Miss Jane was thinking, sleepily, about the utter unpredictabilities of life, even for a Scottish-Memphremagog woman of a certain age and with second sight. Henry was daydreaming about old treasure and new airplanes.

"Well, Henry," Jane said, feeling oddly as if she were still talking to him through the grate in the ceiling, "I believe that you and I find ourselves on a different footing than earlier in the day."

"Yes," he said. "We are indeed on a different footing. We are on a — a sublime footing. Tonight has been the most sublime night of my life."

"Why, Henry, I quite concur. Yet to one who is, perhaps, not unfamiliar with the matchless favors of Miss Lola Beauregard Beauclerk —"

"Miss Jane," Henry interrupted, "please. Do not mention that unfortunate woman in the same breath with yourself. Not to speak ill of the dead, but the favors of Miss Lola Beauregard Beauclerk were, to your charms, as dross is to purest gold."

What most surprised the Duchess was the depth of her own passions. How would she explain this new development to her dear people? Surely they would know, from the moment she stepped into On Kingdom Mountain tomorrow morning, that she and Henry Satterfield were indeed on a different footing. Fine. She would deal with them when the time came. For now, she intended to savor every moment in the arms of her aviator. As usual, she thought, the Nazarene know-it-all had gotten it only half right. Sufficient unto the day were the evils thereof, true enough. But he should not have stopped there. Sufficient, too, were the sublimities. Miss Jane was certain of it.

The next morning the tail of the hurricane curved around and lambasted the county, bringing with it more rain and high winds. By noon the river was lapping at the floor of the covered bridge. The pasture where Henry and Miss Jane had landed the previous evening was under two feet of water by midafternoon. Just before dusk an empty blue rowboat came bobbing down on the current. It was an eerie sight, though what it signified neither of them could say.

Before joining Henry in her bedchamber that night, Miss Jane stepped into On Kingdom Mountain, where she had ensconced the Bride of Ramses on her mother's horsehair love seat. "I want you to hear this from me, not anyone else," she announced to her dear people. "Some of you may be scandalized to learn that Mr. Henry Satterfield and I are keeping company. This is our business and none of you need to concern yourselves with it. I hope you aren't too disappointed in me." None of Jane's people seemed disappointed or even particularly surprised. They had seen much life, and were, perhaps, beyond surprise. They just looked back at Jane with her own level gray eyes. What she had told them was, after all, the way of the world.

"In the meantime, there has been an addition to your number," Miss Jane continued. "I mean, of course, the Bride of Ramses. Please make her welcome."

The following morning the rain abated but did not stop. Throughout the county, pasture seeps had turned into freshets. Hillside rills had become cataracts, the boggy little brooks feeding the Upper Kingdom were torrents. The steam shovel working the cut at the foot of Blue Clay Hill had vanished. In Kingdom Common the village green was a miniature lake. The statue of Ethan Allen stood waist-high in water. The roar from the High Falls behind the commission-sales barn could be heard inside homes on Anderson Hill, and the railroad tracks north of town had been torn up by the flood.

In the middle of the afternoon Eben, George Quinn, and Prof Chadburn made their way back out to Kingdom Mountain in Prof's old Model T, with chains on the tires. They stood in the rain on the far side of the rampaging river holding up a board on which they'd painted, in large black letters, MAKE IT STOP.

"I can't," Henry shouted from Miss Jane's flooded barnyard. His words blew away on the wind, but he held out his hands, palms up, in a gesture of helplessness. The Common had wanted rain. Rain they had gotten. The great hurricane of 1930, Hurricane Ada, was remembered throughout northern New England until it was eclipsed by the big blow of 1938. In the Kingdom, Ada would forever afterward be known as Hurricane Jane.

The rain continued for three days and nights. Then it stopped as abruptly as it had begun. On the morning of the fourth day the sun came out. The sky was an innocent azure. As the water receded from Miss Jane's lower pasture, the grass turned from brown to emerald between dawn and sunset. The stiff-legged carcasses of construction horses and mules hung bloating in the trees along the Kingdom River beside the county road, and for weeks afterward were found in woods a quarter mile away from the river. The missing steam shovel was discovered on its side behind Ben Currier's barn.

As for the one hundred dollars that the town fathers had promised Henry Satterfield to nudge the rain toward Kingdom County, nothing more was mentioned about it by either party, though the glares that the rainmaker and Miss Jane received in the village from the Reverend, Eben, and George Quinn spoke volumes. In the meantime the Supreme Court had scheduled the appeal in the case of *Jane Hubbell Kinneson v. Township of Kingdom Common* for the last Tuesday in August, now less than four weeks away.

31

As much as Miss Jane enjoyed making love with Henry Satterfield, and he with her, they were of the age when most couples, whether long married or recently engaged, enjoy one another's quiet companionship as much as what the Duchess and the rainmaker both thought of as their more sublime moments together. Over the succeeding days, they came to greatly look forward, both before and after their romantic interludes, to their now somewhat more intimate featherbed chats — long, wonderfully unpredictable conversations about everything under the sun from Henry's dream of the brand-new red Gee Bee Racer to Miss Jane's ongoing investigation into the disappearance of her uncle Pilgrim.

One night, as Jane was explicating the Kinneson family genealogy to Henry and lamenting, once again, the sad gap in the family tree left by the vanishing of Pilgrim, Henry mentioned that during his days as companion to and later keeper of his granddaddy, the old man, a devout churchgoer, had taken up door-to-door Bible selling. At the same time he had dabbled a bit in drawing up family genealogies. For five dollars he could show nearly any trusting widow from Georgia to North Carolina who happened to let drop the name of a long-deceased or, better yet long-lost, second or third cousin exactly how, through that long-deceased or long-lost cousin, she and her descendants were related to Stonewall Jackson, Robert E. Lee, Thomas Jefferson, or very nearly any other celebrated personage back to George Washington. Under the grandfather's tutelage Henry himself had become adept at genealogical work. It was plumb amazing, he said, how many descendants Jeff Davis had scattered around the South-land.

"Why, Henry," Jane said. "You should be ashamed of yourself. Imposing on those poor women in such a way."

"I am ashamed of myself, Miss Jane. If it was to do over again, I would never dream of it."

"Didn't your mama, the Sunday school teacher, and your daddy, the gentleman farmer, teach you that it was wrong to take advantage of the bereft?"

"They did. But I fell in with the old captain and his cronies, who were all bad to tell lies and drink whiskey and loaf away their days. Fortunately, I saw the error of my ways."

"Is that when you went into the rainmaking profession?"

"Not immediately. After I got out of the RCAF, I took up banking for a time. I worked as a kind of itinerant teller. I didn't stay long at any one bank. Then I turned to stunt flying. One day not long after the fateful plunge into the Tulsa stock-yards of Miss Lola Beauregard Beauclerk —"

"Beauclerk pronounced without the *k*," interjected Miss Jane, who of late had entertained some private doubts about the fate and indeed perhaps the existence of Miss Lola. Moreover, Jane was certain that she knew precisely what kind of itinerant teller Henry Satterfield had been during his abbreviated stint as a banker.

"How did you happen to come to Kingdom County?" she said. "I've often wondered."

"It was very strange. A week or so after the tragedy in Tulsa, I was looking at an aviation map of New England. I'd surely examined that same map twenty times before. But suddenly there it was, right before my eyes. 'Kingdom Mountain.' The mountain of my granddaddy's riddle. That very afternoon I was on my way north and you know the rest. It was the luckiest day of my life."

"And of mine, too, Henry," Jane said.

There ensued an especially sublime interlude, after which Miss Jane repeated sleepily, "And of mine, too."

32

IN THE VILLAGE, small wheels were revolving within great wheels. Eben Kinneson Esquire had assured the town fathers that the Supreme Court would reverse Judge Allen's ruling in favor of Miss Jane and her mountain. After the debacle of the flood, however, which the fathers blamed squarely on Jane and her guest the rainmaker, they decided, in a secret meeting, to assail her on two new fronts.

Every Friday night in those days Miss Jane operated the projector at the weekly picture show at the town hall, a rambling, cracker-box-shaped affair with heaving floors, a small stage with a screen on it, and a balcony where the kids had sat until about ten years ago, when it was deemed unsafe and roped off. The coal furnace in the basement was unreliable, and the previous winter a water pipe in the lobby had sprung a slow leak. It was so cold inside the hall that a glazing of blue-green ice formed on the wall behind the ticket counter and remained there until spring. Miss Jane called it the Great Devonian Glacier.

Since the village could not afford to rent talkies, Miss Jane had dragooned Judge Allen into playing the piano for the silent comedies and cowboy pictures and melodramas. It was an ancient instrument, with several ivories missing, formerly used in a dancehall in Pond in the Sky. At some point it had been stored in a barn and still had wisps of straw inside. Judge Allen, who had worked his way through Harvard Law School playing the piano in Boston speakeasies, was an accomplished amateur musician, but nothing he did could make the town-hall piano sound like anything other than a demented Victrola. The melodramas were the worst. The judge hammered out ominous low off-key chords when the villain appeared, and the audience would hiss like a hall full of vipers. Ira once confided to Jane that he could never quite get it into his head that they weren't hissing at him. "Jim Dandy to the res-cue!" the moviegoers roared as the words appeared on the screen. Or "Along came Sam. Slow-walking Sam. Slow-talking Sam." "*Fortissimo*, sir," Jane cried out to the judge from the projection booth, cranking the projector handle for all she was worth.

The year Miss Jane turned fifty and Henry Satterfield came to Kingdom Mountain, a gang of high-spirited junior high boys had established themselves as the bane of the Kingdom Common Academy. They began referring to themselves as the Dalton/James Boys, and in an odd way the village was proud of them, since they enhanced the Kingdom's reputation as a last frontier. Twice during the past school year the Academy trustees had sent a delegation to Jane's mountain to beg the Duchess to take over as the seventh- and eighth-grade English and social studies teacher and rein in these scalawags. Wisely, Miss Jane said no, thank you, and the bad boys continued their reign of terror. Emboldened by their own reputation, they began to act up at the Friday-night picture shows, engaging in one-sided dialogues with the silent-film actors, raining popcorn down from the closed-off balcony onto the patrons sitting below, and singing falsetto and off-key. Judge Allen, who had been an infantry major in the Great War, said he would forsake the piano for once and go up to the off-limits balcony and sit with the boys. That, he assured Jane, would end their insurrection. Over her dead body, said she. Jane Hubbell Kinneson had never had to call in reinforcements before, and she didn't intend to now. On the Friday evening after the flood, armed with her redoubtable scrub broom, she descended from the projection booth just before the movies began, as the Dalton/James Boys were stomping and catcalling and chanting "Start the show," and laid about right and left as vigorously as Friar Tuck with his quarterstaff. But the boys were as agile as young bobcats, and very nearly as feral, and they dodged and ducked and dived under the cracked wooden seats. Miss Jane could make no headway with them at all.

Then came the letter from the town fathers suggesting that the Duchess had more than fulfilled her civic duties over the years, and it might be time to graciously step aside for a younger projectionist. Their true purpose, of course, was to hector her into agreeing to the high road. They hinted that if she wished to sit down and talk with them about the Connector, they might assign the low high sheriff to police duty at the town-hall movies, thereby enabling her to stay on.

"Be at this coming Friday's show," Miss Jane tersely replied by return mail.

Word immediately spread throughout the Common that something momentous was going to happen at the town hall the following Friday evening. A huge crowd turned out for *The Perils of Pauline,* and the Dalton/James Boys rose to the occasion. There were screeching catcalls, squealing pig calls, boys jumping out of their seats to pepper the villain and hero alike with spitwads, boys spilling out of the balcony, pelting up and down the aisles, and generally holding Bartholomew Fair while the patrons tried in vain to watch the movie. "Here now," George Quinn said to them once. Judge Allen would undoubtedly have intervened, but he was in Burlington, where his first grandchild had just been born. Julia Hefner, the church organist, was filling in for him on the piano. When Black Bart appeared on the screen, twirling his oily mustachios, the Dalton/James Boys erupted, cheering, stomping, clapping, and exhorting the villain as he roped Pauline to the railroad tracks. That's when the frame froze on the screen.

Forth from the projection booth issued the Duchess, to a storm of hooting jeers. She proceeded down from the balcony, along the faded crimson carpet on the stairs, past the frayed purple rope and NO ADMITTANCE sign, past the ticket counter and the soggy remnants of the Great Devonian Glacier. Without breaking stride, she switched on the house lights and started down the center aisle in her long black motoring coat, which resembled a cowboy's duster.

Someone sang out, "And then along came Jane." Others joined in, "Long, tall Jane."

It was the hero's refrain from *The Perils of Pauline.* Julia slyly accompanied the Dalton/James Boys on the piano. Popcorn and spitballs and hard candy poured down from above. The refrain rose to a thundering crescendo as Miss Jane walked up the steps to the stage, head held high, as stately as a condemned queen walking to her own execution.

"Slow-walking Jane! Slow-talking Jane!" roared the hall.

Henry, unable to bear another moment of this, rose to go conduct her off the stage and home. Then, in one motion, Jane Hubbell Kinneson of Kingdom Mountain swept open her duster, produced Lady Justice, jacked a shell into the chamber, swung around, and, firing from the hip, put a fist-sized hole through the heart of Black Bart on the screen. The roar of the gunshot reverberated in the old town hall. Later it would be ascertained that the slug had passed through the back brick wall of the building and lodged in the trunk of an elm at the foot of Anderson Hill. Jane wheeled around to face the stunned audience as acrid smoke twisted out of the end of the rifle. She twirled Lady Justice half a revolution by its lever and tucked it barrel-up inside her duster. Then, in the total silence that had fallen over the hall, she walked back up the aisle, past the ticket counter, past the purple rope, up the stairs to the balcony, and calmly finished showing the movie.

"What is it?" Henry said in an alarmed voice. "Are you all right?"

It was several hours later, some time after midnight, and Jane had sat up in bed very suddenly, as if starting out of a nightmare.

"I am not all right," Jane said. "I am all wrong, Henry. I must go into On Kingdom Mountain and have a heart-to-heart talk with my dear people. I did a very foolish thing tonight."

She started to swing her legs over the side of the bed, but Henry reached out and put his hand on her shoulder. "What would you think," he said, "about having your heart-to-heart with me? You could still talk to your puppets afterward."

"They are not puppets, they are family. Some things, you know, should stay in the family."

Henry let this go unanswered, and for a time Jane sat silently on the edge of her bed. Then she said, "Henry, you know and I know that I made a terrible hash of that affair tonight at the hall. I had no business discharging a weapon in a public place. Frightening the children and the grownups as well. If someone had been standing out behind the hall, I could have blown his head off."

"It was the only way to deal with that James outfit, Miss Jane. You did the right thing."

"Horsefeathers. Back when I was teaching I would have dealt with them before they got started. Oh, Henry, these days I scarcely know myself what the right thing to do is."

"Miss Jane, you are under a great strain with the high road and the trouble with your cousin and the town fathers. A very great strain. But you are holding your ground and you certainly do know what is right. Now come back to bed. Tell your pup —

your people — tomorrow. They will no doubt approve of your actions at the town hall."

By degrees, Miss Jane allowed him to enfold her in his arms and draw her down beside him. After some time had passed, she said, "Henry?"

"Yes, Miss Jane?"

"Thank you."

33

ROUND TWO TO JANE HUBBELL KINNESON read the front-page headline of the following week's *Kingdom County Monitor*. In the accompanying story, Editor Kinneson facetiously suggested that the hole in the movie screen was the work of the village's longtime apparition and mascot, Pilgrim's ghost, who had manifested himself in the guise and service of the Duchess, Civil War rifle in hand, to put down the officially condoned insurrection at the Friday night picture show.

"I am curious, Miss Jane," Henry inquired on their way into town to open the Atheneum for its regular afternoon hours the day after Editor Kinneson's spoof appeared in the *Monitor*, "to learn more about your uncle Pilgrim's ghost. How has he come to be the village mascot? I've never heard of a mascot ghost before."

The Duchess explained that for many years, whenever anything unaccountable or untoward happened in the village, especially if the event had a slightly comic flavor, Commoners had attributed it to the ghost of her missing uncle. Sometimes there would be a spate of inexplicable happenings when Pilgrim's spirit seemed especially active. Just the past fall, Judge Allen's five-and-dime-store spectacles had vanished at one of Jane's one-woman symposiums and turned up a week later on the oblong countenance of the Pretender of Avon. A book Jane had tried to get for years, *The Penobscot Man,* suddenly appeared on the shelves of the Atheneum, then disappeared the next day — no doubt Pilgrim's doing.

On Halloween Eve Miss Jane had brought her carved Pilgrim in his blue uniform, carrying his Aesculapian snake staff, from home and set him up by the punch bowl and the orange-and-black-frosted half-moon cookies she'd made for the children of the village. By candlelight she told them how her great-great-grandfather Seth, captured as a boy in Massachusetts by her Memphremagog ancestors, had seen his mother tomahawked before his eyes on the back side of the mountain below the devil's visage because she could not keep up with her captors; how Robert Rogers and Seth's father had, in retaliation, slaughtered a village of Memphremagogs, whose relatives, in turn, had chased and butchered some of Rogers' men, including Seth's father, on the shores of the big lake. The children loved these stories, the bloodier the better, and Miss Jane did not spare them the grisliest details. She ended the evening by telling how Pilgrim had vanished in Tennessee in the Civil War and how his seventeen-year-old brother, Morgan, had set off on foot to find him and had come home with Pilgrim's staff but no Pilgrim, whose sweetheart had gone mad and drowned herself in the Great Northern Slang.

Sometimes passing villagers, glancing in through the Atheneum's mullioned windows late at night, claimed to see, by flickering candlelight, a studious-looking young man poring over Civil War books and letters or Morgan's old law books. That, of course, was Pilgrim's ghost. Miss Jane even hinted to Henry that from time to time, when she was occupied on her mountain, Pilgrim had opened the Atheneum and waited on a customer or two in her bookshop, tendering them their change in Confederate bills. Pilgrim's ghost had even been blamed for the recent deterioration of the Atheneum, as nails continued to rust away, causing the handsome blue and gray roof slates to slide down and nearly brain the library's patrons, as bricks fell out of the ancient chimney, and as floor joists sagged and split under the weight of the ever-increasing number of volumes Miss Jane added to the shelves. What was needed, she said, was a fundraiser, something like the Fourth of July gala but designed to refurbish the Atheneum before it collapsed of sheer neglect.

As Jane and Henry turned left at the northeastern corner of the common and proceeded down the street toward the library, they saw ahead, on the green under the elms, what appeared to be a party of gaily clad picnickers gathered on the grass. It looked as if a group of traveling tinkers had camped on the village green. No — they were not tinkers. The picnickers, Miss Jane suddenly realized, were her own scribblers and scrawlers, who had been unceremoniously removed from the Atheneum and transferred to the common. At first Henry wondered if Pilgrim's ghost might be up to his old pranks. Then he noticed that the front door of the library was padlocked, and nailed to it, like Luther's theses, was an official-looking notice:

THIS BUILDING CONDEMNED
BY ORDER OF THE TOWN FATHERS
OF KINGDOM COMMON UNTIL
FURTHER NOTICE

Henry had the presence of mind to grab Lady Justice and empty the live shells out of its chamber and tuck them into the pocket of his white coat. Miss Jane was so beside herself that she hardly noticed. Henry had never seen her so angry.

"I am sorry, so sorry, that it should come to this," she told Dr. Johnson, the Pronouncer of Litchfield, as she and Henry and now Judge Allen, who had come hurrying across the street from the courthouse, lifted the Great Cham into the truck bed and roped him in beside Jane Austen. "You of all people, sir," Jane said, "who as a starving young author with no place to spend the night walked the streets of London until dawn with Goldsmith and Kit Smart. Never fear. This won't go unanswered. We'll have our day in court. Even you, my poor misguided liege" — patting her great adversary, King James, on his gilded wooden crown — "even you will have your satisfaction."

"Jane, I'm so sorry about this," the judge said.

"Eben's behind it," she said. "He'll pay and pay dearly."

"Maybe," Judge Allen said. "But from what I've witnessed of the behavior of our good town fathers lately, I don't think they need much abetting. Could an old friend offer a suggestion?"

Jane nodded.

"Move your books and your scribblers into my old law office above the hardware store. It's yours, rent-free, for as long as you want it."

Moved by her friend's kindness, Jane began to weep. "Maybe it's time for me to give up the bookshop and the library, too."

"Nonsense. Think over my offer. It would be my great pleasure."

"Well, I'll think about it, Ira. For now I'm going to move every one of my scribblers and scrawlers, and my books, too, out to the mountain, where I can keep track of them. Come along, Mr. Clemens," she said, picking up Mark Twain and setting him in the bed of the truck. "Perhaps all this will give you an idea for another great book. Life, not on the Mississippi, but on Kingdom Mountain. As for Eben and the town fathers" — and here she seemed to be addressing her scribblers and scrawlers along with the judge and Henry — "I shall deal with them in a more fit season. Rely upon it."

Miss Jane was devastated. As she told her dear people in On Kingdom Mountain that evening while Henry tuned the engine of his biplane, since her retirement from teaching, much of her very identity derived from her occupation as a bookwoman. With a book in her hands she felt connected to the story it told and its characters and the places where they lived, to the world beyond Kingdom Mountain, and to her scribblers and scrawlers. She loved the way a well-read old book smelled, loved the fading print on its spine and cover, the different fonts and styles of type. A life without books would be unimaginable.

Yes, she could move her literary operations into Judge Allen's former office, but what hurt her most was that the town fathers, and perhaps the village as a whole, simply didn't care whether they had a library and bookshop or not, didn't appreciate the work Miss Jane had done over the years at the Atheneum. She was surprised by her own vulnerability, her capacity to be wounded by what the village thought, she who had always held herself apart and perhaps regarded herself as indifferent to anyone's opinion but her own.

Later, when Henry tried to console her, she snapped at him, then turned coldly away from the bewildered man. *Back off a mite, boy,* the granddaddy suggested. *A Yankee female is as unreasonable a species as God ever created. Give her a little room now. By and by we will strike behind her lines and take her and the gold both by storm.*

Then, as if to prove the adage that bad news comes in sets of three or even four, the very next morning, Miss Jane received two letters. The first was from the North American Bird Carving Contest award committee, informing her that she had won third place, behind Santiago and Jackson, for her "strange, prehistoric bird." As far as Miss Jane was concerned, placing third was far more ignominious than not placing at all. She was particularly enraged to learn that her beautiful archaeopteryx, Noah, would soon be displayed with the birds of her rivals at the Montreal Museum of Fine Arts, for all to see that she had once again been bested.

The second letter was from Judge Allen's lawyer son, Forrest, confirming that the Vermont Supreme Court would hear the case of *Jane Hubbell Kinneson v. Township of Kingdom Common* the following Tuesday.

Then on Sunday, Eben Kinneson Esquire came out to the home place for his annual chicken-and-biscuits birthday dinner. Over the coffee and apple pie, Eben produced a certified bank check, made out to Miss Jane from the town of Kingdom Common, for two thousand dollars, along with a waiver for her to sign granting the town permission to extend the Connector from the hemlock-plank covered bridge to the home place and the official Canadian line. Miss Jane glanced at the bank check and the waiver, then excused herself and went into her bedchamber. She returned with a sewing needle. She picked up the large, rectangular pink check and poked one corner of it at the eye of the needle. Then she handed the check back to Eben. "I'm sorry, cousin," she said. "A camel won't fit through and neither will a certified check for two thousand dollars."

"The Supreme Court will never rule in your favor, cousin. Your case is a lost cause."

"I love a lost cause. I always have."

"It is hardly something to boast of. This appearance before the Supreme Court in Montpelier will not be like your Pyrrhic victory in the backwoods chancellery of your crony Ira Allen. Rest assured that the justices, before whom I have successfully argued eight cases without a loss, will never in this world allow you to represent yourself. The Supreme Court in Montpelier will most certainly not permit you to transform its proceedings into a charade."

"The Supreme Court in Montpelier will be delighted to hear what I have to say, cousin. It will be a wholly refreshing change from listening to you pettifogging shysters."

"My arguments will smite down yours as the avenging she-bears smote the two and forty children who mocked Elisha for his baldness. Second Kings 2:24."

"The she-bears do no such thing in the Kingdom Mountain Bible, cousin. In the Kingdom Mountain Bible, the good bruins turn on King James's Jehovah and put both him and Elisha to rout. In the same way, I'll rout you and demolish your arguments in court."

"I implore you not to subject the Kinneson family name to further mortification."

"The Kinneson family name will survive very nicely. Look at it this way, cousin. Whatever the outcome, a Kinneson is bound to walk away victorious."

"Aye. For the ninth consecutive time." Eben neatly folded his cloth napkin, folded it again, gave his lips a fastidious pat, and placed the napkin beside his pie plate. "A superior birthday dinner, cousin. I thank you. Your biscuits are unsurpassed. Wouldn't you agree, Mr. Satterfield?"

"I would," Henry said.

"Thank you for coming, cousin," Jane said. "It is always a pleasure to entertain family."

"Thank you for inviting me, cousin."

On the way across the dooryard to Eben's car, Henry said, "Meaning no disrespect, Mr. Kinneson, but how can you torment your own blood relation this way? She cooks you a tasty birthday dinner and then you abuse her hospitality by arguing with her. Why don't you leave her be?"

Eben gave Henry a wondering frown. "Why, sir," he said, "don't you know that Jane had the best time today that she's had since the last time I was here? I've been venturing out to this fastness, checking up on your friend, and arguing her out of her most capricious follies for decades. Who do you think has saved Miss Jane Hubbell Kinneson from herself all these years?"

Henry looked at the attorney. "So I am to understand that you are Miss Jane's benefactor?"

"Jane is a remarkable individualist," Eben said. "Perhaps the last great individualist in Kingdom County. For that I admire her. But she cannot prevent this road from going through. Frankly, I doubt that her archenemy, King James's Jehovah himself, could stop the Connector at this point. Progress has at last reached the Kingdom. It will not be stopped. It, I mean progress, is the one true perpetual-motion machine. In the meantime, who do you suppose persuaded the town fathers to offer Jane twice as much for the right of way as they originally intended to? For that matter, who do you think put Jane in the way of her little jobs as village librarian and projectionist? I respect you, sir, for standing by your friend. But when young lawyer Allen appears in front of the Supreme Court on her behalf, I shan't spare him or her. Nor will the justices. This is no parlor game, Henry. Use what influence you have with the woman to dissuade her from her course of action. It can only end badly for her."

Amen, said the granddaddy in Henry's head as Eben drove off down the lane. *I am right glad to see, boy, that not all Yankees are complete fools. There is a man worth heeding.*

"I've asked you before to stay out of this," Henry said.

I cannot, said the captain. *I have been in it for well over half a century. You have been in it since I told you the first part of the jingle when you was a tadpole in short pants.*

"Why did you give the second part of the riddle to Jane's father?"

To pit you and him against each other for my amusement, why else? But you, boy, are blood. Blood's thick, thick. You and I are in this together. We are as alike as two peas in every way.

"We are not, sir."

Who taught you to cast genealogies? Who tolt you to go into the banking profession?

Henry decided to ignore Captain Cantrell Satterfield. He was under no obligation — he was not beholden to the old man, as the granddaddy would have put it — to reply.

How is it you wear white? the captain said with a mean chuckle.

"Because I'm a showman," Henry replied despite himself.

No, said the granddaddy. *You wear white because I did. Deny it if you can.*

"If you are who you say you are, tell me where you hid the treasure," Henry said.

To this the granddaddy's voice said nothing.

"I declare, Mr. Satterfield," Miss Jane said from the porch. "You remind me of myself, standing out there talking to yourself a mile a minute. Whom are you conversing with?"

"No one, Miss Jane," Henry said. "Absolutely no one. What may I do to help you get ready for your big day in court? Are you really planning to represent yourself again?"

"Come up out of the sun," Miss Jane said. "I'll tell you just exactly what I'm planning."

For the next forty-five minutes Miss Jane spoke to Henry nonstop, laying out her case point by point, exactly the way she would present it to the Vermont Supreme Court. When at last she finished, he thought for a time. Then he said, "Miss Jane, I wish to tell you something."

"Yes, Henry? Do you think my argument has holes in it? Don't be afraid to speak up."

Although Henry was not at all sure that Miss Jane would be

allowed to present her own case, or any part of it, he did not think her argument had holes in it, and had he thought so, he certainly knew better than to say so.

"It has occurred to me that one day, many, many years from now, after you and, I venture to hope, I as well have ascended to the celestial canopy, Saint Peter may ask you to spell him at the gate from time to time. Regardless of what happens with the Supreme Court, that is how highly I regard you and your judgment."

"Why, thank you, Henry. But whom do you think I would admit to the celestial canopy?"

"Everyone."

"Nay, nay, Mr. Satterfield. Surely not everyone."

"Yes, Miss Jane, surely everyone. Every applicant during your watch would receive the most severe and horrible tongue-lashing of their lives, so to speak. After which you would throw open the gates of heaven and, with open arms, welcome every last wretch to the canopy. It is the highest compliment I know to give and it came to me just now as you were telling me your plan."

"Well, it is a fine, original compliment, and I much appreciate it, and I agree with half of it, at least. That, of course, is the tongue-lashing part. I hope the second part would be true as well. But lord, Mr. S., can you imagine spending an eternity with Eben Kinneson Esquire and the town fathers? Not to mention such luminaries as Sneaking Saul and King James's Jehovah?"

"Not really, but when you stop to think of it, it might be more pleasant than the alternative."

"Well, that's so, too," Jane said. "When all's said, however, I must say that I seem to get on better with my life when I dwell less on how I'm going to spend eternity and more on how I'm going to spend today. Come. Let's go write that in the Kingdom Mountain Bible."

34

"The supreme court of the great Republic of Vermont, claiming statehood but not relinquishing independence as a Republic in the year of our Lord seventeen hundred and eighty-six, is now, on this eighteenth day of August in the year of our Lord nineteen hundred and thirty, officially in session. Please rise."

Into the Vermont Supreme Court in Montpelier filed the five black-clad justices. Often in her girlhood Miss Jane had sat in this musty-smelling gallery, watching as her father, Chief Justice Morgan Kinneson, presided. Jane herself had briefly considered pursuing a legal career. Now, looking around the courtroom, she was glad that she had not and that, whatever the future might hold, she had devoted her life to teaching, carving her birds and dear people, and lending and even occasionally selling books to the people of Kingdom County.

The justices took their seats behind the dark, polished bench at the front of the courtroom. One by one their faces began to register reactions ranging from curiosity and surprise to consternation. As they looked out from their hallowed bailiwick, they saw, sitting or standing next to the dark-complected gentleman in the white suit and the attractive, light-haired woman in black, a row of figures with long, narrow heads and painted features, dressed in a variety of antiquated styles, all looking straight back at them with the same grave, wide-set gray eyes as the light-haired woman's. A young man wearing a blue uniform held a two-headed snake staff in his hand. Beside him stood a boy dressed in homespun and carrying a rifle. One figure wore a great wooden ox yoke around his neck. A tall man with a wild halo of white hair held the hand of a black child, herself holding the hand of a black woman escorted by a black man. Next to them was a man dressed as plainly as a Quaker, carrying a woven basket containing an infant with a shock of coal black hair and black eyes.

Otherwise the courtroom was a rather nondescript place, much smaller than Judge Allen's in Kingdom Common, with no pictures on the walls and seating for no more than fifty spectators. At the plaintiff's table sat Forrest Allen, just out of Yale Law School, wearing a broad, light-gray necktie and a dark gray double-breasted suit, waiting eagerly and perhaps with some apprehension, to make his first appearance before his home state's highest court. Across the aisle at the defendant's table sat Eben Kinneson Esquire. In the first row behind him were the town fathers of Kingdom Common, shooting glances at Miss Jane and her dear people. How had she gotten her wooden menagerie into the building, much less the courtroom? Four of the justices wondered the same thing. The court clerk looked significantly toward Chief Justice Hamilton Dewey, now a white-haired magistrate but once, as Miss Jane well remembered, her father's law clerk. It was Justice Dewey who, earlier that morning, had instructed the clerk to allow Miss Jane's people, whom she had transported to the state capital in the back of her Ford truck, to accompany her into the courtroom. If the daughter of his old mentor, Chief Justice Morgan Kinneson, wished to bring her wooden creations from the Kingdom to court with her, that was fine with him. This might be the state capital, but it was still Vermont, and Justice Dewey, at least, was determined not to forget it.

The chief justice nodded at the clerk, who announced in a grave and sonorous voice, "To the Vermont Supreme Court come Jane Hubbell Kinneson and the selectmen of the township of Kingdom Common in the case of Jane Kinneson versus

Kingdom Common. This case came on to be heard on the fourteenth of May in the Shiretown Court of Kingdom Common, in which the court chancellor did order and decree that the town highway known as the Connector stop on the south side of the Upper East Branch of the Kingdom River and not be continued across said river onto the property of Miss Jane Hubbell Kinneson. The defendant in this case, the township of Kingdom Common, has filed a demurrer averring that the ruling of the chancellor is contrary to evidence, not supported by evidence, and contrary to law. Now comes counsel for the plaintiff, Mr. Forrest Allen, Esquire, duly admitted to, and in good standing with, the Vermont Bar, to present the case of the plaintiff, Miss Jane Hubbell Kinneson."

Forrest Allen started to stand but, cutting him off, Jane herself stepped briskly to the podium in front of the bench, cardboard file folder in hand. "Good morning, gentlemen," she said. "I am Miss Jane Hubbell Kinneson of Kingdom Mountain."

"Where is your counsel, Miss Kinneson?" the chief justice inquired. "Is the gentleman at the plaintiff's table your counsel?"

"I'm my own counsel."

"I'm sorry, Miss Kinneson. Only attorneys licensed by the Vermont Bar Association may argue cases in front of the Vermont Supreme Court."

"*Vermont Supreme Court Decisions*, volume XVII, 1892 to 1893, pages 824 to 912, page 825, *Kittredge versus the Grand Trunk Railroad*. I cite: 'It is hereby ordered and decreed that any freeborn Vermonter may argue his own case in any Vermont court.' Mr. Kittredge argued his own case against the railroad, which was trying to appropriate part of his farm, and won. The decision was unanimous, and the court's opinion was written by my father, Chief Justice Morgan Kinneson."

"Hasn't that precedent been superseded by the ruling in the 1901 case of *Vermont Electric, Inc., versus Rufus Hodgdon,* who was *not* allowed to represent himself before the Supreme Court because he had not passed the bar examination?" another justice said.

"It most certainly has not been so superseded," Miss Jane said. "The *Vermont Electric versus Rufus Hodgdon* case, found in volume XXXVI of the *Vermont Supreme Court Decisions,* states on page 418, 'Cases before the Supreme Court must be argued by licensed attorneys who have passed the Vermont Bar Exam and been duly admitted to the Vermont Bar, *with the exception of land-claim cases brought by Memphremagog Abenaki property owners against town, state, or federal government, the presumption being that native landowners know their land best and can, therefore, speak best on behalf of that land.*' Also authored by Chief Justice Morgan Kinneson. My father felt, gentlemen, and very rightly so, that no one but a Memphremagog could speak for the Memphremagogs. My mother was a full Memphremagog Abenaki. I'd like you to meet her." Jane gestured at the carving of the infant Pharaoh's Daughter, wrapped in the red Hudson's Bay blanket, in the sweetgrass basket.

In the meantime the clerk had checked the pertinent volume in the *Supreme Court Decisions* and confirmed Miss Jane's statement. Chief Justice Dewey said, "Let's get this show on the road and move ahead with the arguments. I'm satisfied that there's good precedent for Miss Jane Kinneson, whose Memphremagog mother I remember very well, to speak on behalf of her own land."

Forrest Allen, shaking his head, started to rise.

"Sit down, young man," Jane told him. To the justices she said, "I am here as the last Memphremagog to dwell on Kingdom Mountain. Unfortunately, mountains are inclined to be silent. If it could, however, Kingdom Mountain would tell many powerful stories. It would tell how it was formed long before our puny Green Mountains. How, a mere ten thousand years ago, the great ice sheet deposited on its summit a massive glacial boulder inscribed with wondrous carvings. And how, for many millennia, it was the home of caribou, wolves, panthers, and a unique, now endangered species of fish known as the blue-backed char."

Chief Justice Hamilton Dewey leaned forward. "Taxonomically speaking, Miss Kinneson, is the blue-backed char officially designated as a separate species?"

"She is." Jane consulted her notes. "I cite Professor Louis Agassiz, the Swiss-born naturalist, who in 1860 and again in 1861 journeyed to Vermont with his student, my uncle Pilgrim" — gesturing toward the young man with the snake staff — "to view the rare Arctic plants and glacial phenomena on Kingdom Mountain. In his monograph entitled *Glaciation of Kingdom Mountain,* besides identifying four new species of Arctic saxifrages and a pink and blue windflower previously unknown to science, Professor Agassiz wrote, 'In the three tarns on the north side of the mountain, and in the upper reaches of the East Branch of the Kingdom River, there dwells a bluish fish of the *Salmo* genus, a species I have named *borealis fontinalis Kinnesonian,* found elsewhere only in a lake on Baffin Island.' The Vermont Fish and Game Department lists the blue-backed brook trout as endangered. Benson's authoritative *North American Fresh Water Ichthyology* classifies 'the blue trout of a few cold-water ponds and brooks in remote northern Vermont and southern Quebec' as a *separate species.*"

The justices were taking notes. Henry Satterfield was beginning to feel excited. Whatever self-doubts she might have had when conversing with him or alone in On Kingdom Mountain with her dear people, Miss Jane's public presence was magisterial.

Chief Justice Dewey said, "Miss Kinneson, wouldn't the Connector bring jobs and industry to rural northern Vermont?"

"Certain local businessmen hope to purchase the mountain and turn it into a winter spa so that idle folks can slide down hill by day and roister by night. When it comes to roistering, people can always be counted on to be very industrious, you know."

"Miss Kinneson," a younger justice said, "do you own all of Kingdom Mountain?"

"Every square foot. In trust for the Memphremagog branch of the Abenaki nation."

"I don't believe that the Memphremagogs or, for that matter, the Abenaki nation, have ever been officially granted tribal status by the state of Vermont."

"The Memphremagog nation is nearly extinct. In 1856 thirty-six men of the tribe fell to their deaths in the Saint Lawrence River while constructing the Victoria Bridge. I am their last descendant. If you doubt it, ask Memphre Magog." Miss Jane gestured at her two-headed wooden sculpture of the Creator of Kingdom Mountain, standing erect and tall, drawn up to his full seven feet, and regarding the justices sternly with both his heads.

"I understand that the international border, as designated by the Webster-Ashburton Treaty, actually runs through your home, Miss Kinneson."

"The international border is an arbitrary line on a map, nothing more. But Kingdom Mountain, which is silent, or it would inform you of this fact itself, officially belongs to neither the U.S. nor Canada." From her cardboard folder Miss Jane withdrew an ancient handwritten document. "Your Honors, behold. The *first* Webster-Ashburton Treaty, drafted by Daniel Webster and Lord Ashburton as a letter to my great-grandfather, Freethinker Kinneson. He's the gentleman to my left who looks like John Brown. 'As for the massive wild peak along the border known as Kingdom Mountain, lying between Vermont and Quebec, bisected by the 45th Parallel, and stretching from

Lake Memphremagog on the west to the headwaters of the Upper East Branch of the Kingdom River in Pond Number Three of the Chain of Ponds on the east, and from the Grand Bayou du Nord or Great Northern Slang on the north to the Lower East Branch of the Kingdom River on the south, comprising approximately one hundred and fifty square miles of forests, lakes, and streams, this territory shall belong to neither the United States nor Great Britain but rather to Freethinker Kinneson and his heirs, to be held in trust for the Memphremagog branch of the Abenaki Nation, for as long as the summer sky over the mountain is blue, its waters flow north to the Saint Lawrence, and the grass on its slopes turns green in the spring.'"

"Miss Kinneson, does this interesting provision appear in the ratified Webster-Ashburton Treaty?"

"It does not. It was struck out by politicos in Washington and London at the last minute. But this document predates the final treaty by eight months and was signed by both Daniel Webster and Lord Ashburton."

"Where is its legal validity if it wasn't incorporated into the final treaty?"

"It was intended to be in the final treaty or it would have been invalidated in that treaty. Frankly, Kingdom Mountain was so remote and forbidding that originally neither the United States nor Great Britain wanted it. Now that it has some potential value, the town of Kingdom Common wishes to steal it from me."

"Miss Kinneson, can people — the public — visit your mountain and see these natural wonders you've told us about? Isn't it all private land?"

"Private, certainly. But open to anyone who wishes to fish, hunt, hike, look for birds. Not a square foot of Kingdom Mountain is posted."

"Are you yourself an American or a Canadian citizen?"

"Neither. I'm the last member of the Memphremagog tribe and the last of the Kingdom Mountain Kinnesons, speaking on behalf of the rights of Kingdom Mountain."

"How can a mountain have rights? Does the United States Constitution stipulate such rights?"

Once again Miss Jane dived into her cardboard case. "I now read from the Constitution of the Memphremagog Tribe of the Abenaki Nation, dictated by Chief Joseph Hubert, my Indian great-great-grandfather — whose name was subsequently anglicized to Hubbell — to my Kinneson great-great-grandfather, Seth." Miss Jane gestured at the figure in the ox yoke. "'The domain of the Memphremagog, including the lake and mountain of that name, belong to Memphre Magog, our Creator, and to his Memphremagog children, in perpetuity.' Since the domain in question belongs to another nation, not Canada or the U.S., neither the U.S. nor Canada can exercise *eminent* domain. Kingdom Mountain *is* an eminent domain. It belongs to itself. If it were not obliged to keep its own counsel and remain silent, it would readily enough say so."

"This is all intriguing. But could you please clarify, Miss Kinneson, what the *legal* issue is here? Are you arguing that the town can't exercise eminent domain on your mountain because of your ancestors' aboriginal rights?"

"Take care, sir, whom you call an aborigine. This case has nothing to do with aborigines, though in 1759 Robert Rogers and his so-called Rangers hunted down many of my ancestors and slaughtered them, even as the poor aborigines on the far side of the world were hunted down and slaughtered. I am arguing that the state has no right to appropriate property outside its own boundaries. Eminent domain, a term I have never much cared for, is, of course, the so-called right of a government to appropriate private property for public use, just compensation being given to the owner. But there can be no just compensation for destroying the last original wilderness in

Vermont. And how, pray, do you compensate someone for taking away her history and traditions? How do you propose to compensate me for taking away and defiling the place that binds me to my family?"

"I assume, Miss Kinneson, that you pay taxes to the state of Vermont? And to the federal government as well? And property taxes to the township of Kingdom Common?"

"I pay taxes to no one. Kingdom Mountain is an unincorporated township. No Kinneson has ever paid a penny of taxes to any governmental entity — town, state, or federal. Seth Kinneson saw to that."

"Miss Kinneson, how do you propose that people travel by road from Kingdom County to Canada without the Connector?"

"That's not my lookout. They may go in a handbasket for all I care."

Two or three of the justices smiled.

"Doesn't your mountain lie directly in the way?"

"Let travelers go the long way round then. In the Kingdom people have always gone the long way round to get nearly anywhere. Look you, my friends. Do you see this young gentleman? This is Morgan Kinneson, my father, as a boy of seventeen, setting out to go south to find his brother, Pilgrim, missing in action in the Civil War. Morgan had no paved high road to follow. He went the long way round. So too did this worthy, Venturing Seth, who helped his ox pull the sled carrying his family through trackless wilderness to settle the mountain. This gentleman in gray is one of the Confederate raiders who carried away a fortune in gold from the bank in Kingdom Common. To return back to the South, he first traveled north. Here is Canada Jane Hubbell, my Memphremagog mother's mother, a basket maker who traveled from the Saint Lawrence to the Atlantic and back each summer. She needed no high road to complete her annual migration. Let Kingdom Mountain remain as these good people all knew it. Let it remain itself, as Judge Ira Allen of Kingdom County has determined it should."

"What significant damage will a narrow corridor of paved roadway do to an area of one hundred and fifty square miles?"

This was the question Miss Jane had been waiting for. Out of her cardboard file came photographs she had taken of the scalped hillsides of East and West Round Hill, the deep ruts filled with muddy water, and the brush-choked spawning pool of the blue-backed trout. The Gate to Canada looked as though a meteor had crashed into it.

"Mountains are silent," Jane said. "This sector of Kingdom Mountain will be silent for a long time to come."

The courtroom, too, was silent, as the Duchess of Kingdom Mountain sat back down beside Henry Satterfield and her dear people.

Of course, Eben Kinneson Esquire did a very able job of presenting the township's case, arguing that that part of Kingdom Mountain lying south of the forty-fifth parallel of latitude designating the border belonged officially to the township of Kingdom Common and always had. He emphasized that the projected Connector had already been rerouted around the spawning grounds of the "so-called blue-backed trout" and that the right of the people of Kingdom County to be "connected" to the rest of the world transcended any supposed right of the mountain, based on suspect, unofficial documents and heathenish notions, to block progress. He argued that Judge Allen's decision on Miss Jane's behalf had no basis in evidence or law.

The justices had some tough questions for Eben. One wanted to know if the state could guarantee that the Connector wouldn't eradicate the Arctic saxifrage, unique windflowers, and blue trout? And wouldn't the blasting for the highway jeopardize the stability of the balancing boulder on the summit?

"Justice Smythe," Eben said, "I know of no such guarantees in this world. Every precaution will be taken not to disturb the native flora and fauna and the natural geological configurations on the mountain. Some change is inevitable. Are we worse off today because thunder lizards no longer stalk the land? Which of you would care to discover one browsing in your backyard? Change is a condition of the natural order of things."

"A tiny pink and blue windflower is hardly a dinosaur," Justice Dewey said. "How is a concrete highway that will bring noise and fumes and roadside trash and cut hundreds of acres out of the heart of Vermont's last wilderness part of the natural order of things?"

"It will also bring tourism to an impoverished and isolated corner of New England. It may attract good jobs. It will lead to the salvation of the Kingdom."

"From what does the Kingdom need to be saved?"

"From economic stagnation," Eben Kinneson Esquire replied. "Seventy-five percent of our young people leave the area after graduating from high school. There's no sustainable work for them locally."

"I don't understand how the Connector will bring sustainable work," a justice said. "Do you mean construction work on the new highway itself?"

"Yes. As well as jobs in industries attracted by cheaper transportation as the area continues to be developed."

"That's just the issue, isn't it?" the chief justice said. "Development of the last unspoiled corner of Vermont? Isn't this a matter of two competing rights, Mr. Kinneson? The right to develop the economy of a depressed area — if, in fact, the Connector will accomplish that — versus the right of Miss Jane Hubbell Kinneson and the people of Vermont to retain some wilderness?"

"That's exactly what our recently established national parks are for, Justice Dewey."

"It looks to me as though the clear-cutting has already ruined some of the wilderness. How could *any* fish spawn in that mud-choked river? Much less trout?"

"As for the blue-backed brook trout," Eben continued, "no such subspecies has ever been officially recognized by the U.S. Fish and Wildlife Service. They're blue from eating blue crawfish, a slight regional differentiation in pigmentation."

"So it's all right to exterminate them? Because we can't agree on whether they're a separate species?"

"They have not been exterminated, Justice Chittenden, nor will they be."

"How do you respond to Miss Kinneson's contention that Kingdom Mountain belongs to the Memphremagog Indians and to neither Canada nor the United States?"

"As pointed out, no such provision exists in the *ratified* Webster-Ashburton Treaty. Everyone knows that Dan'l Webster was a famous practical joker. He got Lord Ashburton drinking my great-grandfather's applejack, then drew up that spurious document and tricked him into signing it."

"How do you explain the fact that each Kingdom owner has left the mountain to his heirs in trust for the Memphremagog nation?"

"They felt remorse for Rogers' near-annihilation of the tribe. Seth Kinneson's father was one of those Rangers. That was, perhaps, unfortunate. But what's done is done. The tribe is extinct or nearly so. The dusky Memphremagogs are a moot point."

"Isn't your cousin, Miss Jane Hubbell Kinneson, part Memphremagog?"

"I advance no such grand claim on her behalf. For all I know, her mother may have had some native ancestry. Let us admit that Jane Hubbell Kinneson does not much resemble an Indian."

"You have five minutes left, Mr. Kinneson."

"The township of Kingdom Common, which indubitably encompasses Kingdom Mountain as far north as the forty-fifth parallel of latitude, designated as the international border between Vermont and Quebec, has offered Miss Kinneson two thousand dollars for the right of way for the Connector. The Connector itself will follow a long-existing road, the Canada Pike. The township has promised to make every effort to preserve and protect the trout and other native animals and plants on the mountain. The Connector will bring much-needed jobs and tourism to Kingdom County and provide its residents with much readier access to the outside world. No winter resort is planned for the slopes of Kingdom Mountain at this time. Thank you."

"Miss Kinneson, you have five more minutes if you or your attorney would like to make a concluding statement," Chief Justice Dewey said.

Miss Jane rose and approached the lectern. "As I said at the outset, mountains are silent. Likewise rivers, ponds, and forests. I must speak for them. Kingdom Mountain has seen a great deal over the past three billion years. It stood watch as my great-grandfather Freethinker" — gesturing to him — "barricaded it and the lake it overlooks, during the War of 1812, against all incursionists, American and British alike. It was the site of Vermont's northernmost Underground Railroad station. Guided by my grandfather, Quaker Meeting, hundreds of fugitives from the Southland passed over the mountain to Canada and freedom. Once a seal came up the river from Lake Memphremagog and the Saint Lawrence and bided with us for a season. Let the mountain's last tale not be its own destruction at the hands of those with a shortsighted notion of progress. To a true Kingdom Mountain Kinneson, progress is saving the last of our dwindling wild countryside for future generations so that they may know where they came from and who their ancestors were and, knowing that, have a clearer idea of who they are and who they may yet become. On Kingdom Mountain, the past lives on as part of the present. Indeed, it *is* the present. Let us do it, and our forebears, the honor of permitting it to be part of the future as well."

"Mr. Kinneson, you have two more minutes."

"The Connector will bring thousands of people each year to see the wonders of Kingdom Mountain. A highway pull-off will be built on the west saddle of the mountain, over-looking the balancing boulder to the east and the lake to the west. Sturdy fences will be erected to keep wild animals from wandering into the traffic. Moreover, the township will offer to purchase and preserve Miss Jane Hubbell Kinneson's little wood-carver's museum and to purchase and reestablish her farm as a working nineteenth-century Vermont homestead, a fascinating slice of living history. A ski slope, should one ever be built, would bring in considerable revenue for our hard-pressed local schools. Its alteration to the mountain would be quite minimal. But that is up to Miss Jane Kinneson and her heirs. For the time being, the Connector would scarcely change the mountain at all. Let us graciously accept some change in Kingdom County, welcoming what is new and helpful, preserving the best of the past that Miss Jane has so zealously guarded and so passionately evoked for us here today. Thank you, gentlemen."

"Well, Miss Jane," Henry said as they loaded Jane's dear people into her truck a few minutes later, "I believe you have won a great victory today. No one who heard you could doubt the outcome."

"We can only hope so, Henry."

"Why, did you see the old judges' expressions? You had them eating out of your hand from the very start of the proceedings."

"Perhaps. My father often told me that the law was a unique species of animalcula. That you could never predict how a case would turn out. I fear, sir, that we must hope for the best, expect the worst, and be prepared for anything in between. That, of course, is why I moved my grandparents' graves."

The Far Side
of the
Mountain

35

Miss Jane was fond of remarking, as her father had before her, that while you could never, under any circumstances, tell a Kingdom Mountain Kinneson what to do, you could *ask* a Kingdom Mountain Kinneson to do nearly anything. Except, perhaps, to attend church. But while she did not hold with churchgoing, which she considered bad for the soul and tedious besides, Miss Jane believed, with nearly evangelical fervor, in what she was pleased to call "educational book-buying tours." Once or twice a week she would point the Model A in one direction or another and strike out, stopping at every secondhand book emporium within fifty miles of Kingdom Common. Miss Jane could happily spend the better part of a morning or afternoon in a falling-down barn or a stifling attic crammed with mildewed volumes, searching for long-forgotten titles. She had a particular interest in Civil War–era books, diaries, letters, and maps, over which she pored by the hour. On their return trip from the Supreme Court proceeding in Montpelier, she insisted that they stop at the Blue and Gray Bookshop in Plainfield, a secondhand bookstore specializing in literary memorabilia from the War Between the States. Here, after a long, thorough search, while Henry sat perusing the latest *True Detective* under a dooryard maple, she came across a locally printed tome called *Union Engagements in East Tennessee and the Western Mountains of North Carolina, 1863–1865.*

Back at the home place, after unloading Jane's people from the bed of the truck and replacing them in On Kingdom Mountain, Henry, still decked out in his elegant white suit and shoes, sipping Miss Jane's delicious switchel and swaying gently in the porch hammock, thumbed idly through Jane's latest purchase. He knew that before she relegated *Union Engagements* to the Civil War section of her library, she would study it carefully, tracing her father's and uncle's presumed routes through the war-torn southern mountains and wondering aloud whatever had become of Pilgrim. Somewhere in the back of his head he heard his granddaddy laughing sardonically. Henry wondered, Could Captain Cantrell Satterfield have met Pilgrim during the war? It was a most intriguing speculation.

Late that night, after Miss Jane had fallen asleep, Henry rose, tiptoed into On Kingdom Mountain, lighted a lantern, and looked long and searchingly into Pilgrim's oblong wooden face. Suddenly the door of On Kingdom Mountain swung open, and Henry gave a terrific start.

"Why, Mr. Satterfield," Jane said. "What are you up to? I thought I was the only one around here foolish enough to consult with my dear people."

"I think, Miss Jane," Henry said, "that we need to find out exactly what happened to your uncle Pilgrim."

"I've been trying to do just that for the past thirty years. Come back to bed, Henry. We'll study more on the matter in the morning."

For many years the Duchess had advertised regularly in genealogical newsletters, historical society bulletins, and local papers in such far-flung places as Asheville, North Carolina, and Knoxville, Tennessee, for information about her lost uncle Pilgrim. Family was everything to the Duchess, especially now that she was the very last of the Kingdom Mountain Kinnesons and, for that matter, of the Memphremagog Abenakis. Even her beloved mountain, for all of its natural marvels, perhaps meant most to her as the place where her ancestors had lived their hard, worthwhile lives, helping all who came there, preserving the wild country intact for their heirs and theirs. As she had told the Montpelier justices, it was Kingdom Mountain that enabled her family history to live on into the present.

The next morning at breakfast, she confided to Henry that it was all but unendurable to her to reflect that if Pilgrim did live through the war, she might have family in the South whom she didn't even know about.

"Your father was what, just seventeen when he went to look for Pilgrim?" Henry said skeptically.

"He turned eighteen on the way," Miss Jane said. "He was no boy, Henry. Not by the time he started to Tennessee. He was a young man who had been conducting Underground Railroad passengers over the mountain to Canada since he was ten."

As had often happened on Kingdom Mountain, help arrived from an unexpected quarter and in an entirely unpredictable way. That afternoon the dog-cart man showed up with his wagon and bright paints and mongrels and went to work painting a beautiful tree of life, bearing an array of ripe apples, pears, peaches, oranges, and tropical fruit, on Miss Jane's front door. Henry, in the meantime, decided to make friends with the painter's dogs, lying with their heads on their paws, watching their master as reverently as if he were another Michelangelo. When the pilot offered them a few bites of venison steak left over from supper the night before, they ignored him until their master signaled that it was all right to accept the scraps. What interested Henry most about the dogs was that never once had he heard one of them bark. Like their owner, they made no sound at all, though they wagged their tails, ran and played with each other, and behaved like any other happy-go-lucky country mutts.

After finishing the tree, the tiny artist carried Jane's home-made spruce-pole ladder to the east wall of the barn, facing the house. For minute after minute he surveyed the weathered boards, as if summoning up an image of what he wanted to paint. Finally he climbed the ladder and began, with astonishing rapidity, to paint a picture of a middle-aged man and a little girl riding in a train carriage over a great railway bridge into a snowy city framed in the background by a high hill or a low mountain. The man and the girl both had light hair and gray eyes, and they wore dark clothes, as if headed for a funeral. "What does it mean?" Henry asked Miss Jane.

"It means that he wants to help us in our search for Pilgrim," she said. She gestured at the epigraph on the lintel above her door. "That works both ways, you know. Though he lives in no house, at the end of the road or elsewhere, the dog-cart man, too, is a friend to mankind. Kingdom Mountain Kinnesons have no monopoly on generosity, Henry."

Henry remained mystified about what the painting on the barn might signify, but that evening after supper, there came into Miss Jane's eyes the faraway expression that sometimes preceded a Kingdom Mountain moment. "When I was very small, Henry, I couldn't have been more than six or seven, my father took me on a train ride. It was in the wintertime. We went over a great railway bridge into a city very much like the one in the dog-cart man's painting, and we took a horse-drawn sleigh through snowy streets to a large house where there were calling hours for someone who had died. While my father paid his respects to the deceased, a beautiful young woman picked an orange from a tree growing inside the house and gave it to me. That's all I can remember. For years I've assumed the city was Boston, but just now I had a different thought. I don't know if it was a moment of second sight or not, but it suddenly occurred to me, while thinking about the painting, that perhaps I've been looking for information about Pilgrim all these years in the wrong direction."

"How so, Miss Jane?"

"I think, Henry, that we should turn our attention north-ward. Toward Montreal."

The word was hardly out of Miss Jane's mouth before an electric thrill ran up Henry's back. He could scarcely have been more excited had he just stumbled onto the Comstock Lode. Montreal had been the jumping-off point for his grandfather's strike against the First Farmers and Lumberers Bank of King-dom Common as well as the city to which the captain had fled after the Great Raid. Montreal, with its churches and cathe-drals and basilicas and King James's Jehovah alone knew what other earthly emblems of the heavenly host, was where the treasure was undoubtedly hidden. True, it was a good-sized city, large enough to cast a red glow on the sky above the mountains visible on some nights from Miss Jane's porch, one hundred miles away. But Henry had little doubt that with her second sight and her great determination, she would be able to locate the large house with the orange tree growing inside it and, thence, the fortune hidden by Cantrell Satterfield. If they happened to learn something about Pilgrim's fate as well, so much the better. On the spot, the magnanimous Texan made up his mind that if — no, *when* — they found the gold, Miss Jane would have not ten percent but twenty. She had more than earned it. *You are a prince of a man, Mr. Satterfield,* he heard her saying to him, with tears of gratitude in her eyes as he pre-sented her with a flour sack bulging with twenty-dollar gold pieces. And he would merely bow slightly and say, "Not at all, Miss Jane. But you are a true duchess." It was a moment he looked forward to almost as much as the actual discovery of the treasure.

"It still seems to me a very great coincidence that the dog-cart man should happen by with his helpful painting, if it does turn out to be helpful, just when we needed it most."

"When else would he choose to help us, Henry? When we

least needed it? No, sir. You must understand that on Kingdom Mountain there are few coincidences. Only consequences. You will see what I mean soon."

"How soon?"

"Very. In the meantime, life being as short and unpredictable here on the mountain as elsewhere, let us enjoy every last moment of our time together."

"I second that motion," Henry said, following Miss Jane into her bedchamber. Though he feared that the granddaddy, seeing an opening here, would add his own two cents, the old captain held his peace for a wonder. Cantrell Satterfield was merely biding his time, however. He had told Henry that he would strike at the time and place of his choosing, and Henry had absolutely no doubt that he would and that he himself was as apt to be the target as Miss Jane. Blood relation or no, that was the way the captain operated, and always had. Henry, too, knew a thing or two about consequences and family. The price of being Cantrell Satterfield's grandson was undeniably steep, and for this reason, among others, the aviator felt that he had already earned his share of the treasure several times over. He shot the bolt on Miss Jane's bedroom door with a satisfying click, hoping that would keep the old devil at bay. Whether he had come to Kingdom Mountain by chance or design, as a result of sheer coincidence or as a consequence of his grandfather's actions three-quarters of a century ago, Henry intended to take Miss Jane's advice and enjoy every moment of his time with her, beginning right now.

36

August 28, 1930

Jane Hubbell Kinneson
Kingdom Common, Vermont, U.S.A.

Dear Miss Kinneson,

I saw your notice in the personals column of Sunday's Ga-
zette. I believe that my mother, Mrs. Slidell Choteau, may
have had a connection with your father, Morgan Kinneson. I
would be very glad to discuss this matter further with you by
mail or to entertain you here in Montreal at your convenience.

> Most sincerely yours,
> Elisabeth Choteau Dufours
> 256 Côte des Neiges
> Montreal, Quebec, Canada

For all his great faith in Miss Jane's capabilities, even Henry
was astonished by how quickly the response to her inquiry in
the Montreal paper had arrived. It was a fine late-summer
morning in the mountains of the border country, with a touch
of fall in the slanted light and the mist over the river as they set
out in the Model A with the letter from Elisabeth Choteau
Dufours tucked into Pharaoh's Daughter's sweetgrass basket
with their lunch, and Morgan's Lady Justice between them in
the front seat, barrels up, under a blanket. Henry drove, and although he was terribly excited about heading to Montreal to
find the treasure, it was time, he knew, to think about getting
back on the road. Or, in his case, back in the air. Like the black-
birds beginning to flock in Miss Jane's fields, he was not meant
to stay in one spot too long. He would miss Jane, but there

would certainly be opportunities to visit her, and he took great satisfaction in thinking how well provided for she would be with her twenty percent share of the money he had come to regard as his rightful legacy from his grandfather.

As they approached the border, a large green and white sign announced, WELCOME TO CANADA. ALL TRAFFIC MUST STOP HERE.

Miss Jane frowned. "Canada," she said.

A man in a blue uniform approached the Model A and asked their names and the purpose of their trip. "I am Jane Hubbell Kinneson of Kingdom Mountain," the Duchess announced. "This is my friend Henry Satterfield from the Republic of Texas. We are en route to Montreal. As to the nature of our business, we travel on a private matter, which, I assure you, concerns no one but us."

At first the countryside across the border was mountainous. As they drove down into the St. Lawrence River valley, the terrain flattened out. The farms looked neat and flourishing. Each village had a soaring church spire sheathed in metal and visible several miles away. The houses were painted pastel pink, lavender, even chartreuse. Miss Jane remarked that the splashy colors relieved the bleakness of the long Canadian winters. What, Henry inquired, relieved the winters of Kingdom County?

"Nothing," she replied.

Around noon they crossed a bridge over the St. Lawrence River. A railroad track ran between the inbound and outbound lanes. Halfway across, as a train thundered past, they could see people in the carriages reading or looking out the windows a few scant feet away. "That's how my father and I came into this city when I was a little girl," Miss Jane said. "I'm sure of it."

They ate lunch sitting on Pharaoh's Daughter's red Hudson's Bay blanket on the grass of a downtown park near a domed cathedral. Over deviled egg sandwiches and Miss Jane's own pickles and still warm baked beans, she again told Henry the story of Morgan and Pilgrim. "My father, Mr. Satterfield, thought the world of his older brother. It was Pilgrim who taught him to hunt, to fish, to track, and to tell the name of every animal and plant on the mountain. Pilgrim enrolled in medical college, then came war. When the strife broke out, my father's brother had a dilemma. Like his father, Quaker Meeting, he was a fervent abolitionist. But also like his father, he was a pacifist. He wasn't sure what to do, but the star-crossed love affair with Manon Thibeau made up his mind for him. He enlisted in the Grand Army of the Republic as a medical adjutant. Pilgrim survived Gettysburg and several other battles, but toward the end of the Rebellion, he came up missing. There was no body, and my father didn't believe that his brother could be killed that easily."

"So he went to find him," Henry said. "But what happened next?"

Miss Jane looked at him. "I'm hoping that Elisabeth Choteau Dufours will be able to answer that question."

As Henry threaded the Model A through the narrow city streets, horns blared and drivers shouted in French. In a traffic jam downtown a young woman in a short red dress leaped onto the hood of the Ford, banged her hand twice on the roof, and jumped down again. Henry laughed. Miss Jane called out good-naturedly, "You, young lady, should have your behind paddled."

On Sherbrooke Street Jane directed Henry to pull up in front of the Museum of Fine Arts, where the winners of that year's North American Bird Carving Contest were on display in the great foyer. First prize had gone to the insufferable Santiago for "Two Harris Hawks Chasing a Jack Rabbit." The runner-up was Jackson's "California Condor, Soaring." Henry, while no judge of bird carvings, found the winners rather ordinary. He was disappointed for Miss Jane, who had spotted her beloved Noah, looking out fiercely over its many-toothed bill from the Honorable Mention display. A hand-printed message on a note card said, "Superb execution but carver DID NOT FOLLOW DIRECTIONS. This bird is extinct!"

Miss Jane swooped up her bird, crumpled the card, and headed for the exit.

A uniformed guard came running. "Ma'am!" he called.

"I am Jane Hubbell Kinneson of Kingdom Mountain, Vermont, the creator and owner of this archaeopteryx," she said. "How dare you mark me down for not following directions? In my career as a teacher, I never once marked down a student for not following directions. That is the last resort of the mediocre teacher. Where do the contest instructions stipulate that a bird cannot be extinct? Is it Noah's fault — this is Noah — that his tribe is no longer? Extinct, indeed. I won't have it. Better no mention at all than honorable mention. Better no prize than third prize."

Back in the Ford, Miss Jane set the much-maligned Noah on top of the sweetgrass basket between herself and Henry. Though he didn't say so, Henry thought that she could scarcely have been more satisfied with herself had she won first prize. He felt in the side pocket of his white jacket to be sure the paper was still there. Reassured, he smiled to himself. With its help, he was quite certain that Elisabeth Choteau Dufours would be able to solve the mystery of the missing gold, if not that of Jane's missing uncle Pilgrim. He had already decided to reward her for her assistance with a five percent commission. After Miss Jane's cut, that would leave him with a cool seventy-five thousand dollars. While there might be some slight trouble with the granddaddy in his head over giving away twenty-five thousand dollars of Satterfield family money, his percentage should tide him over quite nicely.

37

THEY LOCATED Côte des Neiges and followed the house numbers to an imposing half-timbered stone residence overlooking the city and the river below. Certainly, Henry thought, Elisabeth's residence was located *on high*. Now to find the *blessed sweet host* and *Holy Ghost*. A greenhouse extended from the southeast side of the house. The woman who met them at the door had dark eyes and dark hair with a little gray in it. Only when Henry looked at her very closely did he realize that she was almost certainly in her middle sixties, fifteen or so years older than Miss Jane. She was tall and slender and, like Miss Jane, she had a kind face and kind eyes. She was quite dark-complected. "Miss Kinneson?" she said, extending her hand.

"Yes," Miss Jane said. "And this is my friend the celebrated aviator Henry Satterfield. It's good to see you, Elisabeth Dufours."

"It's good to see you, Jane Kinneson," the woman said warmly. "And you, as well, Mr. Satterfield."

Elisabeth Choteau Dufours escorted them into the conservatory. In the center was a low flagstone-lined pool with a waterfall hung with ferns and a *host* of colorful tropical flowers — hibiscus, birds of paradise, bromeliads, and orchids. Henry looked around for an orange tree. He didn't see one, but this had to be the house Miss Jane had visited long ago with her father. They sat on white lawn chairs arranged around a glass-topped coffee table and sipped iced coffee through glass straws tinted with swirls of color.

For a few minutes they chatted politely. Then, as the water

murmured over the little falls, Elisabeth Dufours told her guests a story. "My mother," she began, "grew up as a slave on a plantation near Memphis. She had been well educated and worked as a kind of governess. Her job was to teach the young children of the plantation owner their letters and numbers and manners. In fact, my mother was the daughter of the owner, whose name was Dinwiddie, and a slave named Minerva. My mother's name was Slidell Dinwiddie.

"At sixteen," Elisabeth continued, "my mother ran away. This was during the War Between the States, soon after the North took New Orleans. She made her way north using contacts in the Underground Railroad. When she reached Virginia, she found herself entirely on her own. While she was hiding from patrollers in a great cave, she met a boy from the north."

Elisabeth paused. Then she said, "This boy was going south to find his brother, who was missing after an action in Tennessee."

"Pilgrim," Jane said softly. "The brother's name was Pilgrim."

Elisabeth nodded. "I believe so. And the boy's name was Morgan. Your father, Jane. And mine."

"Yours!" Jane exclaimed. "How yours, Elisabeth?"

"While they were hiding in the cave, Morgan somehow saved my mother from slave catchers. He and she had known each other only a few days, but they became deeply attached. And here I am. Here we are, sister."

Miss Jane shook her head. "All the best stories are about love," she said, thinking of the Bride of Ramses.

"They are, aren't they?" Elisabeth agreed. "While my parents were in the cave, Morgan gave my mother the name of his family's Underground Railroad contact people in Montreal, which was Choteau. The rest is history. My mother married a

Choteau, my stepfather. He knew she was pregnant with me at the time but he loved her. She died when I was in my early twenties. You came to her funeral, Jane. I gave you an orange. Do you remember?"

Jane had tears in her eyes. "I remember very well. I should have given you something, too, Elisabeth. You were very kind to me."

"I take it that our father never found his brother?"

"It's a great mystery," Jane said. "He brought back Pilgrim's walking staff. That's all. I had hoped to learn more about Pilgrim from you."

Elisabeth smiled. "And I from you, Jane."

Henry, who had been sitting on the edge of his white chair with his hand in his jacket pocket, was speechless. For once Miss Jane herself seemed somewhat at a loss for words.

Finally she said, "Your mother, Elisabeth, must have been a remarkable woman."

"She was. Witty and outspoken, a born mimic. She could talk several different ways when she told stories. Creole, Québecois French, High-Church English. She even mimicked our father's New England dialect. She made fun of herself and everyone else. My stepfather worshipped her."

It was quiet again in the conservatory. It occurred to Henry that for such a ready talker, Miss Jane was an uncommonly attentive listener. As quick as she was to state all kinds of notions and opinions, she had a way of pondering what was said to her and then nodding as if she understood exactly what you would most want a sympathetic listener to understand. So much about this remarkable woman was admirable, he thought. But the time had arrived to produce the paper.

Reaching into his jacket pocket, Henry said, "Madame Dufours, my grandfather, Captain Cantrell Satterfield, may have had a connection with Pilgrim Kinneson and Miss Jane's mountain. He left me this riddle, or part of it, which may hold the secret to a great legacy. A legacy I am prepared to share with you and Miss Jane."

"Henry!" Miss Jane protested. "The money stolen from the bank in the Great Kingdom Common Raid is hardly a legacy." To Elisabeth she said, "My friend is referring to one hundred thousand dollars in gold plundered from a Vermont bank during the Civil War by Confederate soldiers. It has never been recovered."

Henry handed Elisabeth the riddle. "I have reason to believe, Madame Dufours, that the treasure may be hidden here in Montreal."

Elisabeth took the sheet of paper and read the riddle aloud. "'Behold! on high with the blessed sweet host, / Nor Father, nor Son, but Holy Ghost. / The soldier stands vigil, where the rood is rove, / Over the golden trove.'"

To Henry's disappointment she shook her head and handed back the riddle. Miss Jane gave the pilot a look of school-teacherly disapproval. "We did not come here, sir, to speak of twice-tainted gold."

She turned to her newfound sister. "And the rest of your family, Elisabeth? They're all well?"

"Thankfully, yes. My husband and I have two sons, grown up now with children of their own. One lives in Vancouver, the other in Ottawa. Soon enough we'll probably have to sell this old place. We have no family here in Montreal to leave it to."

Miss Jane nodded. "Everything changes," she said. "They want to drive a highway through my property."

She summarized the story of the high road and her long-standing feud with Eben Kinneson Esquire and the town fathers. Henry, in the meantime, was taking furtive, sidelong glances around the greenhouse, looking for soldiers standing vigil, riven roods, heavenly hosts, and he didn't know what. The granddaddy's cackling laughter caused him to start. *It's gone, boy,* the old man chuckled. *Found and spent, every last doubloon. How else would the quadroon woman have financed this great manse? Whilst you wracked your brain to cipher out the jingle and old Morgan hid his half of the rhyme away from the world in a vault? Two fools well met!*

"I don't believe a word of that," Henry said aloud to the grandfather.

"Why, Henry," Miss Jane said. "Whatever ails you today? You've been right there all summer to see it all happening with your own two eyes. Henry has not been quite himself lately, Elisabeth. You must excuse him."

"I'm sorry I didn't get in touch with you sooner, Jane," Elisabeth said. "I wasn't sure — it seemed awkward, but I should have done so anyway. I take it our father was a magistrate?"

"He was chief justice of the Vermont Supreme Court," Miss Jane said proudly. "A great champion of women's rights and other forward-looking causes. He very much hoped to preserve the mountain where I live in its wild state forever."

Elisabeth picked up a magazine from the glass-topped coffee table and handed it to Miss Jane. It was called the *Appalachian Land Trust Monthly.* The land trust, Elisabeth said, was dedicated to conserving the Smokies, the Blue Ridge, and other ranges in the Appalachian chain. Recently, she and her husband had made a sizable contribution to the organization to buy and protect the cavern in Virginia where Slidell and Morgan had met.

"The matter of my mountain and the high road is now being reviewed by the Vermont Supreme Court," Miss Jane said. "We can only hope that the ruling is favorable. I don't have the funds to take it any further."

Henry seemed unusually quiet, but Jane and Elisabeth talked away the afternoon as if they'd known each other forever. They planned to meet again soon in Vermont. As Jane and Henry prepared to leave, Elisabeth excused herself briefly and reappeared with a cardboard box. "I wish I had some oranges to give you and Mr. Satterfield, sister Jane. But I'd like you to have this."

She handed Jane the box. "These are letters from our father to my mother, Slidell. He wrote to her quite regularly after he returned from the South and until he was married. Each year after that he sent her a birthday card. All very proper, of course. Yet you can tell he still loved her."

"But Elisabeth. These letters belonged to your mother. She left them for you."

"I've read them all many times. I'd like you to have them. Who knows? Maybe there's a clue in them about Pilgrim. Or Mr. Satterfield's riddle. Something I missed."

Miss Jane thought for a moment. Then she asked Elisabeth to wait in the conservatory while she fetched something from her Model A. When she returned she was carrying her archaeopteryx, whom she placed in a pink-blossoming bougainvillea vine beside the waterfall. "I carved this gentleman and named him Noah," Miss Jane said. "I think he fits in perfectly here. Do come and visit me, sister. I'd like you to see my mountain. Come soon. We've a great deal to talk about."

The sisters embraced with tears in their eyes. Elisabeth promised to visit Miss Jane and also to take her to the cave in Virginia where their father had met Slidell. Then, as the shadow of Mount Royal crept out over the city toward the great river, Henry and Miss Jane headed back to Kingdom Mountain.

On the way home, Henry found himself thinking again about Miss Jane's assurance that the recent apparent coincidences on the mountain were in fact consequences. Certainly everything that had come to light that afternoon — the family connection between Jane and Elisabeth, the purpose of that long-ago train ride, the box of love letters now in Miss Jane's possession — seemed the result of human actions. He now had no doubt that his own presence on the mountain was the result of his grandfather's participation in the Great Raid. But why hadn't Cantrell Satterfield returned for the treasure? Or had he? And what had happened to Pilgrim? Why, for that matter, had Miss Jane chained herself to her solitary life on the mountain after vowing as a teenage girl not to do so? Could her motive have something to do with the treasure? Most of all, where *was* the damnable gold if not in Montreal? Consequences aside, they had resolved few of the great mysteries of Kingdom Mountain today, only learned a new family story that would doubtless raise new mysteries of its own.

With the lights of the Ford cutting a swath through the woods covering the northernmost extension of the mountains that Morgan Kinneson had followed south to Tennessee in search of his missing brother, Henry said, "Miss Jane? Why did you stay on the mountain? You could have been a high-up professor or an ambassador or whatever you wished to be."

"Why, Henry, I have been, and am, exactly what I wished to be. A teacher — a former teacher, to be precise — a bookseller and librarian and a bird carver. Not to mention the custodian and protector of that mountain."

Slowing for a pair of eyes beside the road ahead, a raccoon or a skunk, perhaps, which melted into the woods, Henry said, "I've been thinking about what you said to me, Miss Jane. About there being few coincidences on Kingdom Mountain. About the far-reaching consequences of human actions. I was thinking about your decision to stay on the mountain."

Miss Jane remained, like her mountain, silent.

"I hope you know that you can trust me, Miss Jane, never to repeat anything said to me in confidence."

Jane reached out and placed her hand over Henry's on the knob of the steering wheel. Then she said, "It was the day I turned eighteen, my last year of high school. Early in the morning I slipped into my rubber boots and went out to the barn. I fed and watered our six Jersey cows, milked them, then fed the oxen, Seth and Freethinker Kinneson, named for our ancestors. Seth and Freethinker were a matched pair of Red Durhams, like Ethan and Ira Allen. They were yoke mates and brothers and more like members of the family than beasts of burden. They were just four years older than I, and of all the animals on the farm, they were my favorites. I'd grown up with them. I proudly rode to high school in an ox cart in good weather and boarded the animals during the day at the livery stable. Oh, how I loved those steers! In the winter I tapped balls of ice and frozen snow out of their cleft feet with a wooden mallet. I curried them every day. And that morning I gave them each a maple-sugar cube. For there was much to rejoice over. Three days before, I had been given notice that I was to receive the full scholarship awarded by the state university in those days to the first scholar of the graduating class of each high school in Vermont. It had been a hard time for us because my mother had died quite recently and my father was now ill himself, but I would be going to college and I was delighted.

"I gave Seth and Freethinker each a hug and set the milk cans in the cooling tank in the milk house, then returned to the kitchen and busied myself making breakfast. I put a freshly sliced loaf of salt-rising bread, warm from the Glenwood, on a plate and set it and two lovely soft-boiled eggs in my father's favorite periwinkle blue egg cup at the head of the applewood table, in front of him.

"'I'm not hungry this morning, my girl,' he said.

"'It's salt-rising bread, Father. Your favorite.'

"'Perhaps later. Is the wind still out of the south?'

"I nodded.

"'Mud time,' my father said. 'So many people die in mud time, Jane. It's the natural course of things. Mud time, death, then spring.'

"'Tell me a story,' I said, quickly. 'Tell me the story of Grandpa Seth pulling in the yoke with the ox.'

"'I've told you that story a hundred times. But not this morning. This morning, Jane, I must have your promise. You must promise me, as I promised my father.'

"'They will never leave this farm, Father,' I said. 'I give you my word.'

"'Can you give me your word that you won't leave yourself?' Father said. 'And that Seth and Freethinker and the dairy cows won't be auctioned off to someone who might abuse them? The animals are mine to do with as I please. On this matter, daughter, you'll do as I say. We'll start with the oxen. Fetch them around.'

"You see, Henry, my father had gotten it into his head that after he was gone, with me away at school, Seth and Freethinker might be sold to someone who would mistreat them. His father made him promise never to let an animal leave the home place. His father promised the same thing to his father. Father wanted me to shoot the oxen before I left for school."

"Shoot them? Why, that's crazy, Miss Jane!"

"Aye. So I said again, 'I swear to you, Father, that the oxen won't ever leave this farm. I'll care for them myself.'

"'And how will you do that, my girl? Aren't you off to college? Lead the oxen into the dooryard, if you please.'

"'What could I do, Henry? The brass balls on the tips of Seth's and Freethinker's horns glowed in the spring sunrise as I brought them out into the muddy barnyard. Their coats gleamed a deep, rich red. Then I had an idea. I would lead the oxen behind the barn, out of sight of the house, take Lady Justice, and shoot twice in the air. I'd tell father that they were dead. Then, when night came, I'd drive them into the village and sell them to Stevens, the auctioneer. He'd see to it that they didn't fall into the wrong hands.

"Just then the kitchen door opened. My father stepped onto

the porch, pale and gaunt. He was wearing his black judge's robe and carrying Lady Justice.

"'Damn it, father,' I shouted. That was the first and last time I ever swore in my father's presence. 'All right,' I said, 'I'll take care of them. Behind the barn. Give me the gun.'

"'No,' he said. 'Do it here, my girl, in the barnyard. Where I can see that it's handled properly. Otherwise, I shall tend to it myself.'

"'You don't have the right to make me do this,' I shouted.

"'I promised my father,' he said. 'He his.'

"Henry, I would have given anything, including the mountain, had my father come to his senses and told me to put the oxen back in their stalls where they belonged. He handed me the rifle he had carried all the way from northern Vermont to Tennessee and said, in his stern, calm voice, 'They will never leave this mountain to be abused by another owner, Jane. Do it now. Do it now or I shall do it myself in accordance with the promise I made my father.'

"'I promise you that I won't let them leave,' I cried. 'I give you my word, Father.'

"'Can you give me your word that you won't leave the mountain yourself? You, who are college-bound?'

"Oh, Henry! Just eighteen. Just accepted at the university with a guarantee of that scholarship. I looked at my father, standing in his judge's gown on the porch, and then at Seth and Freethinker, waiting placid and trusting in the barnyard. And I cried out, 'I won't go to college. I swear to you that I will never leave the mountain.'

"'Will you swear with your hand on the Bible?'

"'Yes,' I cried. 'Anything. If you wish to imprison me here, fine.'

"'I don't wish to imprison you, my girl,' he said as I followed him into the kitchen. 'I want you to have heirs to inherit the mountain from you. Just as you'll inherit it from me.'

"So I swore, and for better or for worse, I stayed on Kingdom Mountain, attending the county normal school, where I trained to become a teacher. That very night, the night of my eighteenth birthday, I started my great life's task, to revise that pernicious book upon which I had been compelled to vow away my future. The oxen lived out their natural days, and so too did my father, and so will I. But I will tell you this much, Henry. If I decide, for whatever reason, that I wish to leave the mountain, I intend to do so."

Henry, thinking of the black-robed old chief justice, Jane's father, standing on the porch with Lady Justice, was less sure of this than she. But he nodded and said quietly, "Thank you, Miss Jane, for telling me the story. You may rest assured that it will go no further."

Later still, just before they crossed the hemlock-plank bridge over the river, Henry heard Miss Jane murmur, "Well, Father? What shall we do with our old mountain, eh? What do you think?"

She paused, then said, "Yes. I think so, too."

"You think what?" Henry said. He had been doing some careful thinking himself and, despite the old grandfather's mean laughter and the implication that Elisabeth had discovered and spent the gold, he was inclined to believe that Cantrell Satterfield had never taken it to Montreal at all. The grandfather was merely having sport with him, as usual. The gold had to be somewhere on Miss Jane's mountain. It simply *had* to be. The question was where.

"I think we're home," Miss Jane said. "As my father always said, the best part of leaving Kingdom Mountain is coming back to it again."

A few minutes later, comforted by the familiar scents of wood shavings and paint and varnish, Miss Jane got the Kingdom Mountain Bible out of the Currier and Ives safe in On Kingdom Mountain and opened it to the book of Proverbs. At the end of the sentence "All the best stories are about love," she added an exclamation point.

"Isn't it strange, Henry?" she said, closing the great book. "How, looking for one thing, we so often discover another?"

"It is, Miss Jane. What discovery were you thinking of?"

"We went to Montreal hoping to find out what happened to Pilgrim. Instead, I found a dear sister."

"And I came to Kingdom Mountain hoping to solve a riddle and found, instead, a dear friend. It goes to show, I reckon. In both cases."

"Goes to show what?"

"That, as you wrote in your great Bible, all the best stories are about love. Shall we put your proverb to the test?"

"Let us do so," Miss Jane said. "Let us do so indeed."

38

EARLY ON IN HIS sojourn in Vermont, Henry Satterfield realized that Miss Jane loved not only most birds but nearly all of the wild animals on her mountain. More than once she had told Henry that it was great good luck to have almost any woodland or meadow creature show up at the home place, with the exception of usurping cowbirds, whining mourning doves, and shambling moose, which, she was certain, competed with her beloved white-tailed deer for feed. Soon after their return from Montreal a colony of striped garter snakes, some as big around as Miss Jane's hoe handle and fully as long, quartered themselves in the back stone foundation of the house. Henry, having grown up in a region where poisonous serpents abounded, was deathly afraid of all snakes and hinted that these lithe intruders might have spared him their visit. But the Duchess was delighted by her good fortune. She would no more kill a snake than a songbird.

Miss Jane deemed red squirrels in the house partitions auspicious. Every evening Henry could hear them rolling last year's butternuts around in the walls as if they were playing at tenpins. The brown summer weasel in the woodpile augured equally well. Weasels, Miss Jane assured Henry, were the best mousers in all the world. A family of swifts took up housekeeping in the disused chimney of Henry's former bedchamber upstairs. More good fortune. Under the eaves of the kitchen dwelt several extended families of bats, and in June a saucy raven with a glittering yellow eye had soared down from the mountaintop cliffs and plucked up half of Jane's sweet corn as soon as it sprouted. Instead of chasing him off, she taught the raven to warn her when Eben Kinneson Esquire came driving up the lane. "Here's the shyster, here's the shyster."

But nothing, so far as Miss Jane Hubbell Kinneson was concerned, betokened so much felicity as a swarm of honeybees.

Like many Appalachian mountain folk, from Georgia north to Quebec, Miss Jane maintained an apiary. Her Kingdom Mountain honey came in several flavors. From the hives near her buckwheat patch she obtained a rich honey that was sweeter than most. Her clover fields yielded a light and delicate honey as pale as fancy-grade maple syrup. But Jane's favorite was the dark, syrupy, delicious wild honey that she procured on her occasional beelining expeditions. Every few summers she went "a-lining bees," an adventure that Henry Satterfield might well have enjoyed for the opportunity it afforded to explore new territory on the mountain where he might stumble across the treasure. However, as a small boy, he had been severely set upon by yellow jackets and ever since he had been terrified of every member of the stinging tribe.

"Why, friend Satterfield, the wicked bees that assailed you as a child were no Kingdom Mountain honeybees," Miss Jane declared. "Kingdom bees are noble creatures. Their ancestors were brought here by Seth's wife, Huswife Kinneson, in a thatch-roofed hive. For all we know, they might be the descendants of those regal bees Samson discovered nesting in the dead lion. No Kinneson, I assure you, was ever afraid of a little bee. Nor was young Samson. Nor need you be."

Henry refrained from reminding Miss Jane that young Samson had also blithely squared off against an entire regiment of Philistines with no other weapon than the jawbone of a donkey. He had once watched his grandfather sell a family Bible to a burly moonshiner in Tupelo, Mississippi, whose genealogy, for an extra three dollars, the captain obligingly traced back to Samson. He didn't tell Miss Jane this, either. When the Duchess of Kingdom Mountain said it was time to go beelining, a-beelining they would go.

"A swarm of bees in May is worth a load of hay," Jane announced as they headed out on their latest mission one very fine morning. Why she repeated this old saw Henry had no idea. It wasn't May, it was early September. And they wouldn't be looking for a swarm but for one individual bee to line back to its tree, which Miss Jane would then, in entirely good conscience, cut down and plunder of its contents.

Nor did Henry understand why they had to traipse all the way around to the far side of the mountain to locate a bee tree. There were bees by the hundreds in the multicolored hollyhocks right beside the high drive of the five-story barn, and the golden glow growing eight feet tall around Jane's immaculate outhouse was abuzz with them. But she was not interested in harvesting honey from dooryard bees, which probably lived in her hives behind the barn. Nothing would do but she must venture off to the back side of the mountain and find the dark, precious honey manufactured by wildwood bees. She and

Henry would make an overnight trip of the outing and stay at her hunting and fishing camp, Camp Hard Luck, in order to combine their honey foraging with some wilderness fly-fishing. It would all, Miss Jane assured him, be most romantic.

In the sweetgrass basket she brought a pint Mason jar containing a solution of maple syrup, crushed tansy buds, and dooryard honey; a chipped blue tea saucer wrapped in a clean white dishtowel; and a small tin smoker, resembling a miniature bellows, in which a handful of burning leaves and a few strips of cloth soaked in kerosene would produce a stream of thick smoke to pacify the bees. On a flat-bottomed hand sled pulled by a long handle, they brought Miss Jane's two-headed felling ax; Freethinker Kinneson's crosscut saw; an empty beehive with a thatched roof, similar to the hive in which the estimable Huswife Kinneson had conveyed the first honeybees to Kingdom Mountain; two fly rods; Lady Justice; and the brass-bound spyglass that had come down in the family from Seth Kinneson's seafaring Massachusetts father. As fearless as Samson himself, Miss Jane brought no net, bee veil, or gauntlets to ward off stings.

They followed the eastern extension of the Canada Pike past several abandoned farms grown up to barberry, thorn apple, and poplar, out to the blueberry barrens on the remote lower east slopes of the mountain. They continued along the edge of the barrens toward the Chain of Ponds, where the East Branch of the Kingdom River rose. Once again, Henry was impressed by the sheer immensity of Kingdom Mountain and the astonishing variety of its terrain: bogs, a subarctic climate at the summit, vast forests, disused farmland, several brooks, even a cold, rushing river and a unique species of char.

Miss Jane led the way to a leanto hidden in the evergreens near the outlet of Pond Number One. Inside, under a sheet of green canvas, was a boat about sixteen feet long and curved up at both ends like a canoe but fitted for oars. The sides were constructed of thin cedar planks beveled along the edges to fit together so that nowhere were they more than half an inch thick. This elegant craft was Miss Jane's Kingdom Mountain guide boat, patterned on the fabled Adirondack guide boats of the past century. In her day, she told Henry, she had probably brought more fish over its upswept sides than any other Vermont angler had caught in a lifetime. This was not a boast. It was simply what Miss Jane believed to be a statement of fact. She had built the boat with an ax and a North Woods crooked knife, and, like her birds and dear people, it had been a labor of love.

They eased the guide boat out of the leanto and turned it right side up. It was beautifully varnished, with two slim, jaunty racing stripes, one blue and one orange, running around it just under its gunwales. After transferring their gear from the hand sled and propping the sled in the bow, they pushed off, with Jane manning the oars. She told Henry that she had mounted the pins on ball bearings, thereby making her boat exceptionally silent. She could slip up on a rising char or a drinking deer as quietly as in a canoe and much more swiftly.

The guide boat had a name inscribed neatly in black under its bow. Miss Jane had christened it the *Sairy Gamp*, after the tippling nurse in *Martin Chuzzlewit*. Like Dickens's red-nosed Nurse Gamp, Jane's craft took no water. "Troll your flies along behind us, why don't you, Henry?" Jane said. "Let us see what we shall see."

Henry dragged his flies thirty feet behind the boat as they glided across Pond Number One. Jane had rigged a leader for him with a Duchess of Kingdom Mountain lead fly and two droppers, a Green Drake and a Queen of the Waters. This was how her Scottish ancestors had fished in their deep lochs, with a cast of three different flies. Today the surface of Pond Number One was choppy, which often made for good fishing. But the sun was very bright on the water, which didn't. This was fine with Henry. After the hot walk up the pike and across the barrens, he was content just to sit on the cane seat of the guide boat and enjoy the breeze over the water. He couldn't help thinking, as they skimmed across the little lake, what a very attractive woman Jane was, with her light hair, gray eyes, and strong, shapely arms working like an extension of the oars. "Miss Jane," he said, "I hope you will not think me forward if I tell you that you are a fine figure of a woman."

"Why, sir," she said, turning pink, "I don't think you forward at all. It is kind of you to say such a thing to a woman of my age. You are the living picture of a gentleman."

"Well, I truly mean it," Henry said. "Perhaps we should just sit on the porch of your cabin enjoying each other's company and leave the bees to their own devices."

"Ah ha," Miss Jane said. "I see where you are headed with your blandishments. We will indeed sit on the porch and" — she gave him an arch look — "enjoy each other's company. *After* we line our bee back to its tree."

"Of all crafts, give me your flat-bottomed guide boat," she said a minute later. "It's responsive to every impulse of the oars yet much more stable than a canoe. One sudden movement in a canoe, and you're in the drink."

Not being much of a swimmer, Henry was glad to be riding in a craft that was much more stable than a canoe. The portage to Pond Number Two was only about an eighth of a mile. Henry offered to help carry the guide boat, but Miss Jane easily swung it up to her hip and from there upside down above her head so that the gunwales rested on her shoulders. Kinneson women were all rugged, she assured him. Huswife Kinneson had discovered the flume on the far side of the mountain on a solitary fishing expedition when she was ninety-three. Even so, as Henry poked along behind, pulling the hand sled and picking his way around wet spots to protect his white shoes, he was amazed at how easily Miss Jane managed the guide boat, which must have weighed close to a hundred pounds.

Pond Number Two was smaller than Pond Number One. The fishing conditions were the same, direct sun on wind-ruffled water, but Henry had a strike almost immediately, then another, then a third, and he played and boated three handsome blue-backs, the largest about a foot long. Ahead a loon whooped, a big, low-riding bird with a large black head and a black-and-white-checked back. Miss Jane said the bird was vexed with Henry for stealing his fish. Soon it dived out of sight. Jane pointed to where she thought it would come up and Henry pointed in the opposite direction. Neither of them came close to guessing correctly. The bird gave a long, hooting laugh, and Miss Jane said that they might as well try to predict the weather on Kingdom Mountain as predict where a diving loon would come up. Her father had once told her that a loon was one-third bird, one-third fish, and the rest mostly laugh.

After another short portage they reached Pond Number Three, where Bad Brook came rushing down the steep cataract known as the flume. Running along beside it was the wooden logging chute down which Miss Jane and her father had sent her first buck. Jane said that the great slide, which rested on stone-filled cribs spaced about forty feet apart, was more than a thousand feet long. In recent years the last hundred or so feet had rotted away. Now the chute ended at the foot of the mountain in a grove of young fir and spruce trees.

At the head of Pond Number Three the flume dropped over a twenty-foot-high waterfall into the pond. When viewed from below, the falls seemed to jet directly out of the side of the mountain. Nearby was Camp Hard Luck. Beyond it to the north lay the Great Northern Slang, a vast expanse of cotton grass, wild cranberry bushes, bog rosemary, tamarack trees, and dead water, relieved here and there by beaver and muskrat lodges, eventually leading out to Lake Memphremagog.

Camp Hard Luck was constructed from matching American chestnut half-logs facing each other across the main room of the cabin. As a little girl Jane had been delighted to discover that whenever she located half of a knot on the west side of the room, she'd be sure to find the other half directly opposite it on the east side. She loved looking at the ruddy-colored wood, which had come from the last stand of chestnuts in northern Vermont, high on the north side of the mountain, near where she had shot the huge deer as a teenager. Mounted on the log wall was the ridge runner's sixteen-point rack. Henry could see where one tine had been snapped off when Jane and her father had sent it down the chute to the frozen pond. Below the deer was nailed a small rectangular box, open at the top, and inside was a pencil stub and a notepad on which someone had scrawled, "Used camp in June took six trout to eat shot yearling mouse Canvasback Glodgett ps left woodbox fulle." The "yearling mouse" puzzled them until Miss Jane deduced that Canvasback probably meant that he'd shot a young moose.

A clearing in the woods behind the cabin was choked with late-blossoming daisies, buttercups, paintbrush, and jewelweed, all of which had sprung up after the overdue rains. Miss Jane set the saucer from the sweetgrass basket on a ledgy outcropping bright with summer wildflowers, shook up the concoction in the Mason jar, and poured a few drops of the amber-colored treacle onto the saucer.

"Teatime, Mr. Satterfield," she announced.

Honeybees seemed so well adapted to Kingdom Mountain that Henry had been surprised to learn from Miss Jane that like the purple lilac bush growing at the opposite end of her porch from the Virginia creeper, they were not native to northern New England. Over the century and a half since domestic bees had been introduced to the mountain by Huswife Kinneson, however, many colonies had emigrated from their hives to dwell in the woods. The opening in the woods behind Camp Hard Luck on the far side of the mountain was alive with them.

"My goodness, hear them converse," Jane exclaimed.

"What do you think they're saying?" Henry asked uneasily.

"Why, I know perfectly well what they're saying. They're telling each other where the best nectar is."

Just then a bee appeared beside the blue saucer. It climbed over the rim and loaded up with the sugary concoction, then flew off in the direction of the flume. "Let the lining begin," the Duchess said. Out came her ancestor's spyglass, which she trained on the departing bee.

Replacing the lid on the Mason jar, Miss Jane struck off up the mountainside with the reluctant aviator tagging along behind, pulling the hand sled with the saw and the sweetgrass basket. The understory was a tangle of wild blackberries, virgin's bower, mullein, and evening primrose. Miss Jane lost sight of their bee a couple of hundred yards above the camp. She stopped and repeated the process, unscrewing the lid of the jar, pouring out some of the cloudy liquor, setting the saucer on the floor of the forest. After three or four minutes a bee appeared. Whether it was the same one or another was impossible to say. Jane said it didn't matter, they were all likely from the same nest anyway.

"I didn't see him flying in," Henry said.

"Her," Miss Jane corrected him. "The workers are females, Henry. And you rarely do see them arrive. One of their most charming ways is that they seem just to materialize. My father used to tell me that all the best gifts in life arrive by surprise," she continued. "Like my mother, Pharaoh's Daughter, who just appeared in the barn one Christmas morning."

"Miss Jane," Henry said as they continued up the mountain after the bee, "I am interested in your mother. She had a most unusual name."

"If she had been a boy, my grandparents would have named him Moses. I suppose that her mother, the itinerant basket weaver Canada Jane Hubbell, wished her to have advantages not available to her, and therefore left her in the sweetgrass basket, like the infant Moses, for my grandparents to raise."

"You mentioned that she had no Indian ways."

"None at all, Henry. My father said I inherited all of the Indian ways from Canada Jane and her people."

"Were your father and Pharaoh's Daughter raised as brother and sister?"

"Well, that was a rather delicate point. Of course, Pharaoh's Daughter was my father's stepsister — I've lost sight of our bee, Henry. Let us pause and see if we can lure it back. They were of an age, and inseparable as children, the greatest chums in the world, I judge. Then he went off to war and she to Mount Holyoke College. After the war, Pharaoh's Daughter married my father, and they were very happy together. They had me rather late in life. I think my arrival was a great surprise to them both. As I told you, they had their own little Kingdom Mountain particularities, but I know this much. Neither of them would have stood still for a minute for Eben's ridiculous high road. Here's our honeybee, right on schedule. I don't think their nest can be far from here."

"Miss Jane, I don't mean to pry, but I have to ask. Do you think your mother knew about Slidell? And Elisabeth?"

"I expect that she did, Henry. My parents were lifelong friends as well as man and wife, and they had few secrets from each other."

"Do you believe he divulged to her what he discovered when he went south to find Pilgrim?"

"I don't know," Jane said, capping the Mason jar and starting up the steep, wooded slope. "If so, I'm sure neither of them ever told anyone else."

Through gaps in the trees above them, Henry could see patches of gray cliffs and, high above them, the devil's visage on the north face of the balancing boulder. This was not a place he would care to visit alone after dark. There was something forbidding about the far side of the mountain. Jane's determined bearing as she set off up the steep slope under the trees made Henry wonder if she might sense it herself.

The flume roaring through the nearby gorge made Henry dizzy. Miss Jane showed Henry where, over the millennia, sand and pebbles had scoured out a deep pool she called Satan's cauldron. Upstream was a black rock shaped like a foot. Satan's boot.

Here in the deep woods the derelict log chute had an eerie look. Miss Jane said that because of the great speed of the logs hurtling down the chute, and the friction they created, the lumbermen had sprinkled sand on the boards to keep them from catching on fire. The man charged with sending down the logs was called a kedger. In Jane's grandfather's time Jean "Kedger Jack" Riendeau had somehow tumbled onto the chute. As he hurtled down the mountainside, his clothes caught fire. Kedger Jack hit the pond at an estimated one hundred miles an hour and was killed on impact.

With this inspiring image in mind, Henry followed Miss Jane higher into the Limberlost. They came to fresh blowdowns where the tail of the recent hurricane had roared through. The few trees still standing were mostly hemlocks, though here and there grew a few lone beeches. Miss Jane pointed out where black bears had climbed them to eat the beechnuts in the fall, then slid back down the trunks like great sooty firemen coming down a pole, grooving the smooth gray bark with their claws. She remarked that very probably the honey tree they were searching for would turn out to be a basswood.

"Look for that linden, Henry," Jane said, peering into the thick green canopy overhead.

"Say what, ma'am?"

"Linden tree. A basswood. Bees dearly love an old basswood tree. So do I, for that matter. It's my favorite wood to carve."

Sure enough, a few yards away stood a soaring hardwood tree that Miss Jane identified as a basswood. That's not where they found the bees, though. They were nesting in the tallest of the last three remaining American chestnuts on the mountain, beneath which Miss Jane had shot the great ridge runner.

The limbs of the bee tree were longer on the east side of the trunk, indicating that the prevailing winds were from the west. High overhead, two major horizontal branches jutted out opposite each other at right angles to the trunk. Ten feet below them another large branch appeared to have broken off long ago. Perhaps the missing branch had been struck by lightning. Where it had once grown, a long, dark cavity bisected the trunk. A steady squadron of bees flew in and out of the fissure.

"Well, Henry," Miss Jane announced, "the hollow tree ought to come down anyway. We'll cut it."

They collected some damp wood from old chestnut stumps and a few handfuls of last year's fallen leaves and built a smudge fire under the tree to calm the bees. Miss Jane notched the chestnut tree with her ax so it would fall up the mountainside, away from the bee cavity. Then they fell to with Freethinker's crosscut saw. The maple handles were worn to a glassy smoothness from generations of use, and Miss Jane had kept the teeth filed sharp and shiny. Smoke from the fire curled up through the leaves of the towering old chestnut. Agitated bees zoomed past their heads. "Cower not, Henry," cried Miss Jane. "The bees won't harm us if we don't harm them."

How, Henry wondered, were the bees to know that he and Miss Jane posed no danger? Two gigantic marauders who were choking them with thick black smoke in order to level their home and pillage their larder?

The straight-grained chestnut wood cut easily, and the two sawyers made quick progress. In a quarter of an hour they were halfway through the trunk. As they worked, the smoke stung their eyes. They stopped once to add more wet wood and leaves to the fire.

"Soon you'll have a fine new home," Miss Jane called up to the bees. "Be patient a short while longer, my friends."

Henry shot a wary look at the crease high in the tree trunk. It looked large enough for a good-sized bear to come out of. An enraged bear, he thought, was all they needed. An entire battalion of bees now hovered just outside the opening. Miss Jane chuckled. "Saw on, Henry. All we need fear is our own trepidation. The bees can scent it."

If so, thought Henry, he was a goner. But at just that moment the massive chestnut gave out a long creak and started to sway. As they scurried out of the way, it toppled, crashing down through the smaller trees around it, hitting the ground with a tremendous metallic clang, as if the trunk were petrified and had landed on a boulder. The bees were now buzzing all around the opening, but as Miss Jane approached with her hand-held smoker and gave them several friendly puffs of smoke, they rose as one and alighted on a low branch of a nearby striped maple tree, from which they depended in a great inverted, humming cone.

The Duchess, carrying the hive, stepped boldly up to the cone of bees. "I am Miss Jane Hubbell Kinneson," she told them. "Come, friends, dwell with me on my side of the mountain. No thieving, flyblown bruins with rooting black snouts will pilfer your honey. I'll leave plenty to tide you over for the winter. You'll meet my swarms and make powerful new alliances."

The bees hummed louder, as if they were considering Miss Jane's proposal. Then out of the throbbing heart of the swarm crawled a pale-colored individual, larger than the others.

Miss Jane held out the thatch-roofed hive, and soon enough the pale queen walked inside on her six legs at a stately pace, followed by her subjects. For better or for worse, the bees from the far side of the mountain had cast their lot with the Duchess.

Now it was time to gather the honey. Miss Jane stepped up to the fallen chestnut with her double-bladed ax. Just below the bee hole, she dealt the trunk a powerful blow. It shattered apart, laying bare comb upon comb of dark wild honey. That wasn't all, though. Inside the hollow tree, encased in honey and beeswax, were the perfectly preserved remains of a butternut-clad soldier, still holding his rifle. The soldier had a ragged dark beard and long dark hair. His gray eyes were wide open and he was or, rather, had been at the time of his death, very young, no more than twenty or twenty-one. Spilling out of eight large white linen sacks wedged into the hollow beside him, covering parts of his uniform like the bejeweled armor of some ancient and fabulously rich emperor, were hundreds upon hundreds of honey-coated gold coins.

Henry was beside himself with glee. He was fairly capering at the sight of the long-lost treasure, dancing a jig on the forest floor, whooping and throwing his white hat high into the air.

"Sir, please, desist!" Miss Jane cried. "These antics are beyond unseemly in the presence of the dead. The Confederate dead, I might add."

"Who in thunder is he?" Henry said when he regained some control over himself.

Miss Jane had been staring at the soldier's tattered uniform jacket bedizened with coins. Gently, she turned him on his side and pointed at a small hole, about the size of a quarter, in the back of his tunic. Then she showed Henry, in the front of the soldier's jacket, what he hadn't seen before. Just below his breast pocket was a second hole, filled with honey and beeswax and somewhat obscured by double eagles, but considerably larger than the hole in his back. Whoever the soldier standing vigil over the Treasure of Kingdom Mountain might be, he appeared to have been murdered.

39

THAT NIGHT AT Camp Hard Luck, in the camp journal recording the blue-backed char and great-racked deer and fabled bears that she and her Kinneson forebears had taken on the far side of the mountain, Miss Jane wrote, "Found a swarm of bees, the Treasure of Kingdom Mountain, and one (1) preserved Rebel soldier in hollow American chestnut tree below devil's visage." Then, from Pharaoh's Daughter's sweetgrass basket, she handed Henry a folded sheet of stationery. He unfolded it and read the following letter written in faded brown ink.

September 5, 1864

My dear Slidell,

A most astonishing event has transpired here on the mountain, an event that I plan to divulge to no other living soul. Last month, soon after I returned to Vermont from my long trek south, during which I was fortunate enough to meet you in the cave in Virginia, our local bank was robbed by Confederate raiders. They rode out of Canada, hoping to augment the

Rebel treasury and, at the same time, spread panic throughout the North and, possibly, divert Union troops away from the fighting to New England. It is believed that the raiders made away with nearly one hundred thousand dollars in gold! It was a most brazen action, carried out in broad daylight by only two men. At any rate, the day of the robbery, when I went to the barn to milk in the evening, I heard moaning from the haymow above. There, to my great amazement, I discovered a young man, a Rebel captain, lying wounded in his gray uniform. Oh, Slidell! Here was a dilemma. However, bearing in mind my grandfather's motto on the lintel of our door, "They lived in a house at the end of the road *and were friends to mankind,*" which I well remember telling you of in Virginia, I felt obliged to hide and care for this Rebel, with the help of my dear young wife, Pharaoh's Daughter, and to nurse him back to health, then send him on his way back to Canada. What a traitor I felt, until *he happened to let drop that he had done the same for an injured Yankee soldier, hiding in the mountains in North Carolina, named Pilgrim,* who had told him about the wealthy little bank in Vermont and, without dreaming what he was doing, put the idea of the robbery in his head. The last the captain had seen of my brother, he was headed up into the high peaks of Carolina to live with and doctor the mountain people of that region! You know from my earlier letters the outcome of my search in those mountains for my brother. The wounded Reb then told me a tale stranger yet, which I did not, and do not, know whether to credit. He was a wild, ranting fellow, and his injury, which, I believe, will leave him with a ball in his leg to remind him of Vermont, made him no less so. He said that as he and his partner were headed over the mountain, the other man suddenly drew his pistol, threw down on him, and fired, wounding him in the leg, then rode off over the summit to Canada with the gold.

To cut a long tale short, in a week's time he was well enough to return to Canada and, thence, I suppose, to the South. What became of the gold from the robbery I don't pretend to know, and though I am grateful to him for helping my brother, if that story be true, I never did trust the fellow, who was all full of talk about the end of times and final judgments and I don't know what. Yet I do not feel that, in befriending him, I transgressed. My great-grandfather's motto on the lintel particularly stipulates that we are to help *mankind,* which I take to mean *all mankind.* Whoever the man was, I am glad I helped him, and nearly as glad that he is gone. I remain, with warm, best wishes, your dear friend in Vermont,

Morgan Kinneson

"The wounded soldier," Henry said, "was my grandfather, Captain Cantrell Satterfield. He always walked with a limp. But what about Pilgrim, Miss Jane? Your father's letter mentions another letter telling about his search for Pilgrim."

"It's not in the box Elisabeth gave me," Jane said. "I fear it's lost."

"How long have you known where the treasure was?"

"I've suspected for some time," she said. "Since soon after the second half of the riddle appeared so mysteriously on the slate, actually. A few days ago, when I read my father's letters to Slidell, I was less sure. I thought your grandfather's partner, whoever he was, might well have escaped with the gold."

"He was shot in the back," Henry said.

"So it appears."

For a time, neither of them spoke. Miss Jane seemed lost in thought, no doubt wondering if she would ever learn what had happened to Pilgrim. Henry kept expecting his granddaddy to say something to him, offer some explanation concerning the preserved soldier in the tree or pass one of his famous sarcastic remarks. But the granddaddy was as silent as a stone.

Jane was the first to break the silence. "For ever so long, Henry, I dismissed your grandfather's two-part riddle as the addlepated rant of a demented old man. Now, of course, it all comes clear to me. The hollow chestnut has no doubt always been a bee tree, at least since the Civil War. The blessed sweet host on high must be the honey. The Holy Ghost would be the honey tree. The Father and the Son are the two other chestnuts. Together, the three trees make up the Trinity. The soldier standing vigil is our preserved man. The rood is the cross formed by the two horizontal limbs above the cavity. The golden trove is the treasure."

Henry made his small, polite bow. "I think you are exactly right, Miss Jane. But who under the sun would the poor soldier-boy in the hollow tree be?"

"I think it most unlikely that we will ever learn his identity," Miss Jane said quickly. "Or, for that matter, exactly what became of Pilgrim. I'll tell you what. Let's call our bee-tree soldier Pilgrim and let the mystery go at that. What do you say?"

Henry nodded. Outside a cricket chirped, the first of the year. They could hear the constant hush of the waterfalls dropping down the mountainside into Pond Number Three.

"So Miss Jane. How do you propose to get the gold down the mountain? Gold is very heavy, you know."

"Mr. Satterfield," she said, "means will be found. For the time being, let us not fret ourselves with worldly concerns."

Soon enough, Miss Jane and Henry found themselves once again in that sublime state in which Henry actually forgot about his new red plane and all other temporal matters as well, with the possible exception of the five thousand double-eagle gold pieces, glittering softly, like so many lovely fireflies, under the moonlight high on the mountain. The moon shone on the surface of Pond Number Three and through the window of Camp Hard Luck, bathing Miss Jane's lovely limbs and light hair in its glow, and to the enraptured pilot, the great round moon looked uncannily like a large gold coin, hanging in the night sky, ripe for the picking.

*   *   *

The next morning Miss Jane and Henry climbed the mountainside in the bright early sunshine to consider the best way to transport Pilgrim, the bees, and the treasure back to the home place. With care, the soldier and the beehive could be pulled down the slope on the hand sled, then carried across the ponds in the guide boat. The gold was another matter. As Henry had remarked, gold was heavy, and Miss Jane supposed they would have the devil's own time getting it back to Camp Hard Luck. Then Henry suggested that they send it, like the great deer she had shot as a girl, down the wooden chute to the evergreen grove below. From there they could transport it in the guide boat across the three ponds to the blueberry barrens, where Ethan and General Ira Allen could haul it the rest of the way.

"Trust you, Henry, to solve any practical problem," Miss Jane said fondly, and they spent the rest of the morning dispatching the coins down the chute, several dozen at a time, ringing showers of sun-drenched gold which they picked up under the evergreens and plucked out of the branches where some of the coins had lodged like Christmas tree ornaments. In all, it took three trips over a three-day period to transfer the bees, the honey, Pilgrim, and the boodle to the home place.

After scrubbing the honey off the coins in her zinc washtub filled with hot, soapy water, Miss Jane and Henry stacked them inside the Currier and Ives strongbox in On Kingdom Mountain. Jane gently shut the massive iron door embossed with the scene of Lake Memphremagog, pulled down the heavy black handle, spun the dial, then wrote out the combination numbers for Henry in case "something untoward should happen to me." Henry protested that nothing could possibly happen to her as long as he was on hand to prevent it. Jane smiled and asked him for a moment alone with her dear people.

"Now, then," she announced when Henry had departed. "This handsome young gentleman" — motioning at the preserved Confederate soldier, whom she had placed on the horse-hair love seat beside the sarcophagus containing the Bride of Ramses — "is our guest. Who he was originally, I don't know. Truth to tell, I'm not entirely sure I wish to know. Whoever he was, he came to a tragic and violent end, and I want you to welcome him to On Kingdom Mountain, and to be kind to him, as you would be to any stranger. Perhaps he and Ramses' bereft young widow will come to know each other and even begin keeping company. The heart, as we have recently seen, works in its own mysterious way. In the meantime, you're not to breathe a word to anyone about the contents of the safe or, upon pain of being taken immediately to the burning barrel, to tender me a single word of advice about its disposition. That's all. I thank you for your understanding, my dears. Sleep tight."

40

ON KINGDOM MOUNTAIN summer was quickly fading. In the cool evenings Miss Jane and Henry sat out on the porch, Henry sometimes playing the old mountain tunes of his Satterfield ancestors on his fiddle. Sometimes they played catch in the dooryard with a couple of ancient three-fingered baseball mitts and a grass-stained baseball. They pitched horseshoes in the mountain twilight, their ringers and leaners clanging against the stake like the purloined gold coins clanging and ringing down the chute on the far side of the mountain. Henry allowed as how, next to Miss Jane as God made her, that was the greatest sight he had ever seen. Recently he had been pondering a grand scheme by which he might wind up with both the gold and the Duchess. It would be by far the boldest venture of his life, and it would depend on her willingness to live at least part of every year away from the mountain. But he was prepared, he thought, to make the proposal, the first such of his life, and to leave the rest to Miss Jane and, as he thought of it, the roll of the dice.

"Gold generally appreciates in value, Miss Jane," he began one evening, lying in the old rope hammock under the Virginia creeper with his stocking feet in her lap. "The boodle in your safe is no doubt worth several times its original value. With it you could save half a dozen mountains." Henry took a deep breath. Now that he was airborne, there was no sense landing until he had accomplished his mission. "You are not only a very beautiful woman, but a very wealthy woman as well."

The words were scarcely out of his mouth before he realized that this was probably not the best approach to the momentous proposition he was about to make to a woman who had little concern for money. "But let us not speak of gold tonight. Let us speak, rather, of each other and our future together. All I meant to say was that the gold, you know, will pave that future and remove any little bumps in the road."

"What can you be driving at, Henry?" Jane said. "Aren't your feet getting cold? Here, let me slip your shoes on your feet."

"I am certainly not getting cold feet, Miss Jane. In Atlantic City, where I am scheduled to perform later this month, there is a small chapel near the fabled boardwalk along the ocean. Present company agreeable, I would very much like to make you Mrs. Henry Satterfield in that chapel. We could then," he plunged on, "divide our time between touring the world and living here on your wonderful mountain."

A look of distress came across Miss Jane's face. It was not that she did not wish to travel the world, much less that she did not wish to marry the dashing aviator. The problem was leaving her mountain, even for part of the year. Who knew what Eben and the town fathers might do while she was gone? And which seasons could she bear to be away from home? She loved them all, from mud time through the roaring Canadian blizzards of January and February. Yet she could not, she absolutely must not, lose Henry Satterfield the way she had, long ago, lost Ira Allen.

"Mr. Satterfield," Jane said, "I am honored and moved by your kind — most kind — proposal. I will return to it momentarily. But first, I could not consent to burdening you and your tours with my presence unless I could contribute in my own right."

"Oh, but you can," Henry said, nearly blurting out *with your gold*. Catching himself just in time, he said, "With your *presence*."

"I appreciate that," Jane said. "But I am quite interested, Henry, in what you have told me about Miss Lola Beauregard Beauclerk."

"I meant it from my heart, Miss Jane. Not to speak ill of the departed, but her charms were as dross to your —" He had nearly done it again. "Charms," he said lamely.

"I am not speaking of Miss Lola's charms, though I have no doubt they were not inconsiderable," Miss Jane said in her driest manner. "I am speaking, sir, of her skills as a wingwalker. What, pray, does wingwalking require?"

"Oh, a fearlessness of heights. Exceptional balance and a certain delight in performing for an audience. It helps to have a shapely set of legs."

"Very well," Miss Jane said. "Later this month, on the weekend of the autumnal equinox, the village will be celebrating the one hundredth anniversary of its Harvest Festival. It is the major annual event in Kingdom Common, held over a three-day weekend on the county fairgrounds. The festival opens two weeks from this coming Friday. That should give me sufficient time to master the art."

"The art?"

"Of wingwalking. Mr. Satterfield, I plan to be walking on the wing of your Burgess-Wright biplane on the opening day of the Harvest Festival when you land on the racetrack in front of the grandstand at the fairgrounds. We will make a bargain. If you teach me to wingwalk, I will seriously consider your most kind proposal to become Mrs. Henry Satterfield."

"I goddamn!" Henry exclaimed, very nearly tumbling out of the hammock. "Miss Jane. Only a few people have ever attempted to walk on the wing of a flying airplane. It is far too dangerous. I myself have never done it. It is madness. You know what happened to Lola."

"Lola, through no fault of yours, was ignited by a lightning bolt. Are you suggesting that I am not up to the mark? That I am not capable of doing what Lola Beauregard Beauclerk, pronounced without the *k*, did?"

"Miss Jane, I beg you. Many a wingwalker has met a similar q-u-i-e-t-u-s to Miss Lola. We must not consider this further."

"I am a strong and agile woman, Henry. You of all people should know that."

"And a most lovely woman, Miss Jane. You would grace the wing of any airship. The problem is the great hazard."

"In this life it is sometimes a great hazard to climb out of bed in the morning. I will wear a tether and hold fast to the guy wires between the wings, and there will be very little risk. Then, present company willing, I will very seriously consider accompanying you on your upcoming tour. With the proviso, of course, that like Pluto with his dear Persephone, you will agree to my spending half the year here on my mountain."

"Oh, Miss Jane," Henry said, pulling her down beside him so that the hammock sagged nearly to the porch floor, while she laughed and protested halfheartedly. "Present company is very willing. Hold out your hand, please. No, no, the other one."

"This one will do for the time being," Miss Jane said, presenting Henry with her right hand. "Are you a palm reader? Did you read palms when you and your grandfather were selling Bibles and family trees to the unsuspecting old ladies? Are you going to read my future?"

"No, Miss Jane. I leave your future entirely up to you. Turn your hand over, please."

Without quite knowing how it happened, Jane, who was still flustered from their little hammock tussle, saw, on the third finger of her hand, a narrow gold-colored band set with a small sparkling stone.

She could not help smiling. The ring Henry had placed on her finger bore more than a passing resemblance to the dime-store bauble he had found in the belly of the leviathan steam combine, King James's Jehovah, now converted to a carnival kiddie ride. Yet inside the bit of glass affixed to the ring, she could see the high fall colors of Kingdom Mountain glowing red, orange, and yellow like no other foliage on earth. She could see the northern lights flashing silver and blue and crimson over the summit of her mountain on a clear and icy night in January. And the regal purple of the sunset behind the Green Mountains, viewed from the home-place porch on a midsummer's eve when the sky still held color at nine o'clock.

"For my duchess," Henry said.

"Let us hope," Miss Jane said as the ring threw a fiery arc of color onto the porch railing, "that I will be your first and last duchess."

"You are and you will be," Henry said. "Shall we set a date? For the ceremony?"

"Slow down, sir. I said that if you would teach me to wing-walk so that I could make a contribution to your business, I would consider your proposal. And I shall. But you must first fulfill your end of the bargain."

247

"Then *you* must agree to let me be the judge of when, if ever, you are ready to go up on a wing."

"That's fine," she said. "I am entirely confident that I will master the art. We will take the Harvest Festival by storm, Henry. Then, perhaps, away to Atlantic City and the world beyond. We will commence our lessons first thing in the morning."

Miss Jane spent the next two weeks practicing wingwalking, sewing her costume, arranging for Ben Currier, her neighbor, to care for Ethan and General Ira Allen while she was touring with Henry, and transferring the rest of her books from the defunct Atheneum to her five-story barn. She found walking back and forth on the broad lower wing of Henry's old Burgess-Wright not much more difficult than skipping across the hemlock-plank bridge as a girl. Like her Memphremagog grandfather, a high-steel worker, she had no fear of heights, and so long as she wore the tether Henry had rigged for her, he was no longer worried for her safety.

The trees began to turn color. First the swamp maples along the river, then some of the sugar maples on the mountainside. One morning a light frost covered the home pastures. You could trace the course of the river through the woods by the winding cloud of mist above it. A partridge, drunk on drops from Miss Jane's twenty-apple tree, flew into the west window of her kitchen and broke its neck. Jane fried it for supper.

In the sheep meadows along the burn, New England fall asters were in bloom. "'Asters by the brookside make asters in the brook,'" Miss Jane cited. "It's a riddle, Henry. Can you guess it?"

"Please, Miss Jane," he said, thinking of the hole in Pilgrim's back, "let us have no more riddles on Kingdom Mountain. I fear that I am riddled out for the rest of my life."

Goldenrod choked the disused fields along the Canada Pike.

To Jane, fall was never a melancholy time but rather a season of beginnings. The beginning of a new school term, of the harvest, of the splendid fall fishing for blue-backs in their spawning pool. Miss Jane would miss deer hunting this fall. But she hoped and trusted that becoming Mrs. Henry Satterfield and touring the world would more than make up for it.

41

ON THE FIRST DAY of the Harvest Festival, just as the cattle judging had concluded, Henry came zooming in low over the racetrack with Miss Jane, in black tights, walking on the lower wing of the plane. They swooped high above the fairgrounds, cut a large figure eight, and landed on the track in front of the grandstand to a great roar from the crowd. Henry was resplendent in his white jacket and trousers, white ruffled shirt, red velvet vest, and gleaming white shoes. Jane, in her new tights, with her abundant light hair piled high on her head, looked as vain as a peacock. "Why, it's Miss Jane Hubbell Kinneson!" Eben Kinneson Esquire said as they taxied up to the judges' stand in front of the grandstand.

For fifty dollars per day Henry agreed to perform twice daily, with barrel rolls, sideslips, loop-the-loops, and more figure eights. He and Miss Jane had a wonderful run of clear fall weather for flying, and each time they went up, the village's brass band played "Come, Josephine, in My Flying Machine." As word of their exhibition spread through the county, the crowds swelled. The grandstand was packed, with the more daring young boys scrambling up onto its tin roof. A few even ascended the water tower on Beech Hill.

Yet like the fisherman's wife in the old tale, the town fathers would not be satisfied. "We hear, Mr. Satterfield, that some veteran pilots are willing to fly upside down," George Quinn said on the second day of the festival.

"Flying upside down is an extremely hazardous maneuver," Henry said. "There are veteran pilots, Mr. Quinn, and there have been pilots who have flown upside down. To the best of my knowledge, there are few veteran pilots who regularly fly upside down."

But when the town fathers offered to increase Henry's fee to one hundred dollars if, for the finale on Sunday afternoon, the day of the fall equinox, he would fly in over the racetrack upside down, he agreed to consider their offer.

That evening at the home place, sitting on the porch after supper, watching the sun go down over the multicolored mountains and admiring what Miss Jane believed to be the finest prospect on the face of the earth, she asked Henry what he thought George Quinn and the fathers wanted, that they could never be content with Henry's performances but must always ask for more.

"Why, Miss Jane, they want the same thing that the crowds I have performed for from New York City to Rome, Italy, have secretly wished for."

"Which is?"

"To see me have a spill. Me especially."

"I can't believe it. That would be a terrible sight to witness. And why you especially?"

"Just think who I am, ma'am."

"Who are you? A respected pilot and exhibition man from Texas. That's all."

"An exhibition man from Texas, yes. But begging your pardon, Miss Jane, that is not quite all. No. An exhibition man who is also a man of color and a stranger. What, pray, would the crowd like better than to see the likes of me fall from a great height and be dashed to pieces?"

"Henry! I won't endorse such a notion. As you very well know, I've had my own dustups with the village of Kingdom Common. As a schoolgirl, I was sometimes known as 'Miss Jane Trouble.' But the spectators at our little fall festival are no bloodthirsty mob. As for your Creole ancestry on your mother's side, no one here in Vermont, of all places, would think it any kind of handicap at all."

"Oh, Miss Jane, my ancestry is always a handicap. Always. It is why, in order to fly against the kaiser, I had to leave this land for Canada and join the RCAF. If you are truly considering becoming Mrs. Henry Satterfield, you must understand that. It is a fact of life."

"I assure you that your color is no factor here in the Kingdom. Nor is it at all a factor in our engagement. As you know, I'm half Indian myself."

"That's different. The fact that you were born and bred here, and no stranger, counts heavily in your favor."

"For many decades, Henry, Kingdom Mountain was the last station on the Underground Railroad. For all its many faults, the Kingdom is still a community of civilized people."

"Begging your pardon once again, Miss Jane. In all my travels, I have never yet encountered such a place."

"As?"

"A community of civilized people."

"Then, sir, we must agree to disagree."

Henry nodded, tipped his white hat, and made his small bow. "We must," he said. "As for flying upside down tomorrow, I think I will decline. I have done it once or twice, but at the time I had, let us say, less to live for."

"I am glad to hear you say so." Miss Jane turned her dime-store ring so it caught the last rays of the sun, and they smiled at each other fondly, as if they were already a long-married couple. But that night Henry was a long time falling asleep. He did not doubt his own feelings for Miss Jane, or hers for him, yet he remembered the promise she had made to her father, never to leave the mountain. Whether she could be truly happy away from it, even for part of the year, was doubtful. Suddenly the old captain started up again in his head. *You, boy. Henry. I put in your hands and in your safekeeping the clue to your birth-right, your legacy. Now you propose to bestow it upon this woman wedded to a hill. Shame on you. Shame on you for betraying your old granddaddy and your destiny. I set you up, boy, grand and proud as a riverboat whore. Do you think you can spurn your legacy and your granddaddy so? Do you think you can dwell with these devilish Yankees? Even for part of the year? You'll find out, my boy. You'll find out different.*

"When?" Henry said aloud.

Soon, the evil granddaddy said, chuckling to himself. *Very, very soon. In the meantime I want you to take the old fathers up on their offer. I don't want it said any grandboy of mine was afeared to fly upside down or inside out or whatever which way. Then you'll receive your marching orders from old Captain Cantrell. After you put on your show for those devils.*

"Go to hell," Henry told him.

Too late, I'm there already, cackled the granddaddy, who always managed to get in the last word, even at his own expense. Henry, holding Miss Jane close, firmly put the captain out of his mind. But late the next morning, on the last day of the festival, when the foliage on the hillsides around the village was at its most vibrant and Kingdom Mountain seemed on fire, he thought of the captain's dire prophecy. As he flew in low over the fairgrounds, with Jane walking on the lower wing, then soared up and up, into the clear blue firmament, to begin their loop-the-loop, Henry noticed the crude red heart painted on the side of the water tower. Inside, in red letters three feet high,

were two names. MISS JANE TROUBLE + DARKY SATTERFIELD
= THE FLYING LOVEBIRDS.

42

IT WAS ALL JANE could do not to pitch off the wing like flaming Icarus. She was mortified. Mortified for herself, for Henry, and for the village she had called civilized. Nor were the words on the tower all of it. When they touched down and came to a halt in front of the judges' stand, the town band struck up "Dixie." The grandstand was about half full of fairgoers eating picnic lunches. Some cheered and some laughed, and there were even a few catcalls. But Henry Satterfield, ever the gentleman, gave no indication that anything was amiss as he climbed out of the plane and approached the town fathers.

"We apologize for this," George Quinn said, waving the band quiet. He made a vague motion toward the water tower. "That is a most unfortunate jest. We mean no disrespect. There is, of course, in every town, a certain element . . ."

Henry Satterfield glanced up at the tower on Beech Hill, as though noticing the message for the first time. "Best to just ignore it, no doubt."

Miss Jane, however, regarded the town fathers with a baleful, dangerous fury.

"I was only wondering," Henry said, "about the affront to the lady?"

"We tender our apologies to you and to my cousin," Eben Kinneson Esquire said quickly. "But you are a gentleman, Mr. Satterfield. And we assume that as a gentleman, you will still be

253

willing to consider flying upside down this afternoon just before the grand cavalcade of prizewinners. The show, you know, must go on."

Henry made a small bow of acquiescence. "The show must go on, then. I will fly upside down for the one hundred dollars."

But Jane, her eyes flashing, said, "I won't be so treated, gentlemen. I won't be so treated by any of you. Mr. Satterfield, I am surprised, after this usage, that you are willing to go ahead with your show. I will have no further part in it. I will meet you back at the home place this evening, and you and I will discuss matters further."

There, the captain's voice said in Henry's head very clearly and with finality. *There is your answer, boy.*

Henry looked as though he wished to say something more. But before he could, the Duchess turned on her heel and marched off the track, leaving the aviator standing alone by his machine.

There is your answer, the captain repeated. *How many times did I tell you when you was a shaver?*

"Tell me what?"

That it weren't over yet. Now get in your machine. It's time we finished what I begun.

"What are you talking about?"

I am talking about why I dispatched you up here in the first place. I am talking, Henry, about your destiny.

No one knew where Henry Satterfield went next. He was sighted in so many parts of the Kingdom that some swore he must have managed, like the devil, to occupy more than one place at once. He was glimpsed flying out toward Miss Jane's, again at the Ford agency in Memphremagog, and again at the egg farm on the road to Kingdom Landing. Some said it was the dog-cart man who painted the emblem on the top wing of the Burgess-Wright, but if so, no one knew where or when it was done. No one was absolutely certain how Henry did spend the afternoon other than, it was generally agreed, apart from Miss Jane.

It was Jane's old friend and fishing partner, Judge Ira Allen, furious about the slur on the water tower, who escorted her about the grounds that afternoon and later handed her gallantly up into the grandstand to sit beside him and see the cavalcade of prizewinners. In fact, Miss Jane was determined that it would never be said, after the affront of the message on the water tower and the humiliation of a public spat with her betrothed, that she did not have the courage to face the villagers. Courage was one commodity that the Duchess possessed in abundance, and no one could deny it.

First came the high-stepping band, followed by the Reverend with his big pulpit Bible under his arm, then Eben Kinneson Esquire and the town fathers in their high black silk hats, then the Academy directors, and the Masons. Bringing up the rear were the proud winners with their bright blue championship ribbons pinned to their coats.

The band struck up a spirited marching number, and there was a little strut in their walk as they approached the cheering grandstand, swinging their gleaming instruments first to the right and then to the left. Even Miss Jane seemed caught up in the excitement for a few moments and did not at first see the plane approaching. She heard the Burgess-Wright at the same time the members of the cavalcade did. As the thunder of the engine drowned out the music, the parade came to a ragged halt. The startled processioners looked up to see the airship swooping toward them, with two large metal barrels lashed to the upper wing.

As the plane dived in low over the racetrack, it rolled over so that it was briefly flying upside down, just as Henry had promised. Emblazoned on its upper wing, the red and blue colors scarcely dry, was a large Confederate flag. Then one of the drums seemed to spring a leak. Or, more precisely, a dozen leaks. Out of the barrel gushed ten or twelve jets of a dark and viscous substance, blackening the marchers from head to toe. Henry Satterfield was spraying the parade with used motor oil from the Ford agency.

As the dignitaries and prizewinners tried to flee, they slipped in the grease and pitched headlong in the oily dirt. Down went the band members in their gaudy uniforms, down went the town fathers and Eben Kinneson Esquire, down went the Reverend with his holy book, all sprawled in the sludge on the track like so many greased hogs. In the meantime, back came Henry Satterfield's Flying Circus. This time, as it passed upside down over the people, displaying the Stars and Bars of the Confederacy, the airship seemed to burst into ten thousand pieces. Out of the second drum flew a blizzard of chicken feathers, yellow and red and black and white. It was a plague of feathers from the local egg farm, and whatever they touched, they stuck to. The Reverend's great Bible, the brass instruments of the band, and the blackened faces of the town fathers and other dignitaries. The civilized people of Kingdom Common had become a minstrel show.

Miss Jane was surprised but certainly not alarmed, when Judge Allen dropped her off an hour later in her dooryard, to discover that she had gotten back home before Henry. With the days noticeably briefer, it was too late to leave for Atlantic City that night, and she supposed that he had flown up to Memphremagog to return the barrels to the Ford agency or run some other errand before their trip the next day. As the judge rattled back over the covered bridge and headed down the new right of way toward the Common, she shivered slightly. The sun had already disappeared behind the mountains. A fire in the Glenwood would feel good tonight. In her garden the scattered brown stalks of corn she'd left standing for the raccoons rustled in the sharp fall breeze. She would not be amazed if, on the summit of the mountain, it snowed tonight.

She went into the kitchen, past the faded riddle on the slate. Now that she knew what it meant, she couldn't believe that she hadn't deciphered it sooner. It was so plain to her. Consequences, she thought. There seemed to be no end to them. As she had told Henry, every human action, past, present, and future, had consequences. If she had not invited Henry to come home with her six months ago . . . Shaking her head, she kindled a small fire and made batter for flapjacks, Henry's favorite supper. Before coming to the mountain he'd never tasted real maple syrup. Now he used it on everything you could possibly think of — pancakes, Miss Jane's homemade ice cream, her homemade bread, which, ladled over with maple syrup, he called "poor man's cake." She looked out the window, down across the water meadow to the river. Dusk was falling. It was already dark under the applewood table. Her father had liked to say that when it was dark under the table, it was time to light the lamps.

Only when full darkness had settled over the mountain did Miss Jane allow herself to consider that Henry might not be coming back, and it was half an hour later when, taking a deep breath, then another, she stepped into On Kingdom Mountain to break the news to her dear people.

She lighted the kerosene lamp on the table beside the horsehair love seat where she had propped up Ramses' bride and Pilgrim. She looked around the parlor at her people, and then, for the first time since the night of the great deluge, when she and Henry had collapsed laughing into each other's arms and later gone swimming in the river, she began to laugh. Her laughter did not last long, perhaps a second or two. But when she saw that the door of the Currier and Ives floor safe was open and the safe was empty, she could not help laughing at her own perfect lack not only of second sight but of the slightest amount of foresight. She realized she should have known from the start, from the moment she found the coin in the fish, that the stranger destined to come to Kingdom Mountain was, in the end, like all strangers, also destined to leave, probably with something that belonged to her. Her gold, her heart, whatever. Yet a part of her, she could not deny, felt a certain relief, for she was already homesick for the mountain she would now never leave. The nature of found money was that you would surely lose it again. Maybe that was the nature of love as well. Like strife, such might be the way of the world. As for Henry, she told her dear people, she was glad to think of him soaring off into the sky, headed south with the geese, in possession of the gold that had been his heart's desire, free as the birds she carved.

Only later, alone once more in her bedchamber, did she give way to her grief, made still more unbearable, if possible, by her realization, correct or otherwise, that she, and she alone, was responsible for all that had happened to her in the half year since her fiftieth birthday.

ON KINGDOM
MOUNTAIN

43

To THE ALL-KNOWING Commoners, it was evident that Henry Satterfield had marked Miss Jane from the start. All the blame fell on the outsider from Away. The Duchess, for her part, seemed to have retreated to her mountain in a state of despair. What advancing age and loneliness and the threat of the Connector and hardscrabble living and feuding with her cousin Eben and the town fathers and King James and his Jehovah had not been able to do, namely, break her spirit, had been accomplished by betrayal in love.

As for the Connector, work on it had temporarily stopped after the flood. But Eben Kinneson Esquire remained confident that the Supreme Court would rule in favor of the high road and that construction could begin again in the spring. Even Miss Jane Hubbell Kinneson of Kingdom Mountain, he told the town fathers, could not simply declare her private independence from Vermont and the United States on the strength of an ancient family document of questionable provenance and authenticity. The fathers, enraged at being tarred and feathered in full view of the townspeople, billed Miss Jane for fifty thousand dollars in unpaid back taxes on her mountain, claiming that the provision supposedly arranged by Daniel Webster and Lord Ashburton had never been incorporated into the final treaty and that the mountain had always been part of the township.

And what of the daredevil Henry Satterfield of Beaumont, Texas, who stole Miss Jane's heart and stole away into the clouds with the Kingdom Mountain Treasure? While the

Duchess never said one hard word about him, in the Common talk became gossip, gossip rumor, rumor myth. In time that myth would become legend. The low high sheriff, Little Fred Morse, read in the October issue of *True Detective* that Courteous Clyde had been sighted in Tonawanda, in western New York State, buzzing in low over the New York Central rail yards. Other reports had Clyde making an emergency landing on a commercial cauliflower farm near Bakersfield, California, and in Halifax, Nova Scotia, preparing to cross the Atlantic alone in a new red Gee Bee Racer.

One report was unsettling, at least to Miss Jane, because it had a certain bizarre credibility. On the early evening of the last day of the Harvest Festival, an hour or so after Henry tarred and feathered the dignitaries of the Common, a low-flying yellow biplane was spotted by Ben Currier's two teenage boys, inveterate poachers at sixteen and fifteen, gill-netting the fall run of brown trout coming up into the East Branch of the Kingdom River past the old town farm. Without mentioning what they were doing at the time, the brothers claimed that the plane was coming from the old Canada Pike and Miss Jane's mountain, heading southwesterly out over the lake and flying quite low, with the wings wobbling, as if very heavily loaded. They said the pilot did not appear to notice them and, though he was alone in the plane, his mouth was going "like a whippoorwill's ass in black-fly time," and they saw him shake his fist as if in the middle of a heated argument. It was a misty evening, and the boys lost sight of the biplane about halfway across the lake. A minute later they spotted it again, this time headed back in their direction, as though for some reason the pilot had decided to return to wherever he'd taken off from. Almost immediately, the dense fog on the lake closed in and the boys lost the plane once more, though they could hear it, still coming their way, the engine sounding as though it was laboring. Then it passed out of earshot, lost in the enveloping fog. Had Henry Satterfield, if it was Henry, changed his mind and decided to return for Miss Jane? Or was the gold too heavy a cargo for the old Burgess-Wright? A search turned up nothing. If the plane had gone down in the three hundred feet of water off the foot of the mountain, no one would ever know. Though the Currier boys swore to the truth of their tale forever afterward, they were both notorious storytellers as well as accomplished poachers, and in time no one, including probably the brothers themselves, knew what they had claimed to see.

No place on earth is as fickle as a small town, and soon enough cruel tongues in the Common proclaimed that the Duchess was certain that the rainmaker would return later in the fall to marry her. It was confidently retailed throughout the village that one stormy October midnight, Miss Jane held a black wedding at the old church in Kinnesonville, walking into the roofless chapel all overgrown with woodbine and wild cucumber vines and inhabited by mice, bats, and snakes, and marching down the aisle carrying a life-size wooden sculpture of Henry Satterfield, dressed all in white, as she was. At the altar in the pitch-black darkness inside the ruined house of worship, she said all of the sacramental words, answering for both herself and her betrothed. Then she carried the sculpture home over her shoulder and from that night forward slept with it in her own bed as she would with her beloved.

The facts, of course, were entirely different. There was no wedding, black or otherwise. And though she was indeed carving a new figure, it was not Henry Satterfield. As she announced to her emerging sculpture, and to her dear people in On Kingdom Mountain, King James's psalmist had been right about one thing, at least. There was a season for all things, and, while it had lasted a full spring and summer, her season of foolishness was thankfully over.

44

MISS JANE WOKE to the bellowing of General Ira Allen, alone in the barn, and the harsh calling of crows from above her sugar orchard. It was mid-November on Kingdom Mountain. The leaves had been down for a month, and though there had been no significant snowfall yet, just very cold weather, the air this morning had the smell of an oncoming storm.

It had been a fall of dramatic changes in the Kingdom. First, the ruling had come down from the Supreme Court and, just as Eben Kinneson Esquire had predicted to the town fathers, it was not good news for Miss Jane. Unable to find any reference to the Kinnesons or the Memphremagog Abenakis in the ratified Webster-Ashburton Treaty, the justices had ruled unanimously in favor of the township. They found that Kingdom Mountain lay partly in the town of Kingdom Common and that the old Canada Pike Road over the mountain had never been officially abandoned. Therefore the Connector could legally follow the pike road up to the Canadian border running through Miss Jane's home place. What happened from that point on was up to the province of Quebec, but Eben and the town fathers had effectively won their case. Characteristically, Miss Jane was particularly offended by the legalistic language of the finding, which, to her outrage, stated that "the demurrer of the Town of Kingdom Common is sustained as to all particulars and the injunction against said township and the Connector is dissolved."

That fall the first electric wires were strung out the county road along the right of way of the Connector, though Miss Jane did not choose to become wired up. Then Eben Kinneson Esquire sold his paper mill in the Landing to the Brown Company, which was planning a huge expansion in Vermont. More small farms had gone under, and the human landscape of the county had begun to change as well, with the deaths of some of Jane's closest friends in the village. In early October Sadie Blackberry and Clarence Davis died within a week of each other, played out like the little hill farms and four-corner sawmills and riverside mill towns of Kingdom County. Later that month A Number One slipped up to the Ford agency in Memphremagog, siphoned the radiator fluid from several cars on the lot into an empty fifth of Wild Turkey, drank it off, and died on the spot. A week later Canvasback Glodgett fell into the bay and drowned. Without the fishmonger's cry ringing through the streets, the village seemed as empty as a desert. "Fish for sale. Fresh fresh fresh. Pickerel and pout, pickerel and pout, pickerel and pout but nary a trout." The dog-cart man moved on, perhaps heading south for the winter. Whether he would return was as unknowable as the fate of the departed rainmaker.

Then Jane's twenty-five-year-old ox Ethan Allen died. She found him in his stall, where he had expired in his sleep. General Ira was inconsolable, moaning steadily, throwing his head around looking for his brother and lifelong yoke mate, refusing to eat, and, generally, breaking Miss Jane's heart all over again.

"Did you hear the crows?" she asked her new figure when she came into the kitchen. "They've found that poor steer's carcass up on the mountain, no doubt."

He stood at the foot of the applewood table, one foot on each side of the yellow line representing the border that no Kingdom Mountain Kinneson had ever acknowledged, looking at her expectantly. Miss Jane knew what he wanted her to do. She knew she should put him away in On Kingdom Mountain with her other dear people.

Outside it was just getting light. Over the crows she could hear General Ira, alone and bereft in his stall, bellowing. She took a drink of Who Shot Sam.

She put on her red and green lumber jacket and felt boots and wool cap and mittens. She slipped a lump of maple sugar into her jacket pocket, then headed out to the barn, hoping to entice General Ira into eating something. The dawn sky was pink behind the mountaintop, where Jane was still surprised to look up and not see the fire tower. The crows were cawing. She could make out ten or a dozen of them circling over the soft-woods above the sugar orchard, where, two days before, she and General Ira had taken Ethan.

Ira refused to eat the maple sugar. Back in the kitchen Jane took another long drink of Sam. She sat at the applewood table, her head in her hands.

"Why not return to teaching now, my girl?" the figure said kindly. "Where you belong. You never should have left the Kinnesonville schoolhouse."

Miss Jane could not bear to tell him there were no longer any children on the mountain to teach, that the schoolhouse was an empty shell.

"Did you hear the crows?" she asked him again.

"No," he said. "I heard the grieving ox. Seth Kinneson, your great-great-grandfather, came to Kingdom Mountain in early April of 1775. He had a yoke of Red Durham oxen and a pung on runners. His wife and boy of five, Freethinker, rode in the pung. At the foot of the mountain the off ox cut its hoof badly on the river ice. To spare the poor animal, Grandpa Seth stepped into the yoke himself to pull with the near ox. He couldn't bear, you see, to see the off ox suffer. Now, Jane. You promised me never to let an animal suffer on this mountain. I promised the same to Quaker Meeting. He to Freethinker. He to Seth."

"Maybe Ira will recover."

"And maybe that rounder from Texas will return with your gold and maybe my brother is still alive in the Southland. No, my girl. You'll do as I say. I want it done by the end of the day. The animal must not suffer."

At least, Jane thought, she could drive the crows away from Ethan's carcass. If necessary, she would shoot one of the birds and hang it up in a tree as a warning to the others. Once again she stepped outside into the bitter cold. This time she headed up the mountain.

Above the sugar orchard she came out of a thick stand of softwoods into a clearing. Atop the limbless spar of an old pine tree struck by lightning, looking down at the hulking carcass of the dead ox, sat the largest owl she had ever seen. It was gray, and its immense yellow eyes had eerie white spectacles around them. Twenty or more screaming crows were diving and swooping at it. A murder of crows, Jane thought. A murder of crows, mobbing the first great gray owl she had ever seen on Kingdom Mountain. Without hesitation she fired both barrels of Morgan's gun into the air, scattering the crows to the four winds. Unperturbed, the owl continued to watch her, and at that moment Miss Jane knew, as surely as she had ever known anything in her life, exactly what she must do next. It was not an experience of second sight so much as an experience of her imagination. Maybe that's what her second sight had always been.

Just before she headed back down the mountain, the owl lifted off its perch. Spreading its vast wings, banking and rising like Henry's biplane, it soared off over the mountaintop toward its home in the far north. That was where it belonged, Miss

Jane thought, as certainly as she belonged on Kingdom Mountain. Now it was time to go to work.

45

THREE PEOPLE STOOD beside Miss Jane Hubbell Kinneson's applewood kitchen table. Around their feet were chips and shavings from her latest carving project, a very large bird, already recognizable as an owl.

Miss Jane looked a little pale, a little thinner, and a little older, especially around the eyes, but otherwise the same. "Gentlemen," she said, "let us repair to On Kingdom Mountain."

The safe with the beautiful Currier and Ives lithograph of Lake Memphremagog on its door was unlocked, the massive iron door partway open. On the top shelf was a folder with a white slip of paper pasted on the upper left corner. Written on it were the words LAST WILL AND TESTAMENT OF JANE HUBBELL KINNESON.

"Ordinarily," Miss Jane said, now addressing her dear people as well as her two guests, "the reading of a will is preceded by the death of the person who wrote it. That, of course, is in the normal course of events. But when, on Kingdom Mountain, have events ever followed a normal course? I've decided to read you my last will and testament myself, lest it be supposed I did not have the courage to disclose its contents in person."

Judge Allen interrupted the Duchess. "Jane, this is nonsense. You'll live another thirty years."

But Eben Kinneson Esquire wondered, What new, entirely unwelcome surprises could his cousin's will contain?

"First," Jane said, "I'd like you to meet someone who will be joining us for the reading." She gestured at a tall, elderly figure dressed in a black robe, with snow white hair, a white mustache, and Jane's gray eyes. "Gentlemen, my father, Morgan Kinneson."

Although the likeness was rather impressionistic, with its oblong head and painted features, Eben drew in his breath sharply, as if the old patriarch, who as a boy had walked to Tennessee in search of his brother, had actually come back to life before their eyes.

"Now," she continued, her voice slightly harsh, quite cheerful, entirely in command of what she wished to say, "hearken to my last will and testament. 'I, Jane Hubbell Kinneson, being of extremely sound mind, will to my cousin, Eben Kinneson Esquire of Kingdom Landing, the house I currently dwell in, known as the Kinneson home place, my five-story barn, and the ten acres on which these buildings stand, to hold in trust for the Memphremagog Abenaki nation in perpetuity. I will all of the contents of that house and barn and all of my other moveable possessions, including my blockheads, birds, books, and dear people, to my sister, Elisabeth Choteau Dufours, of Montreal, Canada, to hold in trust on Kingdom Mountain for the Memphremagog Abenaki nation in perpetuity. Signed, Jane Hubbell Kinneson, Kingdom Mountain. Thanksgiving Day, 1930.'"

The room was silent. Outside, a few small flakes of bright, crystalline snow fell. They could hear the wood fire in the Glenwood ticking. Miss Jane looked quite satisfied with herself, quite at peace.

"Your *sister?*" Eben said. "What sister? You have carved yourself an imaginary sister? Like your imaginary father here? And what about the mountain? What becomes of it?"

Jane looked out the parlor window. "I imagine he'll be just where he has been for another few billion years."

In the Thanksgiving snow flurry, the summit of the mountain was indistinct. Through the small flakes, Miss Jane could see that the hardwoods on its lower slopes were already reddening slightly with next spring's buds. Soon the mountain would be white. Then gold with tiny new leaves, then, for a few short months, deep green.

"But what do you intend to do with it, Miss Jane?" Judge Allen said. "All that land?"

"I gave it away, Ira. Lock, stock, and barrel."

"Gave it away? To whom?"

"An outfit called the Appalachian Land Trust, out of Asheville, North Carolina. My sister, Elisabeth Dufours, has conducted satisfactory dealings with them in the past. They have pledged to take the battle over the high road to the United States Supreme Court. And they will win that battle and keep the mountain just as it is forever."

"Cousin," Eben said, "how can you possibly give away what isn't yours to give? According to your father's will, the mountain lies in trust for your heirs in perpetuity."

"Not so," Jane said. "It lay in trust only for my *direct* heirs. Who, fortunately for them, no doubt, never existed."

"I maintain that the mountain was not yours to sell or to give away," Eben said.

"That was indeed my father's design, Eben. That, sir" — now addressing her new sculpture of Morgan, standing by the doorway — "was your plan. To assure yourself that I would hold on to the mountain at all costs and pass it along to my children intact, you left it to my heirs, in trust with me, and to their heirs, in trust with them. But you did not take into consideration the possibility that I might not have progeny. I had so many suitors" — cutting her eyes ever so briefly at Judge Allen — "that it probably never crossed your mind that I might not marry, thus invalidating the stipulation of the will.

"You will remember," she continued, still speaking to her

carved father, "that I was too independent-minded and too proud and half again too picky to entertain those suitors. And there was one more consideration. I genuinely did not wish to defy your wishes, you whom I loved and respected above anyone else in the world. But nor did I wish to make, with any unborn children and grandchildren of my own, any such binding compact as you had decreed. A wild mountain off in the middle of nowhere, belonging to neither the United States nor Canada, from which they could, at best, scratch a wretched living, seemed far more burden than legacy. I have no direct heirs, so the will wasn't binding. Blame me if you will, dear father. What's done is done."

Morgan gazed out over the crowded room as if marveling at how strangely his plans had turned out.

Miss Jane looked fondly at her wooden father, then at his much younger image. "All the way to Tennessee," she said. "All the way to Tennessee and the Great Smoky Mountains you walked. And then you came back, and here you stayed and here you wished me to stay, on our beloved mountain."

"Judge Allen," Eben said, "I implore you to order competency testing for my cousin. I'm sure you'll find —"

The judge sighed and held up his hand.

"Jane," he said, "do you know what day it is? The day of the week and date of the month?"

"Aye. It's Thanksgiving Day."

"How about the date of your birthday?"

Jane gave the judge an arch look.

"I have to ask you these questions to satisfy Eben that you haven't gone round the bend," the judge explained. "When were you born?"

"Long enough ago that you should know better than to ask me such a question, Ira. I was born the same year you were born."

The judge laughed. "What's your phone number, Jane?"

"Why, Ira Allen, are you asking me for a date? My goodness. I've never had a phone in my life and never intend to have one."

"Eben," the judge said, "there is nothing at all the matter with Jane Kinneson's powers of reasoning. Her mind is as clear as a bell. Moreover, for what it's worth, I think it's a damn good will."

"Thank you, Ira." Miss Jane turned back to the figure by the door. "Dear Father, you were deeply suspicious of the world beyond our mountain, and not without reason. That's where poor Pilgrim disappeared. It's where the raiders who robbed the First Farmers came from, and where you feared I would go and somehow come to harm. What you wanted most was to protect your heirs from the dangers of that world by binding them to this place.

"Well, that can't be done. Even if we don't often venture down the mountain into the world, the world will quickly enough come up the mountain to us. It always has, both its malefactors and its luminaries. That's the great irony, you see. There's no hiding from the world. No, sir. Don't cast your reproving look my way. There will be no recriminations on this day of all days. There will be no more such constraining compacts on Kingdom Mountain.

"People," Miss Jane continued, and here she seemed to be addressing all of her dear people, as well as Eben Kinneson Esquire and Judge Ira Allen, "my father bequeathed to me a mountain. Well and good. I gave it away. This Appalachian organization is a sensible outfit, not too smug or self-satisfied with their own fine accomplishments. They'll hold the mountain unchanged, in trust for the future. Anyone who wishes to come here to fish or hunt or just enjoy the seasons and the views may do so."

Jane reached out and took the sculpture's wooden hand. "Father, you saw great horrors. You dealt with those horrors as best you knew how. You were a good son and brother, a good husband and father. But when it came to your descendants, you wished to control their future in a way that the future can't be controlled."

"So the mountain no longer belongs to the Kinnesons," Eben Kinneson Esquire said.

"Cousin," Miss Jane said, "it never did."

Eben shook his head and left the room.

Judge Allen, too, seemed ready to go, but Miss Jane put her hand on his arm. "Ira," she said, "I have a favor to ask of you. A few moments ago, when I inquired if you were asking me for a date? I wasn't entirely jesting. Actually, I wish to ask you for one. I want to ask you to accompany me to the homecoming ball tomorrow night at the Academy. Will you go?"

"With the greatest pleasure in the world," the judge said, and he bowed in a courtly way that fleetingly reminded Miss Jane of Henry Satterfield.

Epilogue

MISS JANE HUBBELL KINNESON of Kingdom Mountain lived well into her eighties. To her satisfaction, she outlived her cousin Eben by several years. He left his very considerable holdings to her and Elisabeth, and she, in turn, left her portion to Elisabeth's children, who, along with their mother and father and her longtime fishing partner, Judge Ira Allen, had become the joy of her life.

Miss Jane won two first prizes at the North American Bird

Carving Contest, once with her great gray owl, once with the northern shrike impaling the redpoll from her exhibit Birds in Strife. In time she resumed work at her bookshop, which she operated out of the five-story barn, and where, by lantern light, she still occasionally hosted literary evenings, roundly denouncing the Pretender of Avon and the Proclaimer of Concord to two or three bemused Commoners. She and Ira Allen took many book-buying day tours and, obligingly affording the village something to talk about, a few overnight tours as well. They never spoke of marriage. Jane and the judge could scarcely have been more companionable, but the Duchess realized that she was, and probably always had been, too independent-minded for married life.

As for the Kingdom, things have continued to change there since Miss Jane passed on. Commoners who were young in the summer that Henry Satterfield came to the county are now old. Interstate 91, though it bypasses Kingdom Mountain, connects the village with the world on the other side of the hills. The ski resort at Jay Peak, fifteen miles west of the Common, gets more natural snow annually than any other resort east of the Rockies. Under "Vermont" in Miss Jane's celebrated 1911 edition of the *Encyclopaedia Britannica,* you may read the sentence, "To the east of Jay Peak lies a beautiful farming country." It's still beautiful, particularly around the spring and fall equinoxes, but the little farms themselves have been amalgamated into agribusinesses, a term Miss Jane would not have cared for at all. The Common, however, with its old-fashioned central green and brick shopping block, looks much the same. Most of the young people leave as soon as they get out of school, returning only to visit. There's nothing here for them to do.

With its long, harsh winters, big woods, and independent residents, the Kingdom remains something of a place apart from the rest of Vermont and New England. Miss Jane's mountain will always be an anomaly, running east-west rather than north-south, officially located, according to the letter from Daniel Webster to Freethinker Kinneson, not in Vermont or Quebec or Canada or the U.S. but in the heart of the land of the Memphremagog Abenakis. Miss Jane said it best. The mountain belongs to itself. There is no high road, or any road, beyond the home place, which is now a small museum containing Jane's Birds of Kingdom Mountain and her beloved blockheads and dear people, including Seth and his ox, Quaker Meeting leading his fugitive friends to safety, the young and old Morgans, the infant Pharaoh's Daughter in her sweetgrass basket, and, of course, Ramses' Bride and the preserved Confederate soldier, Pilgrim.

No one in the Kingdom, including Miss Jane, ever learned Henry's fate or, for that matter, that of the twice-purloined and thrice-tainted gold. In the village, where old men still sit yarning on the hotel porch of a summer evening and old friends meet at the post office or the Harvest Festival or the Thanksgiving homecoming ball, it is sometimes reported that, high on the mountain, near the Kingdom Mountain Cemetery, a hunter or fisherman or a solitary hiker, happening along at twilight, will glimpse a tall, stately woman with light hair, dressed all in black, visiting companionably with a slender man in a white suit and hat, a crimson vest, a black four-in-hand tie, and white shoes. Then the apparitions, if that's what they are, fade off into the dusk and the traveler passes on down the mountain, not quite sure what, if anything, he saw. It is the sort of tale you might hear in any off-the-beaten-track hamlet in New England. Still, as Miss Jane herself liked to say, on Kingdom Mountain, anything is possible.

Sometimes a visitor to the mountain will walk up to the cemetery, past the iron pump of the glacial well, and read the

words carved on Miss Jane's stone. She inscribed them herself a
few years before she died. They're worth seeing.

> Jane Hubbell Kinneson
> The Duchess of Kingdom Mountain
> That which I have learned I leave as my legacy.
> Close all gates behind yourself.
> Every generation should have its own Bible.
> The walls we erect to protect ourselves from early pain
>   often shut us off from later joy.
> To immerse oneself in the natural world is to share a
>   universal thread with every living thing.
> Always declare yourself to the person you love.
> Live each day not as though it is your last, but as though
>   it is the last day of the lives of the people you meet.
> All the best stories are about love.